ALMOST HOME

A SWEET SMALL TOWN ROMANCE

THE BACK TO SILVER RIDGE SERIES

CLAIRE CAIN

Cover design by Emma Robinson

Cover Photography by Abigail Renee Photography

Cover models Christie Tuttle and Alexander Lesch

E-Book: 978-1-954005-30-3

Print: 978-1-954005-31-0

Dear reader,

Almost Home is a closed door romance full of longing and heart that is rooted in a challenging history that deals with miscarriage and past emotional abuse by a parent.

I mention this content since it is sensitive and so many have experienced these hardships. I want you to walk away with only happy, lovely feelings, and hope you'll feel safe proceeding with this information in mind.

My very best to you,
Claire

PROLOGUE

Wilder

Then

I hadn't seen her in four days. *Four. Days.* She'd barely responded to messages. Finally, she'd promised to meet me at our spot today and requested to please give her space until then.

She'd never asked me for space. We'd never needed it. If anything, right now, the last thing I wanted was distance from her. I wanted her right here, in my arms, where I could hold her while she cried. While I cried.

"Wilder, honey, will you be long? Are you taking something to eat?" Mom asked, her tone soothing and low.

Everyone had been talking that way, careful to keep the pity from their glances. Wyatt hadn't said much at all, only clasped my shoulder in his hand, then pulled me into a rough hug. Warrick had no idea what was going on. Six years younger than me, he was eleven. We hadn't told him Sarah was pregnant yet, so there'd been no need to break the news that she wasn't anymore. Grandma Tilda kept him distracted with activities in town and helping with the horses so he wouldn't be around to see me acting like a ghost.

Pain sliced through me once again, and my eyes welled with tears, but I blinked them back. "Yeah. I'll take something."

Mom gave me a warm smile, emotion swimming in her gaze. She'd gone with me to the hospital to be with Sarah. Had stayed while they confirmed the baby was gone and through everything that came after. Then, she'd driven me home after Sarah's parents had refused to let me go with them and held me while I sobbed until I dry heaved and nearly blacked out from how bad everything hurt. I'd never realized heartbreak could come out of nowhere like that. How it had felt like my bones were melting inside my skin, no longer capable of holding me up the same way after losing a baby I'd started to love the minute I knew it existed and seeing Sarah crumpled with so much pain that it had hollowed me out.

"She's meeting you at twelve?"

I shoved a water bottle into my pack, along with the letter I'd written her. I wasn't sure I'd be able to say everything I needed to—had no idea how she'd be feeling, or if we could even talk about this. Words failed me like they often did. I didn't know what to say, didn't know what to want, even. How did we look ahead after this? But maybe she'd just want to move on and pretend like she was okay. Like everything we'd talked about and planned for based off that little pink line wasn't gone.

Except *us*. We weren't over just because we'd lost the

baby we hadn't realized we wanted until eight weeks ago. We'd get through this. Together.

Soon enough, I arrived at the little pull-off on the canyon road that sat thirty minutes from my place and fifteen from hers. It gave us privacy, even though we'd be outside and the January weather was freezing today. The snow would make it impossible to hike to the rock where we sat in warmer months, but I had a full tank of gas so we could sit and talk in the cab of my truck.

Her little white car chugged around the corner and slipped onto the shoulder. She paused, then made the terrifying curve across the two lanes of road to pull behind me. My heart pounded, and I told myself it was because of that—the risk of crossing the road after a blind turn. But she'd done it a hundred times by now, so I knew that wasn't it.

Every twinge or hesitation seemed like a warning—like more bad news would come any minute.

She slipped into the cab of my truck but didn't give me her eyes. I stretched out my hand. Relief flooded in when she took mine with her chilled one, the tensed muscles in my shoulders loosening a touch.

"Are you... okay?"

Her gaze found mine, and the answer lay there in the wreckage of her face. Dark circles under swollen red eyes. A nose raw from being wiped. Lips lined in a darker shade from dehydration. Even her cheeks looked a little gaunt, though it'd only been four days.

"No."

Useless question, of course. If she felt anything close to what I was... I squeezed her hand. "Come here. Let me—"

"I can't."

Okay. I got that. She didn't want to fall apart right now.

She had to drive back. She had already warned me she didn't have long, that her parents wanted to keep her close.

Tension spiraled through me, tightening around my chest and cutting my breath into short, insufficient efforts.

Focus on the tangible.

"What can I do?"

Her lips pressed into a line, firming her chin against a wobble. My heart twisted at the tears that dropped from her eyes without warning. She shook her head like she was fighting for composure. She didn't need it with me—didn't she know that already? She could cry all she wanted. I'd cry with her. Some part of me needed to cry with her, and we hadn't had a chance to mourn together yet.

"I'm leaving town," she said, her voice shaking.

Alarm shot through me, but I stayed calm. For her sake. "How long? To your cousin's?"

She pulled in an anguished breath with eyes closed before speaking again. "No, we're moving."

My mind stilled. The sound of the truck engine idling fell away, and something weird happened in my feet, like they fell asleep, the blood cut off from them. "What?"

"I guess they've been thinking about moving for a few months now, and now that—" She pulled in a breath but pushed through. "So we're moving. Mom, Eddie, and I are leaving this week."

Cymbals crashed in the back of my mind, and none of her words made sense. Her mom, sister, and her... "Leaving? *Moving?*"

"I know it's sudden. I—I'm sorry." She squeezed my hand, then pulled hers out of my grasp.

"What—what is this?" I could hardly speak, hardly see.

What about finishing school together? College together? The baby was... We wouldn't have this baby. He or she wouldn't wear the little outfit we'd bought a few weeks ago that Mom had tucked away when she'd found me staring at it. We wouldn't have to learn about car seats and the right kind of diapers. But we could still be together, build something else together.

I searched her face, but she wouldn't look at me. Tears tracked one after another down her cheeks.

"I'm sorry. I just—I can't."

And then, she pushed open the door and jogged to her car. Started it. Sped off. I stayed trapped in the cab, in this moment, full of disbelief and a fragile, vulnerable feeling like I'd walked over the just-frozen ice of a November lake.

Her taillights disappeared around the corner, and I shifted into drive, unable to let her go like this. She had drowned so far under the grief that she couldn't see a way out. Her parents were moving; she didn't have to. We'd make it through this. We'd had a plan before—we'd go to college, I'd get into ROTC, and we'd marry at graduation and she'd come with me. We'd stay together, never to be parted.

This? Just a bump in the road. A horrible, heartbreaking bump, but we could manage it. We would.

At the bottom of the canyon, she pulled into the parking area that served carpoolers and a few of the trailheads. She must've seen me behind her. I jumped out into the empty lot, and she did, too, car still running.

I grabbed her arms, holding her just lightly enough she could get away with the slightest move. I didn't want to trap her or hurt her any more than all of this had, but I couldn't pretend she was making sense or that I understood.

"You leave this week. So... what do we do?"

Her eyes had grown redder now, her skin splotchy from

crying hard the last few minutes. She really shouldn't have been driving at all.

"I can't do this, Wilder. I'm sorry."

She wouldn't look at me. Still. I shook her a little, just to make her give me her eyes. "Sarah, what is this?"

"I'm leaving and... this is our goodbye."

The words punched into my gut, and my hands fell away from her. A fissure ran along my sternum, severing something vital when it reached my ribs. I said the only word I could summon. "No."

"It's not your choice," she bit out.

"It's not only yours!"

She couldn't do this. This wasn't her. This was the grief talking and showed just how wrong this all was. Every damn second of all this was wrong!

Her eyes, more blue than ever, speared into me without mercy.

"I'm sorry. I really am. But I have to go, and I—" Her voice broke. She pressed a shaking hand to her mouth like it'd hold in the emotion, the destruction she was causing. When she pulled her hand away, I felt the shift in her.

Like she'd stepped back from the moment and extracted herself. She wasn't my Sarah, slogging through the brutality of having lost something so unimaginably precious. She wasn't the woman I'd loved since the time I'd known her and fallen for the minute I knew how to do that, too.

This wasn't the girl who'd shared everything with me and coaxed me into sharing as much of myself as I knew how to.

This was someone else—some mercenary version of her, only willing to take her goodbye and run. My confused, battered heart could hardly beat through the realization that she meant this. She meant every word about leaving, and she had no intention of trying to figure out another way to be together.

"I have to go. It's—it's for the best. Anything we had planned—" She hauled in a breath against that break. "It's gone now. You're off the hook." She crushed her folded arms against her chest, bowing over them, but met my eyes one last time. "I hope you have a really beautiful life, Wilder."

And then, she was gone, leaving me to stare after her and wonder how everything I'd wanted had crumbled to dust in a matter of days. The life I'd imagined with her—becoming more of ourselves together as we grew up, building a family together, growing old together... She'd thrown it all away with those cruel words. Like anything would be beautiful again without her. Without *us*.

That thin ice cracked and I went under.

She wouldn't see me after that—refused to answer when I called. I overhead Mom and Wyatt talking in low tones about how Mom had called Sarah's parents and asked them to let us speak, but they'd insisted Sarah couldn't come to the phone, that we'd already said our goodbyes.

They'd blamed me, as though I'd somehow engineered the pregnancy. Any amount of excitement we'd shared, it'd only been safe to express at my house. They didn't go so far as to be openly happy about our loss, but their refusal to let me see Sarah only sharpened the clarity that they didn't want us together. They wanted this clean break and would do nothing to help us stay connected despite the distance.

By now, Warrick knew something was terribly wrong, but we didn't tell him exactly what, I think in an effort to protect his soft heart. He tried to console me when he saw me cry, but I couldn't take anyone's comfort anymore. The only embrace I wanted was Sarah's.

But I didn't stop calling, and finally, she agreed to let me come to the house—the yard. I realized she was scared I wouldn't leave once I got inside, and I wondered if I had ever given her the sense that I wouldn't leave if she asked, that I wouldn't listen to her. Had I become a different person, too? Had I ever been someone who made sense, or had I always been this jumbled mess of raw emotion?

"I don't want to be off the hook, Sarah. I'm yours and I don't want anyone else. I won't ever want anyone else."

She shook her head, that same haunted, frail look clinging to her. "I can't fight about this, okay?"

The words, a whisper, plunged into my chest and sent me to her.

I pulled her to me, my arms around her shoulders. "Please don't cry. I'm sorry. I just want to help. I want to make this better."

I had to, because failing that, I had no way forward.

She pulled away and her face broke, freezing in an agonized cringe as though physical pain shot through her. "Please don't fight me. I can't."

That look in her eye said she was scared—scared of so many things. Internally, I raged against it, but I'd lived through the hell of the last few days and knew this wasn't normal. This wasn't the way things should be, clearly, and so my clinging to what we'd planned before simply wouldn't work.

I'd heard her. Finally, she'd gotten through. *Don't fight me.*

What she was asking would've seemed impossible if I hadn't seen the visceral pain wreathing her like a gory halo. I could practically taste her agony, and I knew the flavor well since it matched my own.

So, though it shattered my heart into oblivion, I straightened and eased her away from me. "If this is really what you need, I won't fight it. But I'll love you. I will. Stay or go, I'll love you either way."

Her lips flattened, and her jaw flexed. "Okay."

"If this is what you want, I won't stand in your way." Even as I said it, every atom in my body screamed for her to change her mind. To tell me to give her some time and then call her. Write her. Visit her. Move to be near her and see what happened.

She huffed out air through clenched teeth, like she'd been stabbed. "Okay."

My hands slipped away from her shoulders, releasing her, but she grabbed one of mine. "I—"

Her mom stepped in from somewhere I hadn't noticed, arms curling around Sarah's shoulders to pull her out of my grasp and steer her back to the house. "That's enough now, Wilder. That's enough."

And then, Sarah James was gone from Silverton, completely gone.

So I left, too. I quit school, passed the GED, and bumped up my enlistment a full six months. When we'd heard about the baby, I'd decided to enlist rather than wait and go through college. It'd give us insurance and a paycheck right away. I'd never been afraid of hard work and didn't really want to go the college route anyway. Eventually, she could have tuition assistance and, well, none of that mattered anymore.

But I couldn't stay there once she left, in a place that meant only heartbreak and loss to me without her.

Sarah

Now

The voice sounded distant in my cotton-stuffed ears, and I had to be seeing things.

"Do you know Wilder Saint? I'm never certain who knows who in this town." Julian Grenier gestured to my friends and me. "Wilder, this is Quinn Darling, Dahlia Price, and Sarah James."

Did I know him?

At another time, on another day, I might've broken out into a hysterical laugh over the question.

Wilder. *Wilder Saint.*

"Yeah, I think we knew of each other way back when." Quinn's voice emerged tight, and she stepped closer to me.

Coward that it made me, I was grateful.

"Nice to meet you." Dahlia gripped my hand and took a step back.

"Likewise."

Agony crashed through me at the sound of his voice, and I sucked in a breath when our eyes met. The same irises, looking brown instead of blue today, with his black jacket to offset them. The rest of his face was hard to see thanks to the bushy beard, and a hat low on his head gave me no real hints about his hair except that it hung on the long side, curling under the cap at the sides and back.

Just like it had in high school.

Just like it had before everything imploded.

I couldn't read him—he'd become opaque to me, though not expressionless. Not blank and bored looking, but so intense, so charged full of history and feeling, my breaths came shallow and quick.

He didn't speak. Didn't blink. But I did, unable to take it. My friends must've felt my mind clawing to move, because Quinn shoved me behind her right as Dahlia said, "Okay, well—" and yanked me across the street.

I followed, tripping after her and grateful for the tether of her hand in mine to guide me away. I could no more have voluntarily walked away from him than could I have flown, but this was better. No chance I could've spoken—gotten out anything of value.

"Are you okay?" Dahlia asked, taking me by both arms and inspecting me head to toe.

"Yeah." Even that sounded small and shaky, though.

"You look pale. You seem seriously freaked. Come inside the shop, and let's—"

"I swear I'm fine. I just—I didn't expect to see him. I figured I'd hear he was in town—that Sadie would know he was coming or something." I forced a smile to my face, knowing it wasn't convincing but unable to talk about this.

I hurt. My entire body hurt, and my brain was shutting down in shock and self-preservation, blocking out memories as fast as my heart could shoot them into my consciousness.

Quinn dipped her head to draw my eye. "What did he do to you? I want to tear into him for even looking at you, but I need more information."

I studied the ground, wondering if I could just tell them now. Finally explain it and they'd know. We'd been through enough; maybe they wouldn't hate me like I did myself. "It's not what he did to me. It's—"

Tears jumped to my eyes and tracked down my cheeks without warning—though the warning had been seeing Wilder live and in the flesh. I wiped at the wetness, composing myself and determined to get out before I lost it entirely. "It's what I did to him."

I left them behind, both likely shocked, and moved away at just shy of a run until I turned the corner and knew I couldn't see him if I looked back, relieved he therefore couldn't see me either. His unnerving gaze couldn't study me like I was some unexplained phenomenon, wholly unexpected.

Why did it stun me so much to see him? I hadn't expected it. I'd assumed I'd know he was here and could mentally prepare. I'd need to apologize and do whatever I could to atone for all I'd put him through. Because that's what it would be. A simple apology wouldn't cover what I'd done, and even if he'd moved on—he must've—I would never be at peace unless I did it.

But seeing him when I hadn't expected it? Encountering this towering, intense, stupidly appealing man and recognizing Wilder in that body? Behind those eyes?

Knowing that we'd come so close to an entirely different story—a family, with a child, and a life together.

Knowing that I'd destroyed it all?

It tore me apart, and for once, I let it rip me to shreds.

My friends let me be for a full eight hours before the messages started. Within a day, I'd dodged requests for lunch or coffee. By Friday of that week, I had no chance of evading them any longer, so I agreed to join them for lunch at Dahlia's shop the next day.

I'd cleaned my apartment. Called my sister, Eddie, even though it wasn't our normal day to talk. Read a few books and saw two of the ten a.m. specially priced movies. It'd been a while since I'd done that, and it'd been good for me to mentally escape.

"Get in here and tell us how you're doing."

Quinn literally pulled me in through the swinging door that led from the magical showroom area of the flower shop into the work room. Giant paint buckets filled with water and various flowers dotted the space, and Dahlia stood at the far table trimming rose stems.

"Yes. Please. And I'm so sorry. Warrick didn't even know he'd be here until I told him we'd seen him. He showed up at the ranch that night and—well, apparently, no one knew he'd be coming to town, not even Jane."

My heart ached at the mention of Jane Saint, a mother like I never had. It took years to understand her dynamic with her boys, but as I'd gotten older and had the benefit of hindsight, I'd recognized its simplicity. She loved them and wanted the best for them. She'd loved me, too, I'd realized, but I'd never even said goodbye.

I'd seen her but had been too much of a coward to talk to her beyond hellos. I could tell she wanted to say something, but she was leaving it up to me. And it *was* up to me, wasn't it? I'd run away from them—all of them.

Hence why I'd met Wyatt that first time through the RuralMatch app. I'd been so worried about trying to meet them and having the whole family refuse to see me, I'd sought out the oldest Saint brother in the weirdest possible way. Fortunately, he hadn't been bothered and had seemed to understand that I'd needed to approach him that way, even if it barely made sense to me. I'd come here with the goal to heal, and the Saint family played a huge part in that.

"Don't be sorry, Sadie. It's not your job to keep me informed of his plans. And I should've been more prepared. I think I figured if I saw him, it'd be around the holidays, and it snuck up on me." To put it mildly.

"Can you help us understand? I mean, I don't want to drag you through the mud, but can you help us with what had you looking like you'd seen a ghost and could barely keep down your lunch?"

Leave it to Quinn to paint a vivid and brutally straightforward picture. I inhaled slowly, glancing at each of them and summoning the courage I'd worked up over the last few days. I'd need far more than this to confront Wilder, whenever that happened. It would be good practice.

"We were best friends, then dated and were in love. There was a baby, but we lost it. We'd made all these plans, and then we changed them all when we heard. And then... it was all gone. And I couldn't—" I cleared my throat, willing that clog of emotion away. I'd actually done really well keeping it together for this recounting. "My parents flipped out when I got pregnant and decided we needed to move—away from Wilder's bad influence and away from a community who knew about their daughter's downfall."

"What the—"

"That's my wording, but that's what it amounts to. My dad had taken a job in Silverton when I was younger, but supposedly, they'd never wanted to stay as long as they had. So when I lost the baby, they pushed everything up and my mom, sister, and I left within two weeks. And Wilder..." His face, the dark hair and his navy eyes glittering with tears had burned themselves into my mind. "He let me go."

"He didn't fight for you? Or... wait. I'm confused. Did you want him to?" Dahlia asked.

I smiled, understanding the confusion. "He tried to, but I didn't let him. I was a mess. And the momentum from my parents was easier to ride, so I did. In my grief-twisted brain, I thought it was the right thing for both of us. For all of us."

Quiet had settled between us, each of them setting down the bouquets they'd been wrapping with ribbons as I spoke. What a powerful visual counterpoint to this story.

"And now?" Sadie asked, her voice tight with emotion.

I loved her for that—her compassion and empathy.

"For a long time, I've known what an awful choice that was. Not so much the choice to leave with my family but to refuse all contact—to never reach out and see how he was doing. And at some point soon, whenever he's back and settled in, I'm going to tell him how sorry I am that I hurt him, and how I wish I hadn't."

They each nodded or offered small smiles of encouragement, and I knew what they meant. They hoped I would do it, if only to bring myself some peace after so long. I hadn't planned on addressing this part of my past anytime soon, but I'd be a liar if I said I didn't need to. Seeing Wilder was nothing short of a shock, and yet here was the chance I'd been seeking. I'd never placed a limit on my time in Silverton, even if I knew it wasn't forever, but now, I could see that maybe this was part of why I'd come back.

I couldn't imagine he still felt wrapped up on the spool of those events so long ago like I did, but maybe it'd give him some peace, too.

And Wilder Saint deserved all the peace he could get.

CHAPTER TWO

Wilder

Four months later

Tossing the last of my stuff onto the back seat of my truck, I took a quick, calming breath. This next part wouldn't break me.

"We'll miss you, man. Not sure what Wave's going to do without you. Not sure what any of us are." West Wilcox, a fellow team leader, shook my hand and pulled me into a hug.

I held tight, then released him.

Up next came Rob Waverly—AKA Wave. "I'll miss you, you crusty grump. But I've always wanted to ski the Rockies."

"Come find me when you're free," I said, accepting his hug, too.

A small handful of my guys had walked out to the lot

with me, and though it would've been easier to leave by myself and drive off this compound without the memories and relationships cinching my throat tight, this would help. It'd keep me from tricking myself into living in the past in my head like I did sometimes.

"Will do. Stay well, Saint." Wave patted my shoulder, then pulled his phone to his ear as he stepped away, already onto the next thing.

He and my team would be rotating into their next recall cycle in just a few weeks. They'd be the number one response force for any emergent problems the US ran into. As part of the Exceptional Mission Unit, that could mean anything from a coup in a country of interest to US citizens kidnapped in some far reach, and many things in between.

But that was no longer my problem. Not that I wouldn't want to be aware of things, just in case, but life would be very different in Silverton.

My heart kicked at the thought, but I slipped the lid over that particular box and focused on the here and now.

"I've got two months, and then I'm invading. You better keep me abreast." Jaws, also known as Bruce Camden, gave me a little flash of his brows.

"Will do," I said, knowing I'd talk to him more than anyone else in the coming months. Years.

I shook more hands, returned a few more hugs, and then I left. The huge metal gates, topped with barbwire and foreboding, inched back to reveal the pine-lined road ahead. I nodded at the gate guards who flicked their fingers at me, knowing me well since they'd been here nearly as long as I had.

I'd had months to say my goodbyes, and I had used the time. I'd gone out to dinners and nights at the bar. I'd been given awards and recognition and, of course, I'd get my bonus once my terminal leave ran out in a few months. That was maybe the weirdest part—I would still technically be on active duty another three months, but I had enough leave saved up that I could move now, keep getting paid my active salary and housing allowance and already be gone.

Gone.

Not dead. Not depressed or damaged. Just... retiring. At thirty-seven.

But I was losing something. At some point in the twenty years of my career, part of my soul had crumbled into dust. Maybe it'd been the work itself, or maybe it'd been the way I'd lived—or, as my mother had once accused, *survived*.

The psychs had given me their briefings, and I'd promised to see someone when I got settled—not just because I was retiring, but because I'd put off dealing with a few things and it was time.

The time had come for me to pay the debts I owed myself, my family, and my community.

The drive to Silverton would take about thirty hours. As long as there weren't any bad spring storms, I'd make it through Wyoming and into Utah's mountains in about three days. I could try for two, but the brash insistence on doing everything in the most direct, flashy way had long since worn off for me. I might only be thirty-six—fine, nearly thirty-seven—but my soul felt old. Tired.

Or maybe I should say it *was* old, if trauma and grief could prematurely age a person's soul. I'd lost my father at six. I'd lost my child at seventeen, and then the love of my life days later. I'd lost my first friend at twenty-two, and a host of other friends and team mates since. In many ways, I'd even lost my brothers and mom, though that'd been due to my own stupidity.

Miles passed. I stayed the night in the same chain hotels

I always had when I traveled—not crappy roadside motels like one might think. Somewhere along the line, EMU operators had demanded quality when they traveled inside the US, and ever since, any travel meant an upscale name brand with comfortable rooms and free breakfast. I had enough points to travel for months at this point. Maybe my mom would want to go to Hawaii or something. Or Warrick could, not that he needed the help.

Did she even want to travel? Did he?

As though the thought had summoned him, my phone flashed with Warrick's name. In the past, I might've ignored it, shoved away the chance to connect with him. Not anymore. I couldn't keep doing that to him or myself.

"What's up?"

"Just checking in to see how the driving's going. You passed the glories of the Kansas prairie yet?"

A glance showed the Denver airport to my right "Just hit Denver."

"Nice. Making good progress. You pushing through?"

It was only ten in the morning. I'd have at least eight hours of solid daylight left, and the forecasts had been good. "Planning on it, unless I get hung up somewhere."

"Good. Cool. And are you staying... at the ranch?"

He sounded tentative. Treading lightly like he was EOD, and I was a bomb that might go off at any point. I wasn't volatile like that, and he knew it, but in my own way, I supposed I was the opposite. I didn't explode, I imploded. I sank into myself, into my head, and I disappeared. I hated this, him tiptoeing into his questions like any sudden move would spook me and send me back into silence.

But could I blame him?

I'd spent the last two decades keeping everyone I'd grown up loving at a distance. I'd seen him a handful of times, called him only before longer deployments, and had given him so little. I'd pushed him away without realizing, when he'd been just a kid and I'd just lost mine, and we'd never reconnected. Truth, *I'd* never reconnected. He had every reason to be wary of me.

"I lined up a place to rent for the first few months while I get settled."

A pause, then "Cool. Great. Let me know if I can help with anything."

It dawned on me he had a few rentals and maybe more since last we spoke. Maybe I should've used one of his, but I'd assumed they'd all be rented.

Actually, no. I'd trained myself not to rely on anyone but my team, so it hadn't occurred to me to call and ask him for his advice. I'd need to develop that skill—had to. I couldn't keep shutting him or Wyatt or my mom out once I moved back. I didn't want to, but hell if I knew how to do anything else.

"Will do."

"Good. And, uh, we still do family dinner on Sunday nights if there are no other conflicts. I think we'll be on for this weekend. If you want to join us. I'm sure Mom would be over the moon, and I'd like for you to meet Sadie."

"Sounds good."

I could practically hear his smile, that sunny personality and naturally grinning face giving him away.

"Okay, see you Sunday, then."

I hung up without another word and focused on the road. I wouldn't worry about meeting Warrick's girlfriend or what it'd be like to sit down with the family again. We'd done it once, Wyatt and Calla included, when I visited before. This was what I'd been telling myself I wanted for a while now. Might as well get started.

CHAPTER THREE

Sarah

Things were looking up. The last few months had been full of a building sense of destiny, which I recognized sounded hokey as all get out, but there it was. And when Sadie texted to say Wilder was coming back this week, that sensation only heightened.

I'd been barreling toward this moment for almost twenty years—the moment when I'd finally explain myself, my choices, and ask for his forgiveness. Based on the icy greeting months ago, I didn't anticipate I'd be walking up to him *this week* and doing the apologizing. But still. He'd be here.

My stomach flipped with the thought. *Wilder's coming home.* I'd come back a little over a year ago and now—there was that destiny again—he was coming, too. Maybe this would be the last step in my process—the last part of healing the old wounds that lingered in my ragged heart. I'd come with that purpose and just being here had helped. Making friends and repairing things with Wyatt to some degree had done me a world of good. Wilder's return would bring about a kind of closure I'd never dared hope for when I first started planning to move here.

But right this minute, I was heading to my new temp job. There'd been hardly any substitute teaching jobs longer than a day or two lately, and in my quest to figure out what I really wanted, I'd started branching out and using a temp agency to give me exposure to more jobs.

Apparently, this new company had someone lined up as their admin, but she'd gotten placed on bed rest this week due to pregnancy complications. I'd take her place until after her baby arrived—safely, I prayed—and then be on my way to whatever came next. At that point, the school year would be long since over, so it'd likely be another handful of temp jobs, plus I'd spend any downtime in the next few months trolling the school district's website for job openings for next year.

I pulled into the small parking lot just across from the mill building where Warrick had his gym and Sadie her big kitchen. Another bonus there—this job was right downtown and I could totally see my friends for lunches. When I subbed at the school, there was rarely time to meet them, plus the schools all sat slightly removed from downtown— walkable still, but not like this prime real estate.

The façade on my destination showed an old log cabin. I searched my mind for what the building used to be but had no memory of much over this way. For years, the mill buildings had been virtually defunct, and so other than the diner out on this side of town, there wasn't much of anything other than the neighborhood out this way.

It could use some landscaping to create curb appeal,

though to be fair, being only early April, spring hadn't sprung just yet. We'd had snow last week and likely would again before the end of the month, so any real gardening or other efforts would probably come while I worked here. I'd enjoy that. Maybe Aidan Wallace would do their work, or maybe I could assist them with some suggestions. Dahlia would help if I asked, and I could even get Aidan's ideas. He was too generous for his own good anyway.

I knocked on the door, then after realizing it wasn't a home but an office building, and it'd be kind of weird to just stand here until someone came to greet me, slowly opened it. A high-pitched creak coming from the hinge stopped me. *Yikes*. I mean, no offense to the owners, but they needed to do some work. I resumed pushing open the panel and sucked in a breath as the interior came into view. The outside and creaky door notwithstanding, this interior looked gorgeous. Like, what?

Record-scratch-style, my brain took in the space and couldn't quite reconcile the worn, aged exterior with the lush, stylish inside. A fireplace crackled with real wood in a stone hearth to my right, and on the left side of the room sat a polished wood desk. Two high-backed upholstered chairs in a medium gray tone with navy accent pillows faced the desk, and behind it rested a more office-looking chair that I assumed would be my post.

The walls had been done in a pleasing dove gray color, and very unlike the exposed log cabin wood planks I'd been expecting. The room felt remarkably warm and inviting— not at all dingy like the exterior.

Well, this is certainly going to be interesting! I didn't even know what the company did. Something in securities —maybe stock market stuff? Maybe investment banking and such. Not that I really knew what that meant, but I could do basic tasks and would learn whatever I needed to do the job well. The temp agency had thought my skills fit, so hopefully their assessment worked out to be true.

Still no movement or response, though it looked like a light was on in the back hallway. I decided to test out the chair and see how it felt. Good bounce when I gave it my weight. I leaned back and shoved against the backrest a few times, the chair rattling a little. Comfy enough.

"Chair to your liking?"

I froze. Time slowed and curved around me in a weird, dizzying motion.

That voice.

Low, gruff, and almost soft-spoken but with an unmistakably commanding edge. *That* was new, and it sent a flood of awareness through me.

"Um. Yes. I—what are you doing here?" I asked as I spun in the chair and lurched out of it, tripping on my own feet and stumbling into his space. I threw out my hands and backed up quickly before I actually touched him, all in view of his stern, changeless face.

"Okay?"

I nodded, eyes anywhere but on his until the last possible second. "Yep. Fine. Totally fine. Sorry. You were saying? Why are you here?"

"I own the place."

My heart sank, a stone in a pond, and settled in the mire deep inside me. "You—"

A crushing mix of panic, confusion, and a giddy, fluttery feeling smashed into me and stole my words. Heat rose to my cheeks—more heat, because let's be honest, I'd been blushing furiously since I'd heard his voice and tried to face-plant into him.

"Did you need something?"

His face appeared so solemn. He'd always been straight-faced, until he wasn't. Quiet, even withdrawn at times, until that one time I made him laugh and his smile had been... everything. I could still feel the triumph that blazed through me when I'd won that first smile at thirteen. But looking at him now, he'd grown all the more serious. In fact, he was actually, literally war-hardened, and several times over if the rumors were true.

"I, uh, I'm your new admin. I'm replacing Diane while she's on leave."

His eyes narrowed almost imperceptibly, like the lens of his focus zeroed in on me more thoroughly. And he said nothing.

"So, this is where I'll sit?"

His jaw flexed—I detected that familiar movement even through his thick beard. In fact, now that I registered more than just his presence and that same somber air, he looked downright wild, like a mountain man. Maybe he'd been on leave for a while now and had let his beard grow out after retiring from the Army. I could've sworn Sadie had said he'd just moved from North Carolina, where his base was.

Silence stretched long and somehow loud in my ears.

So... apparently, that tendency to not speak hadn't changed in the last twenty years. "If you'd rather I come back another day, I can go."

Though I'd been really planning on a paycheck starting today, so that was about as far from ideal as I could muster, and paired with this being his business? Just so super.

"No."

Horror struck then. "Or, um, you can speak with the agency and have someone else come if you don't feel—"

"You can stay."

Relief rushed in but not enough to cover the nerves

pulsing through me. We stood all of three feet apart. Nineteen years apart with no contact, nothing, and here we stood. By ourselves.

It would've been the perfect moment to get it all out there, wouldn't it? Especially if I'd be working here and seeing him daily, I should've taken the moment and run with it. Explained myself and apologized. Done it all *right now*.

But before I could open my mouth, he spoke again.

"Instructional packet's on the desk. I've got to get to an appointment but will be back before lunch."

With a nod toward said packet, he turned and left. Just like that. No farewell or *see you after my meeting* or *let me know if you have questions*. Nothing.

A minute or two later, while I still stood in that same spot like an idiot, I heard a door click shut and realized there must be a back exit. He'd literally just left without another word. And though I wasn't exactly surprised, I couldn't help the hurt that sliced through me. I had no right to it—absolutely no right to expect him to be nice or excited to see me or catch up. I'd been horrible to him, and we had garbage cans full of baggage.

But it wasn't until this moment, left alone in the fancy front office of what I now knew was his business, that I realized how much I'd hoped maybe the passage of time had done something for us. Anything at all.

CHAPTER FOUR

Wilder

Just like every night for the last three days since she'd shown up in my office, Sarah came to me in my dreams and nightmares. Tonight was no exception, though which tone it took remained to be seen.

In this dream as in real life, she looked far better than the last time I'd seen her. Four months ago and white as the snow around her, she'd looked nothing short of horrified to see me.

Good for a man's ego, that. Particularly when she'd been the one to leave me. But who's counting?

"Hello." I wouldn't say her name. I wasn't prepared for this encounter, even in my dreams.

She tucked a long hank of hair behind one delicate ear. "I'm sorry. Ugh. Hi. Hello. Can I come in?"

This was usually where things went one of two ways. One, I played along like I had in real life, not letting on that her proximity made my spine turn to steel and the ache in my right quad intensify. Or two, I said something awful. Hurled, more like.

That was the nightmare version, but truth be told, either way, I woke up in bad shape. Yelling at her never felt satisfying, especially since she ended up sobbing, and it felt too much like it had when we were younger and she was crying so hard she couldn't breathe. And the welcoming version chafed because it was how I did it in real life, but in the dream, my heartbeat amplified in my ears. Instead of being slow to speak, I could hardly get a word out, and I couldn't find a way out of it. However long it lasted felt like days or weeks, but the scene only went so far as the two of us barely speaking around the giant load of history between us.

I sat up and scrubbed the image from my eyes, relieved that at least in this dream, Wilder wasn't yelling at a defenseless woman. I'd spoken with Dr. Corrigan about Sarah—had found it almost easier than the other crap I needed to deal with, and she'd been front and center on my mind when I walked into that second appointment on her first day of work.

But then, I'd had all these damned dreams. What was the point of them? To warn me away from screaming at her? There existed no scenario in which I'd do that—none. Maybe the point was to simply allow my brain to work out the situation since I'd never imagined her coming to work for me.

Last I'd checked, she had teaching certifications. I'd chosen not to look into her life in a long time, but years ago, in a fit of desperation just after I'd joined the unit, I'd checked in. She'd been teaching middle school for two years at the time, and it'd made my heart twist with a pleasure-pain I'd had to focus to breathe through. Her parents had always wanted her to be a teacher, and I knew she'd be good at it.

So Sarah James showing up as the long-term temp at Saint Securities? Not a scenario I'd planned for. Until I'd seen her in December, not an eventuality that had even occurred to me as possible—not even me *seeing* her, let alone working with her.

But did I turn her away? Did I pretend I didn't need her, or find an excuse to request someone else from the temp agency knowing having her anywhere nearby would be a distraction I did not need?

No. Because I might've been a fairly intelligent man about most things, but Sarah James wasn't one of them. She was a weakness I'd purged a long time ago, and yet here I was again, working my way through the morning with her on my mind like a splinter in my palm.

I couldn't ignore her forever. She'd finish the trainings sometime today, if I had to guess, and then we'd be interacting a bit more. Why couldn't Bruce be here already? Then I could shove him at her and make him deal with all of this.

A couple more months. He couldn't leave Bragg yet, even if his time was up, because of Kiley. So for now, it was on me.

"You ever gonna come work out with me?" Warrick shouted as I jogged past his gym and a line of people flipping giant tires out front.

I tossed two fingers up in a greeting but kept going. I'd join him eventually. The gym was virtually next door to the office, though our building was set away from almost everything in an ideally located spot that had a view on all sides. Exactly what I'd needed.

I couldn't hear what Warrick said, but I'd see him this weekend for family dinner again. I'd gone last weekend, met his girlfriend, hugged him and Mom both, and got an update on Wyatt. I'd talked to my older brother more recently, if only because I'd missed his wedding to Calla, his pregnant wife. And if I hadn't known I was changing before, the genuine regret I felt to miss his day would've made it clear.

I'd missed a lot over the last almost twenty years. One of the most painful was Grandma Tilda's funeral, which happened while I was deployed and entirely out of contact. I didn't hear about it until days after.

And here was one more thing. But Wyatt hadn't pushed or done anything other than say he couldn't wait for me to spend more time with Calla, and he hoped I'd stay safe and get home soon.

He'd meant it. And his sincerity had burned the last threads of reluctance to return away. That hesitation was fear talking, and I'd promised myself, and much more recently, my therapist, that I'd do what I could to stop making decisions from that default self-protecting posture.

Ten minutes after my departure from home and at a downright glacial pace thanks to the altitude, I arrived at the back door to the office. Relieved she wouldn't be sitting at the desk, perfect posture and shiny blond hair glinting in the overhead lights, I unlocked the front door and turned right as it swung open.

"Oh, hi, Wilder."

My stomach twisted. I raised a hand but didn't look back. I had no need to see her to know she'd be beautiful today, just like she had been every day of her life. Having her working here was bad enough—I didn't need to look at her on top of it. If I did, I'd gather up more details about her, packing them away like a greedy squirrel, always aware that the hunger of a winter bereft of her might be just around the corner. Though to be accurate, that squirrel would also need a fair amount of self-loathing as he collected those nuts.

"I should finish up my last online training today. After that, I might need you to..."

I stopped, signaling I was listening without making any move to face her. When she didn't take the cue, I reluctantly turned, careful to keep my eyes a few feet to her left. I notched my chin up and feigned focus on the fireplace, moving there to busy myself with lighting it rather than risk my gaze jumping the tracks.

"Uh, well, I guess I'm not totally sure what I'll be doing? Day to day? So I'm hoping you can give me some guidance. I don't want to waste your time."

"Okay." The kindling I'd wedged into the base between logs fizzed as the fire caught, and I pushed off my knee and set the lighter back up on the mantel. "Let me know."

And then, I bugged out back to my office, where I only managed another twenty minutes before mumbling something about an errand and escaping out the back door.

The spring air was crisp, and I had the fleeting wish I'd brought my jacket, but I wasn't about to go back in there to get it. *Crap*, this was not a good start. I'd created this business to provide myself and my friends a future, but also as a place I could... be. Do work, stay focused on something, but feel it was a kind of sanctuary. My home would be that, eventually, but the build wouldn't start for another month at least due to weather delays.

Thanks to this setup, work was not a relaxing place to be.

I didn't hold grudges. I understood why Sarah had done

what she did—why she'd had to leave. I hoped she understood why I let her go. But whatever the case, however much water under the bridge it all was now? I didn't want to sit down in the middle of it. And having her right there, *right* there, wasn't going to work for much longer.

Our original hire, Diane, was probably a nice lady. She'd come highly recommended by Julian Grenier, so we'd hired her after a phone interview and thorough background check. The temp agency who'd filled the position hadn't given me a name, only said that their candidate fit all the requirements—clear background checks, etc. If I'd caught that it was Sarah before she'd showed up, I would've nixed it. I wouldn't have allowed this proximity to keep pressing on a bone-deep bruise.

But once I saw her, all nervous and eager, however much I hated to admit it, I couldn't send her away.

I'd already requested and reviewed her background checks. Having a small history of her life had proved irresistible, and I'd done it. I'd felt mildly ill the entire time I read through the information, though I couldn't have said why.

Or maybe inside that box I kept tightly sealed shut, I did know. Reviewing that list of moments in her life drilled home how much of it I'd missed. No chance of escaping that that'd been *her* choice. Left to me, we would've spent every bit of it together, but she'd left and then *stayed gone.* Not just physically. She never once called, wrote, or tried to get in touch.

I'd accepted that years ago. Swallowed the bitter pill that was her clean break from me. And yet, being shoved into a room with her, close enough to see the scar at her hairline or freckles on her cheeks and chest, proved agonizing. Like all along, I'd been anaesthetized by time and distance and just now, I was blinking awake, bleary and disoriented, the pain-dulling medicine of artificial sleep receding with alarming rapidity.

By the looks of it, she was determined to stay and finish out her temp contract. The first sign? The three days of online training were pure drudgery. Important in some ways—trainings on basic PPI protection and confidentiality, a few short certifications she'd need to access and understand some of our programs—she'd sailed through them in record time if she really was about to finish.

For now, I'd check out the land I'd purchased just behind the building, where eventually we'd offer self-defense trainings and other education, if things went well. I'd get some fresh air, vitamin D, and I wouldn't feel that crawling sensation I sometimes did when I could feel her on the other side of my office door.

CHAPTER FIVE

Sarah

Wilder came back just as I was packing up to leave for lunch. I would've had to stay put if he hadn't shown, because I didn't know if we closed for lunch if he was out and I needed my break.

"Thanks for coming back before my lunch hour. I won't always leave to get something, but I have to run to the bank and—"

"No problem."

"Oh. Great. Well... see you in a bit."

Before I reached the front door, he spoke again. Not a bit louder than he had before, despite my being farther from him.

"When you're back, I've got a few things for you to review and sign."

I smiled. "Sure. I'll be back soon."

Mercifully, I managed not to smile too widely or send

him a dippy *I clearly don't know what to do with myself* wave. I did, however, let myself marvel at the length of that sentence—at least three times longer than anything else he'd said to me since years ago.

Despite the silly nature of those thoughts, the memories of how close we'd been, how he did talk to me back then, sent a pang of longing and regret through me so hard, my hand rose to my chest and pressed over the ache. I'd hardly spent time with him, and yet he was the same. Different and older, of course, but there was that steadiness, the surety in how he carried himself and the calm, insistent way he spoke when he reluctantly did so. It all felt so awfully familiar.

I blew out a breath, grounding myself into the spring air and away from thoughts of Wilder. They'd do nothing for me other than ratchet up the nerves I already had to beat back daily just sharing a building with him, let alone fully registering how insane it was that Wilder Saint, the man I had loved and nearly spent my life with, was now my boss.

My cheeks burned. I didn't like to dwell on how I'd gotten to this place—emotionally, vocationally, whatever else. But times like this, I cursed myself for the choices I'd made that'd led me to lose myself. I'd taught for years and had never felt truly connected with the work, but now, it felt almost wrong, like a relic from a past life. My parents had wanted that for me, and I'd had no idea what else I'd do, so I'd walked that path without even questioning it.

Until the last few years. I'd taught consistently for the insurance and paycheck until I could move, and I'd found some long-term substitute positions here and there, but in-between, I'd taken any odd job I could in an attempt to unearth what *else* there could be.

After running to the bank and then pacing in circles

outside the building as I ate my sandwich, I reentered after twenty-five minutes.

"You're early."

Wilder's voice carried down the hallway from his open door and caused goosebumps to rise on my arms. The texture and depth of the luscious sound threatened to do that to me whenever I heard it, and my body had apparently missed the memo that we needed to keep my physical response to him under wraps. After setting my purse in the desk drawer, I inched down the hall, unsure whether I should actually respond.

"Uh, yeah. Errand went faster than I expected," I said, inwardly cringing at the overly cheery tone of my voice. I couldn't seem to find a normal, well-regulated mode of speech with him. But then, how did one talk to a man like Wilder? Someone who'd done and seen more than I could imagine, and yet also someone I'd loved to the point of near madness, but who I'd walked away from.

He looked up from a sleek laptop and lifted his chin in a gesture I could've sworn meant come in. But I wasn't about to step into his office without being sure. "Um, should I...?"

"Come in. We'll do the paperwork."

"Okay," I said, relieved to have clear instructions and something to do with myself instead of trying not to stare at him. Because really, he was just... *guh*. He had this brawny, built look, but in a very specific way. Very different from either of his brothers, in fact. Where Wyatt was strong and Warrick was ridiculously fit, Wilder had always been as strong as he *needed* to be. And based on the way his biceps stretched at his T-shirt sleeves, he'd had need of a great deal of strength.

The printer behind him screeched to life and spit out page after page as he clicked and tapped on his trackpad. I wondered if maybe he didn't realize I'd done all the employment paperwork with the temp agency already.

"Francine went over the basics. You should have copies of those."

Without lifting his head, his eyes flicked up to me, then back down to his screen. "I do. These are NDAs and a few other things."

I swallowed. "Non-disclosure agreements?"

He nodded, tapped, tapped, tapped, then looked up. "Yes. We'll be dealing with high-profile clientele. Several people are already on our rosters for the next few months for various security installments and events, and in no scenario would we share any information about them or even the fact that they are our clients. You sign a blanket NDA with us, Saint Securities, in order to avoid having to sign one with each client." He scraped a hand through his long-ish hair and then grumbled, "And even then, you'll end up signing them left and right."

"Oh. Okay. That makes sense." Something niggled at me. It was stupid, and I knew it was stupid, but I had to ask. "It's all... legal. Right?"

I knew that look—that incredulous eyebrow raising just a flash before lowering to his impervious mask. "Of course."

"Okay. Good. I mean, of course. I just don't know anything about this world, sorry."

His brows tipped inward for a second but smoothed again. "No apology needed. You'll learn. And for now, take these, feel free to have a lawyer review them if you like—I can recommend any of the Wallaces."

My heart rate picked up. "That's intense. But okay. Sure."

He eyed me for a beat, then another. His gaze hung there, locked to mine for a moment too long. If it'd been someone else, I would've found myself looking away in discomfort, but I couldn't break from him for anything.

The air shifted somehow, charged with an energy generated from this visual connection between us. My whole body tensed, waiting for whatever came next.

"You can go early today."

Startled out of the electric moment, I sucked in a breath. "Uh, no, that's okay. I'm happy to stay—"

"I'm closing up early. You'll need to leave." He shut his laptop, slipped it into a desk drawer, and stood.

"I'll grab my stuff. Sorry, I didn't realize—"

"I picked up a meeting. It'll be like this—a little unpredictable. But you'll be fine." His eyes flicked to me, then jumped away. "You'll be paid the whole day anyway. Next week, after you've finished training, I'll have you keep the office open."

He didn't look at me for any of that last bit, so I moved to his door. The part about still getting paid had made shame paint my cheeks bright red because the comment was so pointed—like he knew I needed the money. But for someone whose work involved a lot of observation skills, he clearly knew that. I wasn't destitute, but moving from job to job required me to pay attention, and I wasn't about to *choose* to get a smaller paycheck. "Sounds good. I'll... get these to you first thing tomorrow."

"Good. We can't do much until you do."

An edge in his voice had me speaking up before I left his office. "I really could do it today if—"

"It's fine."

My cheeks flamed anew at the words flung over his shoulder as he approached the exit of his office. "Okay. Sorry."

I felt him pause, then take a breath. "Don't apologize."

"Right. Sorr—right."

He nodded, like my catching the mistake had been the right thing, and then he turned back. "I'll lock up after you."

And that was my cue to get out. I hustled forward, grabbing my purse and water bottle and getting gone. My heart and mind rioted as I walk-jogged toward home, working on overdrive to understand what the heck the dynamic between us was. Me embarrassed and him curt, cutting me off when I talked... how was this going to work?

I'd apologize tomorrow. First thing. No time to lose, as soon as I got in, I'd do it, and maybe that would help. Maybe that'd make all this bearable.

Sarah

More nerves. More freaking nerves. I wasn't proud to admit it, but there it was. And the admission? I'd spent extra time getting ready. I'd done so every day after that first one when I realized I'd be working at Wilder's business, not just some random temp job. I both understood this impulse and found it annoying, because what did I expect?

Not that I would've looked like a slob at any other job, but did some part of me expect Wilder to fall to his knees and forgive me and ask for my hand in marriage if I got my eyeliner just right?

Well, no. Maybe not *that*. But I had a good imagination, and I'd also had a long time to concoct scenarios where we repaired the damage done and found a way forward, and... a girl could dream, couldn't she? Granted, until now, those dreams had been harmless. They didn't interfere with my ability to concentrate or even walk without tripping.

Now?

Not so much.

I couldn't even tell how the time passed last night. After reading the contracts as best I could, I understood enough to believe I was safe signing them without consulting a lawyer. Though fairly certain the Wallaces would take a look for a minimal fee, I didn't have that kind of budgetary wiggle room and didn't think I could just waltz in there asking for a consult anyway. Quinn had mentioned John Wallace still did some work for her even though he wasn't practicing law full time anymore now that the brewery took up most of his life, but I didn't want to impose. It'd be fine. The gist? Don't blab about the clients. I could do that.

And today, as I walked to work in black pumps that'd lasted me longer than I ever imagined when I bought them a few years back, a pencil skirt, and a white blouse tucked in with a little black blazer over top, I felt kind of... good. Like, put together, professional, on top of it. And maybe it should embarrass me how infrequently I felt put together, but between general failure, working as a sub at schools where I didn't dress this nicely, and so far, moving through the time at Saint Securities as though it all happened underwater, I had yet to feel truly confident.

But today, I had a file with signed documents to hand over to Wilder, and I'd rehearsed an apology—brief, accurate, sincere—that I would not fail to deliver. Before anything else happened.

As I rounded the corner and saw the lot, more than one car sat there. *Odd.* Normally, Wilder and I both walked. Or, rather, I walked and Wilder jogged the two miles from his house. *Jogged* them. And he still strolled in smelling like soap and clean, fresh air and not of sweat and dirty man. *Not that I'd been smelling him.*

I shook off all those thoughts because that would not be a wise line of thinking and moved to open the door. Upon entering, I could hear voices down the hallway, either from Wilder's office or the small conference room that sat across from it.

My pulse spiked. Was I late? The clock read eight o'clock on the dot as I dropped my purse in the drawer and ran on my toes to the door and peeked in. With his body positioned facing the door, Wilder's eyes landed on me before I even leaned in all the way, as though he'd heard me coming.

He notched his chin up in that short, concise movement, and the two people sitting across from him glanced back toward me.

"Sarah. I hadn't realized you were working here," Julian Grenier said with no hint of confusion, though he likely felt some. Considering his fiancée was one of my best friends, he probably expected to know I was working here.

But thus far, I'd only sent a message to the group with Dahlia, Calla, Sadie, and Quinn that said, *"Interesting new job situation. Can't wait to tell you about it this weekend."* Maybe by then, I would have worked out how exactly I felt about all this—and the apology would be behind me.

"Sarah is temping for us while Diane is on medical leave." Inevitably, Wilder's explanation was the most minimal it could be.

"Okay. Well. Meet my friend Juliet Christensen," Julian said, gesturing to the absolutely stunning woman next to him.

Said woman rose, a giant smile on her face, and cupped my hand in both of her manicured, warm ones as she shook it. "It's so lovely to meet you, Sarah. You're a friend of Quinn's?"

My vocal cords finally kicked in. "Yes. She's one of my favorites, for sure."

Juliet beamed again. "Understandably. And I suppose you're at least a little familiar with my friend Julian here?"

Charmed by the warmth and general splendor of her, I nodded. "Of course. Plus, he knows if he does anything to hurt Quinn, I'll make him a eunuch, so we're good."

Juliet's laugh bubbled up, Julian nodded and I thought I detected a hidden smile between those pressed lips, and Wilder? Wilder just watched, taking every bit of this in, no doubt drawing a million conclusions about all of us. He'd always been exceptionally observant, but even silly little civilian ignoramus me could sense he'd honed those skills in his twenty-year military career.

"I approve," Juliet said with a wink and then returned to her seat and gestured around the table. "Please, join us."

There were three empty seats—two at either end of the table, and one next to Wilder on his side. It felt too weird to opt into sitting at the head of the table, though obviously, it wouldn't be because I thought I was heading things up, but this led me to sit next to Wilder. I couldn't sense whether he approved or not, but I hoped it was okay I'd stayed.

In case this mattered, and I suspected anything involving Julian probably did, I slipped the folder of signed paperwork to Wilder and caught his eye. He nodded almost imperceptibly and then focused back on Julian. There shouldn't have been a swelling of satisfaction behind my ribs, but there it came anyway. Apparently, all it took was his basic acknowledgement of my existence and the sun came out.

"I'm only in town for another week, but Maddie is planning to stay awhile once she arrives. She asked me to set things up since I know Julian and could vouch that anything he's involved with would be quality and confidential."

"Completely," Wilder assured her.

"She'll be arriving in about three weeks, and I'd like to make sure her home is fully outfitted with a good system. She's had some... issues lately."

Juliet's absolutely stunning face with delicate features and piercing blue eyes didn't falter, but somehow, I sensed her unease. Whether due to discussing such things or in concern for her friend, I couldn't tell.

"And those are..." Wilder started.

"I can't tell you that. You'll need to meet with her when she arrives. She's working nonstop and I know you won't be able to pin her down until she's here."

"I can't properly outfit her if I don't know what problems she's having."

Juliet eyed him, an intensity coming from her I wouldn't have expected, before she spoke. "I can't give you details, but she'll need in-person help, as well."

"Good. That's a start. Her assistant already scheduled the meet when she gets here."

Juliet folded her hands on the table. "Good."

Julian stood and buttoned his gray suit jacket. "Anything else you need?"

I looked around, wondering who he was speaking to and startled to realize it was Wilder. But of course it was—this was his business. Still, having Julian solicit a response from Wilder felt like worlds colliding. The billionaire was usually the man in charge everywhere.

My bearded boss—as though I'd ever think of him that way—only said, "All good."

Julian turned to leave, and Juliet slipped out of her seat.

I took that as my sign to follow them to the front and at least pretend to be a proper administrative person by being hospitable.

"If you need anything while you're in town, just let me know. Or, I mean, tell Julian to get ahold of me—whatever works," I offered Juliet, knowing she wouldn't take me up on it.

"Of course. I'm afraid I'm mostly up at the spa this week, but I'm hoping to come back in June while Maddie's still here. Maybe we can get lunch then?"

A thrill shot through me, right on the heels of disbelief. Billionaire heiress and world-renowned philanthropist Juliet Christensen wanted to have lunch with me? I would've laughed if I hadn't recently become friends with Callaway Rice AKA Miss Mayhem and even kind of, at least in a way, Julian.

"Uh, yeah, of course. I'm pretty much always here." Then I did a weird side bend and jazz hands because I knew how to keep things cool.

She laughed lightly, then exited out the front. Julian had left without a farewell, which I knew was more a symptom of his own mind being occupied with his to-do list so he could wrap up and get back to Quinn and Cara after work than a sign of him being rude.

I sank down in my seat, a weird fizzy mix of disbelief and starstruck awe floating through my veins.

"You can't do that."

My spine straightened and I turned in the chair to find Wilder leaning against the wall, arms crossed.

"Do what?"

"You can't offer for people to contact you. You can't be trying to make friends with the clients. It's not appropriate."

I blinked, embarrassment searing through my chest. "I wasn't trying to *make friends*. I was just being nice."

He tipped his head to the side. "Well. Don't."

I felt my eyes go wide but had no ability to tame my response. "Are you insinuating I'm trying to ingratiate myself with your client? Or... I honestly don't even know if she is your client, but you should know, I'm not trying to do that. I wouldn't. I hope you know that."

He nodded fully this time, and wow, that must've taken a great deal of effort for a man who'd thus far only deigned to slightly incline his head in one direction or another when ordering me around.

"Whatever it is, don't do it again."

My jaw flexed and I wondered if it would be too far in the opposite direction of my desire to mend fences and apologize to him if I kicked him in the nuts.

"Yes, sir."

His eyes dulled and he glared at me before turning and saying over his shoulder, "My office in ten minutes."

And even though we were the only ones in the building, I looked around for someone to commiserate with. Someone to help me figure him out. Maybe someone to reassure me that the impending meeting wasn't about to be Wilder firing me for insubordination or... or... trying to be friends with a client.

Disbelief flashed through me before I slumped down in my chair and searched my mind for calm—for that placid, can-do smile I'd worn so often in my life. I wanted this job, and I'd keep it, if I could. I needed to fill the gap of the next few weeks or months, and having something consistent instead of odd jobs through the agency was preferable. The tourist season wouldn't really start until mid-June and even then, it was a shadow compared to winter, so my chances for finding seasonal work were limited. And I couldn't take anything full time that wasn't short-term because I hadn't given up on finding a teaching spot.

Right? I hadn't, had I?

I stared unseeingly at my computer screen while my thoughts chased themselves in circles over whether or not I really was still holding out for a teaching position. My parents had steered me toward teaching since I could remember—my mom and grandmother had both been educators. Two of my cousins were. It was a noble, wonderful profession.

Discovering I didn't love the reality of teaching had gutted me, but I'd hoped it'd been a matter of circumstance. Maybe a change of scene coming back to Silverton would help, I'd thought. Plus, what else would I even do?

If I gave up on teaching now, I'd be starting over. And I essentially was starting at the bottom of the ladder since I'd only managed to sub on and off for a few months at a time since moving here. I had a long way to climb before any kind of retirement or even basic seniority and higher pay would kick in.

I didn't want to feel stuck with teaching as my only option, hence the exploration and even my job in this place. Some of that came from necessity and not having enough work as a sub to keep me living comfortably, but a lot of it stemmed from the need to know I could do something else. I'd slipped into place as an admin for three different offices over the last year, and beyond other kinds of teaching, administration was really all I was qualified to do. I didn't mind it, and compared to subbing, temping as an office admin and not facing down students bent on getting as much leeway as they could out of their unsuspecting sub felt like a cake walk. All of that said, there was the *but.*

I'd taught a lot, and I'd made it known I wanted a full-time position, *but* if I took one, that'd keep me here. And having Wilder back made it feel like something was coming to a close. It had to be my time in Silverton, didn't it? I'd never planned to set down roots, only waiting for some nebulous sense of closure. And now, here came closure incarnate.

If I abandoned the teaching route when all this wrapped up, I'd be wandering in yet another part of my life.

Thinking about that had literally never been a productive line of thought, so I refocused on the matter at hand. For now, I needed to keep my mind on this job. Maybe that meant apologizing sooner than later—before he could even get to the firing part, so at least I wouldn't have to do it after and seem like I was begging.

I didn't like it, but I'd resolved to do the thing today and I wasn't going to let his jerky assumptions about my being nice to Juliet Christensen sway me. And I definitely wasn't going to let it come after he reprimanded me again.

My heart pounded in my chest, the caffeine I'd had through my morning coffee burned to a smoky crisp by the adrenaline pumping through me and making me shudder. I could do this. I would do it. If he was going to fire me, I'd at least have my say and get that over and done with. Then I'd move on.

Hopefully just back here at my desk and not to the temp agency with my tail between my legs after my ex-boyfriend—and still the object of my every desire despite the frigid tension between us—fired me.

____

CHAPTER SEVEN

Wilder

Sarah paused outside my door.

"Have a seat." As usual, I didn't look up.

"I really need to say something before this—whatever this is—happens."

My eyes snapped up to meet hers and a feeling I flatly ignored punched through me. "Go ahead."

She swallowed and inhaled slowly before quickly sitting across from me and launching in. "I apologize for my inappropriate behavior. Juliet is about my age, or close, and I'm used to a more congenial atmosphere in terms of work colleagues and relationships. I understand that I need to create better boundaries, and I can assure you it won't happen again. I—"

"This isn't necessary. You don't—"

"Please let me finish. Okay?"

Her words cut through the air, and silence filled the gap. She hadn't asserted herself like that before—honestly ever before, except when we said goodbye, when she'd left. It wasn't her—or hadn't been. But I didn't know her anymore, so maybe it was now. Either way, I nodded for her to proceed and watched her swallow and straighten in her seat. She was nervous, or maybe *anxious*.

"I realize this setting is not where this should happen, but I can't wait anymore, so I need you to just... hear me. For a minute."

She embodied determination, though her jaw flexed where she clenched her teeth, and her fingers twisted together in her lap. That scar at her hairline was barely visible from here, and yet, I had the vicious need to know how it'd happened, or maybe that was the impulse to avoid what was coming.

A suspicion notched in my gut, and my stomach clenched against it. I nodded again, knowing I couldn't say anything to stop her, especially not without sounding unraveled.

"I'm sorry."

Her big blue eyes doubled in size as she attempted to impress these words into me. She'd already said them, but the lower, steady tone, the way she pressed her hands into the desk in front of her, the way she didn't break eye contact —this was different.

"I know I hurt you when—when we were younger. And I wish I could explain the full extent of how much I regret what happened." She paused here, almost like she expected me to interrupt.

I wouldn't. I *couldn't*. For as many intense situations as I'd been through, I'd never considered what my heart would be doing inside my chest if we had this conversation. I'd imagined it a thousand times in the beginning—her calling, her showing up at my basic training graduation, her being there when I landed after my first deployment. I'd fantasized about letters she'd write, some of them starting out exactly like this. I went through a nasty, resentful phase where all I wanted was for her to reach out so I could reject her and make her feel a sliver of the misery I'd felt and that'd crept up on me whenever I turned my back to it.

It'd been years and years since I'd had any such thoughts, and I'd forbidden my mind to go to any of those old familiar places in the last week since seeing her, or the months since our first encounter. Whatever efforts I consciously made, though, the dreams had done the imagining and fantasizing and horrifying for me.

When she saw I wouldn't be saying anything, she continued.

"I never wanted to hurt you more than you were already hurting. But I was—" A breath gusted out of her. "I was shattered."

Our gazes held, and I could see her as though we'd been transported right back to that moment. Her small body frail from exhaustion and lack of sleep. From grief. The dark circles and grayish pallor to her skin. I'd dreamed of that, too, and those had been so far from fantasies.

"I knew that," I scraped out, needing her to know she wasn't alone in traversing into those memories. No, she'd dragged me there with her. Here in my office. My would-be sanctuary.

She dipped her chin, acknowledging, then cleared her throat.

"I was in survival mode. My parents—" She shook her

head at herself. "No, I don't want to talk about them. I just want you to know that I'm truly, deeply sorry. And I'm sorry for all the years that I've let go by without saying exactly that."

Inhaling slowly, I crushed the rioting slosh of emotions in my gut, my heart, my mind. Enough to unpack from the day already, and I wouldn't do it here, in front of her. "Thank you. But there was no need."

I wouldn't reach for her. I wouldn't allow myself to touch her even though my body cried out for it as though it was right. We'd had a closeness, an intimacy, that was truly unique but that didn't exist between us now.

She'd run away from it, and then she'd destroyed it entirely by staying gone.

"You don't need to thank me. Like I said, it's long overdue."

"And like I said, thank you. You did what you needed to do."

Even in the midst of feeling like I'd lost everything I'd ever loved, part of me had understood that. I'd seen the shattered look of her, and I'd known it wasn't about *me*. I'd wished I could be the one to be there as she put herself back together a thousand times, and it'd hurt like hell not to be—to fear I never would be.

It was later, when the silence from her persisted across weeks and months and then years, that it truly sank in. She was done with me and wasn't ever going to look back. We would never reconcile when she healed.

"Well, thank *you*. For listening and letting me say what I needed to." Her shoulders sank when she let out a big breath—relieved or just out of energy, I couldn't tell.

Every bit of my mind wanted to follow this trail—to talk a bit more, despite never wanting to talk, to understand, to hear what happened to her after she left. I wouldn't. I folded up all the questions and curiosity and the heap of feelings and shoved them into the little compartment in my head where such things went and padlocked it shut.

"Of course. If you're finished, I'd like to debrief you on the meeting we just had and talk through the daily responsibilities in more detail." Anything to distract from the tremor in my hands, a physical manifestation of the unsettling reality of her talking about all the things behind us.

Her blink was the only thing that told me my hard right turn of a topic change had come in completely unexpected. Otherwise, her face stayed calm, eyes clear, and I wouldn't have known anything was amiss except for that blink and the still-pink tinge to her cheeks.

"Okay. So I'm not fired?"

Maybe I'd sunken farther into myself than I'd realized and missed something, though I'd been fighting that very impulse. That said, I had no idea what she meant. "Why would you be fired?"

"Because of the thing with Juliet—I mean, Ms. Christensen?"

Ah. I'd been too harsh with her. She'd always been sweet and sensitive, a kind of foil to my brusque, quiet directness. Time may have passed, but apparently, she'd somehow held onto that part of herself.

I had to get a handle on myself with this woman. "No. And I'm sorry for making you think that was the case."

She relaxed into her chair a bit more. "Oh. Great."

I launched into an explanation of her daily duties— opening the doors if I hadn't already, starting coffee if the same, checking voicemail and a host of other small tasks, and then, account management.

"Is any of this beyond what you believe you're capable

of?" I asked after a laundry list of things I'd need her help with. Most would've fallen to Diane, but some would come off her plate as I hired more staff. I could only do that if we developed a decent clientele list immediately.

"I don't think so. I may need help with the formats for how you want things." She scratched out a few notes on a little pad she'd tucked into the pocket of her skirt.

I gritted my teeth against the pleasure that gave me—the fact that she took notes. I couldn't have explained it for any amount of money. It hit me just right, like so many things about her did, and I tallied it under *things that don't matter.* Because no small amount of delights would erase our past. One heartfelt but thin apology later, there still gaped twenty years and a million miles between us.

"Just ask."

"Will do."

"First up, I'll need to go to the Reynolds home and see where I need to augment the existing system."

Grenier had mentioned what their building contractors tended to install in the neighborhood he'd developed, but that was no guarantee she or whoever had actually built the home had taken the suggestions. One would hope these people would plan to secure their multi-million-dollar homes, but sometimes, people thought of Silverton as a safe haven from the real world. While I approved of that mindset on one hand, the town wasn't without its issues. The continued influx of money and high-profile residents would only increase the need for security.

"Okay. That's Juliet's friend?"

I wouldn't smile or find that adorable. I would not. I needed only to recall the wreckage that was my life for the years following the loss of our child, then the loss of her, and I could maintain a poker face through any inquisition.

"Yes. Madeline Reynolds is our first big client. I've taken over managing Grenier's team and will hope to hire away a few people, but he's been here long enough that he's got everything in place already. She's new, staying for long enough, and as you heard, has some kind of existing security issue we'll need to address." I'd debated pushing Juliet for more information, but she clearly hadn't wanted to divulge what she knew, and I hadn't wanted to make her uncomfortable.

Sarah's eyes flicked back and forth across the room before meeting mine. "Wait. Like. *Madeline Reynolds* Madeline Reynolds?"

Not cute. "Yes?"

Damn. How was I supposed to focus on what mattered when every damned thing she did struck me this way and I had to defend against it?

"The trailblazing woman who wrote *Don't Have it All* and just took a sabbatical from her Fortune500 job?"

I nodded, amused at her little advertisement for the potential client.

A smile cracked and broke slowly over her regrettably gorgeous face. "She's coming here? To this office?"

"Yes."

"I'm going to meet her?"

I narrowed my eyes and despite myself said, "You may need to call out sick that day."

Her gaze shot to mine. "What? No! I've always—oh." Her lids drooped low when she realized I was joking and gave me the most unimpressed glare of my life.

And for the first time in I didn't know how long, I laughed. Just a quiet huff of a sound, but enough for her to notice, too, apparently.

She smiled. "I have a feeling you don't do that often enough."

Something in me twisted at the simplicity and truth of that. "You're probably right."

CHAPTER EIGHT

Sarah

I was the third to arrive at Guac for our girls' lunch, near giddy for the chance to tell everyone about... everything.

"Hey." I slid into the booth next to Dahlia, who seemed to be dealing with a business thing, and across from Sadie who was beaming down at her phone and typing out a message.

"Hey. Sorry. One sec. Warrick was just—" She shut her eyes and ducked her head like something he'd said made her cringe and laugh at the same time. "He's crazy."

Joy for my friend filled me. I loved how happy he made her, and I knew she did the same for him. But more than that, more than a fleeting feeling that could change with the weather, they were deeply in love and so supportive of each other—basically the definition of relationship goals.

Calla slipped in next to Sadie and wrapped her arms around the small blonde. Calla's height and long, dark hair provided a stark contrast to Sadie, but their cheeks smashed together as they both genuinely squeezed with the hug.

"I didn't know you were going to make it!" Sadie said, so cheery and present. Sometimes I forgot she'd once practically run away from lunch with this same group.

Calla laughed. "I think this baby is addicted to Guac. I made sure we'd be back in time for this lunch and tomorrow's family dinner. I think Jane was going to have a heart attack if she didn't get to check on us in person soon."

"You look fantastic," I said, meaning it. She'd just started to show, the tiniest, most adorable little bump. She and Wyatt were Exhibit A on the happy couple loving each other well scale, right next to Sadie and Warrick.

Calla beamed, but then her gaze sharpened. "*You* look fantastic, actually."

Quinn slipped into the seat at the head of the table since the booths were taken and scowled at Calla, jumping into the conversation as though she'd been there from the beginning. "Are you insinuating Sarah doesn't always look fantastic?"

Calla chuckled. "Never. But you just seem... I don't know. Less restless, maybe?"

My brows jumped in surprise that they could see it, even as satisfaction simmered in my belly at the idea it was visible.

"Oh. Thanks. I got that long-term temp job, and it's paying really steady so that's honestly been a huge relief." And as nice as that was, it wasn't even close to the biggest cause of my relief lately.

"Oh, that's right. Your text said you had to tell us something about it. What's the job?" Sadie handed Quinn a menu.

"I'm administrative assistant while the original admin is

on bed rest." My pulse spiked knowing what they'd ask next.

"Where?" Dahlia asked next to me, her focus still on her phone. She'd apologized as I settled in, mentioning a difficult client she was trying to wrap things up with.

Brodie brought baskets of chips and bowls of salsa for each of us. Everyone dug in and so I went for it, too.

"Saint Securities." And then I popped a chip into my mouth.

Everyone stopped. Quinn's and Calla's heads jerked up from their menus and over to me. Sadie's eyes widened.

"Saint Securities as in *Wilder* Saint's company?"

I nodded.

"His business is already open? Julian said he was motivated, but I didn't realize they'd already gotten started. He's been back for like ten seconds," Quinn said, rolling her eyes and crunching down on a chip.

"Well, based on his two brothers, I'm sure he has a decent work ethic. Plus, his identity has been wrapped up in the military for decades. He probably has no idea what to do with himself if he's not strapping on rifles and breaking down doors."

Dahlia's observation hit home. My heart kicked at the thought, stupid as it was. I'd never allowed myself to entertain thoughts about what Wilder had done in the military. I couldn't take it, and apparently even now that he was home and safe, I couldn't tolerate thinking about him in those situations.

"That's probably an exaggeration. But entrepreneurship seems to be catching in the Saint family," Sadie said with a fond smile.

"Aw. True. And considering Wyatt was the closest to a father figure they all had, it's not a huge surprise they'd have their own businesses." Calla took a giant scoop of the guacamole Brodie had just dropped and shoved the heaping chip into her mouth with an ecstatic groan.

Quinn shook her head furiously. "Um, no. No, thank you. You may be pregnant, but let's reserve those sounds for your bad girl music videos and your husband."

Laughter jumped out of me, Dahlia, and Sadie at the same time, and Calla covered her mouth to hide the same without showing us her food.

"Okay but seriously, you're working at Wilder's business? And you're looking like you've not only survived but downright thrived. Tell us what's going on," Quinn demanded, typically impatient to know the details.

I finished the sip of my water, fleetingly wishing it were a margarita to fortify me and, frankly, make the words flow a little freer. We hadn't had an actual girls' night in months—not since Quinn had been agonizing over Julian and I'd had... ugh. I didn't want to think about that high schooler writing inappropriate notes to me. *Ick.*

But I didn't need a margarita to help me feel comfortable with these women. They'd proven their lack of judgement. They'd showed me, time and again, they wouldn't leave me because I did something they didn't like. I hadn't imagined this kind of friendship before arriving here. I'd never had this—maybe not even with Eddie. As sisters, we were close, but we'd had to stay close via phone instead of in-person interactions since she'd left home for college.

"It was super awkward initially, but it has gotten better. And yesterday, I actually had a chance to apologize."

Calla's eyes widened as she chewed, and Sadie's mouth opened, then shut.

Quinn spoke for all of them. "Like *apologize* apologize?"

I nodded. "Yes. I went for the whole thing. I told him how sorry I was about how I'd handled things back then and how I wished it'd been different, but even if not, that I was sorry for not tracking him down and saying as much a long time ago."

"What'd he say?" Calla asked.

"He said 'Thank you, but there was no need.' And I believed him—both that he appreciated it and that he didn't think I needed to apologize. And after that, we shifted gears, and it was almost like we were just... coworkers."

Except for how hard it'd been to stay focused with him right there being all hot and professional and talking about me meeting Madeline Freaking Reynolds, though I couldn't tell them that part, anyway.

And maybe... maybe one small part of me that knew it wasn't enough—that a few minutes saying I was sorry didn't make up for the destruction my choices had caused after we'd both been in so much pain. Maybe that was why I didn't now feel finished here. Or maybe the idea that I'd ever feel like my life here in Silverton was wrapped up in a neat little bow was just foolish.

But he hadn't wanted to talk about it anymore. Wilder was a man now, and I might not have known him like I used to, but I could still tell when he wanted to close the discussion on a topic. He'd stayed stock-still, not shifting uncomfortably like he might've years ago, but something in the way his jaw flexed or he kept himself from blinking gave him away.

So I'd said my piece and we'd moved on. Simple. Easy.

"Why do you look kind of sad?" Sadie asked.

Of course she'd seen it.

"It was weird. I mean, such a load off, and I feel good about it. But at the same time, it feels like something between us is gone. Like in some sick way, all that regret and pain had tied me to him, and now that I've apologized, that tether has been cut."

I hadn't given words to the feeling until just now, and the ache in my chest confirmed it. That was part of it. I couldn't have said exactly what I expected, but it was definitely... more. The confusion of feeling so much relief today, of working to accept the conversation as the one I'd been waiting for, and yet feeling a letdown...

Quinn set her hand on my arm and squeezed lightly. "That's complex."

Calla chuckled. "Ya think?"

"Do you have feelings for him still? No judgment if you do, truly. I just wonder if that's part of it? Seeing him again after so long, and getting this big boulder of emotion out from between you and now..."

My heart kicked and I scrambled for an answer. "I—I honestly don't know. Am I still affected by him? Yes. *Very* much."

Did I ever stop feeling like the lights came on when he entered a room? No. Did I imagine my life and future with anyone else, even in the darkest moments of my despair? Even in the moments I should've had my mind on someone else?

No.

Right on cue, my cheeks blazed.

Calla made a sound. "Aw, honey. That's tricky."

I tucked my lips between my teeth and made an awkward smile. I couldn't figure out what to say.

Sadie's kind smile met my gaze and she spoke. "He's an interesting person. At Jane's house last week for family dinner, he was clearly..." Her brow furrowed as she searched for words.

"A jerk?" Quinn put in.

"No. Not at all. It's just, he was uncomfortable. He was trying so hard to be engaged and talk. I mean, I'm not particularly chatty, but that man isn't a talker. But he made such an effort."

My heart squeezed as Calla eyed Sadie. "I cannot wait to get to know him better. I've had to talk myself down from reaming him for not showing up to our wedding, but at the same time, Wyatt's not mad, so why should I be?"

Sadie nodded. "I would agree that you shouldn't launch into your relationship with your new brother-in-law by chastising him for doing his job and missing your wedding."

Quinn chuckled. "Probably good advice. Plus, doesn't he know like twenty ways to kill a man using only his pinky or something?"

I laughed at that, the twine around my rib cage loosening enough to take a full breath, and finally dove back into the chips and guac. "That might be an exaggeration."

"He's definitely intense and very different, I guess, but I'm inclined to like him. And Warrick was on cloud nine when we left, no joke. I think that man spoke more words to me in the hour after Sunday dinner than he did the rest of the week—and that's not because he doesn't normally talk. He was so hyped up after spending time with his brother. I cannot imagine what'll happen after tomorrow."

Interest piqued, I bit. "Tomorrow?"

Calla answered. "We're doing family dinner at the ranch. It's the first time the three boys have been together since he moved back. And any of the interactions in December were pretty strained. I mean, not awful, but just... a start."

Sadie nodded bigger now. "That's what this feels like. It's all baby steps for them. They've been apart so long that they don't know each other anymore. Warrick's excited, but a little wary. Trying not to come on too strong." Her fond smile made clear how sweet she thought her boyfriend was.

"Wyatt is looking forward to it. And honestly, I am, too. I need to get to know this person and figure him out. And I'm going to do whatever I can to get him to talk about *you*."

My eyes widened and my stomach dropped. "No, thank you."

Calla just smiled. "Yep. And I have a great excuse. We'll just mention how you and Wyatt went out on a date on RuralMatch last year."

The blood drained from my face. "Please don't. Oh, please don't."

"You cannot do that. That's embarrassing for Sarah," Quinn said, shooting Calla a look like she was crazy for even considering it.

"It is not. It's a cute little story that might just get a response from him," she said, pointing a chip at Quinn.

Horror washed over me at the thought of them talking about me with Wilder in *any* way. It just seemed like too... too much. Too obvious, too personal, too invasive.

"You'll see tomorrow, but I am pretty sure even if Wilder had a response to that, we wouldn't see it. He's got a poker face like none other."

Sadie gave me a look, and I read the meaning there. She'd help steer things. Maybe even tell Warrick, who'd do the same. I didn't love the idea of him knowing about my mixed-up mess of feelings for his brother, but he probably already knew.

Calla held up her hands in surrender. "Fine. I won't tell him, I promise. But I'm bringing you lunch next week so I can report back on my impressions."

"I'll agree to that." I held up my water and she touched her glass to mine.

The conversation moved on from Wilder and me and their dinner tomorrow. I let myself be carried away by it instead of stewing over the possibilities of what Calla might say, or what I'd already revealed.

Soon enough, the feelings would fade. All of them. Now that we'd made our peace, as thin as it seemed, we could move on as... coworkers. Friendly coworkers. I'd banish or bury every other impulse I had for him, and we'd be colleagues. Someday, I'd move on completely. On from him, on from Silverton.

And we'd both be better for it.

CHAPTER NINE

Wilder

Upon exiting the theater, I saw her. There was no place in town I could go and not think of her. The initial plan to come back and not think of her would've failed, but at least she wouldn't have been here. She would've been nothing more than an apparition.

Instead, the curse of the small town struck again, hard and fast and stealing my sanity for a moment as I inhaled the look of her every curve and line. I had no prayer of turning away. As though she owned the coordinates of the GPS-guided missile in my mind, I zeroed in on her the second I stepped into shared airspace.

And she did the same, her blue eyes flicking up to meet mine, then widening right as her cheeks flushed. At one time, I would've left without a word, but whether due to my new leaf in retirement or the scenes from Friday's apology and debrief replaying in my head, I headed straight for her despite the knowledge I should go.

She waved as she approached. "Hey, what'd you see?"

Her pretty smile made my stomach clutch. "The new Marvel movie."

She grinned. "I'm heading into that one in a few."

"Getting your popcorn and Coke?"

Lips pressed together, she still managed a smile that sent electricity through me. "Some things haven't changed."

Her gaze met mine, and we hung there a moment, just the two of us connected in the intersection of present meeting past. We'd come to the movies constantly. She always had to have popcorn and Coke, even at a morning showing. That this small detail remained consistent made a deep hunger jab at me and plead for more. More things that were still the same, and the pleasure of discovering what had changed.

"So it seems," I said, knocking those gasping, desperate thoughts away.

"You're off to family dinner now?"

"Yes."

She must've seen the surprise flicker across my face. "Sorry. Didn't mean to be a creeper. Sadie and Calla mentioned it yesterday when we had lunch."

I made a show of checking my watch to gain a moment. "Yes. My first time seeing everyone at once since December, and that time, I only briefly talked with Calla."

She nodded, evidently aware. They must've discussed it.

"She's great. You're lucky to have her as a sister-in-law."

Something had to be wrong with me. Those words struck at a bruise in me I hadn't realized was there. Like two days after a mission finding a foot-sized bruise on your quad you never even felt.

But this was a twenty-year bruise, and coming back here was the discovery of yet another tender place in me.

Her sister, Eddie, would've been mine, too. Her sweet, golden-pig-tailed little sister who'd practically worshipped Sarah the same way Warrick had me would've been my sister-in-law.

I wouldn't say any of that, but irritation and the burn of other feelings I didn't want to be so well-acquainted with jarred me into speech. "Yeah."

Her turn in line came.

"I better..." She tipped her head toward the gangly teen waiting for her order.

I nodded. "See you at work."

"See you then."

Then I left out the front doors, shoving away a rapid assault of memories—the first time we'd held hands at this theater, the many summer days we'd spent the heat of the afternoon watching whatever they had on offer just to escape into the air-conditioned building.

Silverton was full of ghosts for me, and somehow, I hadn't expected so many.

"So, Wilder, can we talk about your business?" Mom asked from the head of the very full table at Wyatt's ranch house.

I'd grown up here, too, but it was unmistakably his, and twenty years away had given me plenty of time to move on from the memories I'd had here, even if they attacked me on and off anytime I visited.

She was likely so used to not being able to ask that she'd hedged with the general question. But for once, yes. I could tell them. At least the basics.

"It's close to Grit. In the old log cabin where the park service office used to be." It'd been a defunct building for years, and I'd purchased it a few years back when I visited and saw it still stood empty. I'd hired out basic refurbishing, and Grenier's assistant had made the last of the changes to my specifications.

"Nice that you're so close. We should catch lunch together sometime," Warrick said.

He'd covered the flicker of upset with that comment, and I wouldn't drill into it now. He'd known about the business only vaguely—that I had a plan for coming back, and I wouldn't be lounging around in retirement. But he hadn't known I owned that building or what I had planned, and as someone so connected in the community, and someone who generally seemed to dislike Julian Grenier, I could tell he was hurt.

Yet another sin to atone for.

"Sure. Sounds good."

"Do you have employees? Partners? What's the setup?" Wyatt asked, dipping his fork into the chocolate mousse Sadie had brought.

"My partner is visiting soon to check things out. He's moving here from Bragg as well, but he's got a few more months to go before retirement. I have an admin. I'll be bringing on security personnel."

"Any luck finding people yet?" Mom asked.

"I have a few people in mind. One guy I worked with who'll be moving this summer."

She nodded, her bright blue eyes and silvering blond hair a mirror of Wyatt more than me or War.

"Do you have clients and such yet? Is that what you call them in your business?" Warrick asked.

"One or two thus far."

Calla spoke up. She wasn't shy, but I got the feeling she didn't like me much. Maybe because I'd missed their wedding, for which she had every right to dislike me. Her nail polish was perfectly painted to match the top she wore, but it couldn't hide the roughened fingertips of her left hand. I'd felt them during an awkward handshake greeting earlier. I could see Wyatt liking that—the shine of the polish paired with the strength and skill those fingers had built over years in her music career.

"Is it like alarm systems or body guarding or other stuff?"

Of all the people at the table, she was undoubtedly most well-acquainted with needing security. "It'll run the gamut. Eventually, we'll offer self-defense and other courses to fill in the gaps."

"Honey, how will you do these current people's work with just you?"

I held in the smile at Mom's endearment. "I'll be doing any outfitting or body work until I can fill out a roster, but I need clients for that."

Everyone nodded and Wyatt mumbled, "Makes sense."

I figured the conversation would move on to something else, but Calla spoke up again. "And Sarah? It's going well with her as your admin?"

Mom straightened in her seat. "Sarah? Sarah James?"

All eyes on me, my pulse spiked at the repetition of her name. At the thought of her. At Calla's pointed inquiry. At the intrusion of her yet again. "All good."

Her eyes narrowed. "That simple, huh?"

Wyatt put an arm around her and pulled her close, pressing a kiss to her temple like it might calm her. The edge in her voice rang clear, and I knew without a doubt Sarah, or someone, had explained our history to Calla.

I nodded. "That simple." Because it was.

And it wasn't. But I wasn't about to tell this newlywed and newly pregnant woman I was all kinds of mixed up over having her friend, my ex, in my space. No one would know that but me. What good would it do to explain to them how irrationally wound up just knowing she lived here in Silverton made me, let alone that she now worked in my business as my only other employee? How could I explain that I'd come home for *them*? Yes, for me, too, but also for them.

And Sarah's mere existence in the space nearly railroaded everything. Logically, she couldn't be blamed for moving back here, though I hated the irony that brought us both in town at the same time.

But the strategic part of me that had planned what came next these last years hadn't planned on Sarah. I hadn't factored her in, and that meant I'd arrived unprepared. By the time I'd found out, things had already been set into motion.

Calla's dark gaze wouldn't intimidate me, but she made a valiant effort. Sadie interrupted the stare down Calla was giving me, her sweet tone pulling my attention.

"She seemed excited about the job when we talked yesterday. She wouldn't give us any details, but she said it was all interesting. It's a big improvement on the last few temp jobs she's had."

A hundred questions ran through my mind, none of which I'd voice. Why had she been going through temp jobs? I hadn't figured out why she came back to Silverton at all, much less to be here without a job to speak of. Why had she come back, then?

I couldn't ask them that, nor would I ask Sarah. If she was happy at my place, great. Fine. She seemed capable and she'd always been smart. She could stay until Diane got back, and I'd keep my distance and make sure I focused on the family, just like I was doing now. She could stay and do the job. Even if it made keeping my mind on the work a bit more difficult.

"Good."

Sadie smiled, evidently approving of my pleasure at her friend's happiness at work. She reached for her water and the small, faded burn streaks on her wrists caught my eye and reminded me of her hidden skill and strength. Anyone who'd been burned by an industrial oven and kept going had some steel in her.

"I'd like to come see your office sometime," Mom said.

I heard the yearning in it—the need to be close to me and know about my life. A sound that used to grate on me so badly, I had to grit my teeth through our conversations in the first few years after I'd left. Her love for me, her insistence on caring and checking in, had pulled at me, chafing against all those places that longed for home.

But now? It was a relief to welcome it in. To accept it, and even if I felt I didn't deserve it, to know she did love me despite my absence. This was why I'd come back. "Anytime. I have some work out of the office first of the week but otherwise, come whenever."

The pleased smile she gave me was reward in itself. Plus, I looked forward to showing her the office. Grenier had spared no expense, and though I'd be paying him back for years to come, it made the right impression. The one we needed to land the high-profile clients to our local service rather than losing out to whoever did their security elsewhere.

That night as I drove home, the conversations from the evening with family filtering through my mind, I felt more settled and at peace than I had in longer than I could remember. I didn't know whether to revel in it or fear it, but for the moment, I let the sense of belonging and good feelings play out against the dimming night sky and dark canyon walls of the commute.

And despite my best efforts, passing the place where we used to meet brought Sarah to mind, just like every other time I'd ever driven this canyon. But where sadness and regret and disappointment and a crushing sense of what might've been had once lived now sat a simmering sense of possibility.

Misplaced though it might've been, all I could think about was seeing her again tomorrow morning—of having her near me, within reach.

CHAPTER TEN

Sarah

Movement behind me made my heart slam into my chest as I whipped around, gasping. "Holy crap, you scared me!"

Wilder stood just inside the break room door, relaxed as could be. If I didn't know better, I'd say a small smile hovered on his lips under that bushy beard.

"Apologies."

"No sneaking up on the poor, helpless temp, okay?"

Hand pressed to my heart, I worked to calm my galloping pulse. But honestly, having him join me in this room first thing in the morning didn't help the situation. Any proximity to the man made everything in me sit up and take notice in a pleasure-pain kind of way that I couldn't seem to stop.

"Never again. Scout's honor." He held up his hand in promise.

"I happen to know you weren't a Boy Scout," I said, turning back to the coffee maker and filling a mug.

I'd decided to just go for it and make myself at home, and part of that was drinking from a mug I'd brought from home and would keep here instead of a metal thermos I would have packed in and out. I'd thoroughly enjoyed the process of opening the building. Not sure why, actually, but I didn't want to ruin the mild buzz I'd gotten from unlocking the doors and flipping on lights and brewing the morning coffee, so I ran with it.

"I suppose you do."

I turned back to him, coffee mug in one hand, and took a sip. His eyes dropped to the mug as I drank, and something lit in his eyes, though they remained seemingly placid. Like the moment before liftoff, his gaze barreled into me, until he pushed off the frame as though compelled by some force akin to magnetic attraction. He covered the ten feet between us and just as I pulled the mug from my lips, he cupped his hand around mine where I held the handle.

This was the first contact we'd had in... in... I couldn't think. I sucked in a breath that sounded mercifully quiet in this near-soundless room. Could he hear my heart thundering in my chest? Could he feel how the rough skin of his palms nearly set me on fire?

I couldn't breathe with his skin on mine so suddenly—my lungs had forgotten. *Is it inhale, then exhale? Or just inhale and inhale and inhale...* I looked up to see him glance up from my lips and meet my gaze. My stomach swooped low and I swallowed.

"Reading is sexy."

I nodded. "Uh... huh."

He squinted and his mouth tipped up. "I was reading your mug."

I shut my eyes and scrunched my nose, making a silly face and neglecting to hide my embarrassment. Why try when my body had flushed from head to toe with heat at his words and then at the realization that he was only reading the mug I held and not just tossing out that fact like a compliment to me?

"Right. Yes. Well. *Fact.*"

Sadly, he let go, and fortunately, I still had some power over my limbs and managed not to let the coffee slosh over the edge or let the mug simply drop to the floor and shatter on the polished wood below once the contact was gone.

"Do you still read?"

I raised a brow. "I find reading pretty essential."

He shook his head, and I could swear he was smiling again. Dang, he needed to shave that beard so I could see. Or at least trim it.

Actually, no. Scratch that. Because if I saw Wilder Saint smile full-out, a Haley's Comet kind of occasion, I'd probably do something ridiculous like burst into tears or kiss him.

"I mean, do you read nonstop? Is it still impossible to talk to you when you've got your head in a good book?"

My heart twisted at the warmth and familiarity of his words and at knowing he remembered. Of course he did, but still. I cleared my throat, willing away the sudden creep of emotion.

"Of course I do. Hence the mug." I raised it in an air toast gesture.

"Fair enough," he said, and then he did the thing.

He'd had this knack ever since he was about fourteen to look at me and make me feel like I was the only person left on the planet. Like I was dinner and dessert and rainbows and every good thing, everything he'd ever wanted.

He did that now—no escaping the explosion of butter-flies and anticipation that shot to every part of me. It poured a triple shot of energy into my bloodstream and sent me buzzing. The spotlight of *this* look had always done things to me, and seeing its effect only magnified by his age and maturity made me actually weak in the knees for the second time today.

He dipped his head closer to me so our heads were only a foot apart—way too far for a kiss or even another brush of his hand against mine, and yet it felt like if I just tipped my chin up he'd move. He'd take my mouth like I'd wanted since I saw him months ago. He'd close the distance between our lips, and in doing so, somehow banish the space that'd filled years between us.

"I can't disagree," he said, then slipped the carafe back onto the warmer of the coffee maker and left.

And I stood there scrambling for what he meant he didn't disagree with. It wasn't until a few minutes later when I finally realized it had to be that he didn't disagree with my mug. Thinking about him finding reading sexy made me all kinds of shifty and unfocused for what felt like a solid hour, until I eventually lost the adrenaline pushing me and had to take a break.

Wilder stepped around the front desk before I even noticed he'd entered the room and began loading firewood into the hearth. "Do you like the fire?"

"Yes. Yeah. I just, I wasn't sure if I should start it or not."

Facing his work, he explained, "Up to you. I'm sure we'll have some no-burn days so not then, but otherwise, whenever you want, go for it. And if you need me to start it, just let me know."

"Or you could show me? Teach a man to fish and all."

He knocked his head to the side, which I realized was

all the response I'd get. Heated moment earlier or no, Wilder still wasn't about to chat my ear off. Ignoring the flutter in my chest, I jumped up and hustled around to kneel where he crouched. He showed me where he'd stuck newspaper for kindling and explained where to stick the match.

"You can also just flip on the natural gas and toss a match in. It'll pretty much guarantee you get it lit."

He must've seen my scowl, because his face split into a smile. My heart exploded in excitement and satisfaction and borderline glee at having elicited that response, and frankly, at how stunningly beautiful it was. Even with his mangey beard and his hat pulled low on his head, his broad, white smile was mind-meltingly beautiful. *Wow.*

The crinkles around his eyes and weathering on his face only served to add to the picture. He'd always been very handsome—broody at times, quiet, and very intense. Just my cup of coffee, always. But now? With maturity and years on him, he was downright gorgeous.

I'd known it'd be fatal to me, and sure enough, his smile had knocked me dead. One flash of his pretty teeth and my flimsy defenses were kindling.

"That's not fair," I whispered to myself as I slipped back into my desk chair.

"What's not?" he said from where he stood watching the fire crackle.

"Nothing. I—yeah. Nothing." Aaaaand definitely not about to explain the utter disaster zone of my brain in the wake of his smile, so I scrambled for something else. "I was just about to review the schedule and make sure I'm on top of everything for meeting Bruce and stuff."

He brushed off his hands and nodded, folding his arms.

"Sounds good. I'm going to check out the Reynolds house and a few other things. I won't be back until later."

"Oh. Of course. Hope it all goes well. I'll hold down the fort!" It only could've been worse with a salute, but at least I stopped myself from doing that. Or maybe I could've said, "Aye, aye, Captain!" and made myself look like even more of a weirdo?

He gave me a nod, and I focused on my computer carefully so as not to blind myself with the view of his retreat. I didn't need to be ogling his backside as he left, even if the temptation was incredible. I'd already had a Wilder smile mind melt, so it was borderline miraculous that I'd managed to keep it together and *not* check him out.

With Wilder gone, I got to work once my brain eventually recovered. I didn't have a ton of tasks just yet, but I could tell that when business picked up, I would. I spent my time reviewing every piece of information I had access to in the shared information drive and then moved to studying everything Wilder had told me about Bruce.

Hours later, I answered the phone on my desk—the first time it'd ever rung as far as I knew.

"Saint Securities, how may I help you?"

"Sarah. It's me."

My pulse spiked. Not *It's Wilder* but *It's me*. That word choice felt like... something.

"Hi. Are you okay?"

A slight pause before "Yes. All good, but I'm not going to make it back in. Can you close up? Feel free to go ahead now—nothing's happening in the next half hour."

"Sure. Sounds good." Normally, I'd hesitate but he'd reiterated that I'd be paid the working hours whether he closed up early or not and that without me there, he'd be closing whenever he left the building, so that gave me some peace of mind.

"I'll be out most of tomorrow, too, but back Wednesday. Feel free to take the day tomorrow, if you want."

"Take the day?"

"Off."

"Wilder, I'm not going to take the day *off*. I just started, and you're a brand-new business. Don't you think it's important to have someone physically occupying the space? To answer questions if they come up or be here if someone calls or needs to stop by?"

Another pause. "Sure. That's fine."

Um. Okay. I guess he didn't really agree with me, but whatever. I wasn't going to take a day off. "Great. Then I'll see you Wednesday."

"See you then, Sarah."

My insides cartwheeled as I hung up, enjoying setting the handheld phone in the receiver. When was the last time I'd called someone on an actual phone instead of a mobile? Kind of crazy and definitely long enough to make me feel old. Thirty-six was by no means old, and yet ever since Wilder returned, I'd had this tunneling feeling. Like time had passed in an instant instead of slowly and sometimes wretchedly over the years.

But maybe that was the simple nature of coming back to your hometown after decades and seeing the man you'd grown up believing you'd spend your life with. The person you'd planned on being with and then ran from.

Particularly when that man turned out to be even better looking than he had been before, a generous employer, and still kind of grumpily appealing despite my best efforts?

Yeah. No wonder I had such a feeling about things lately. And yet... not all bad. I hardly dared acknowledge that glimmering thought way out on the horizon of my mind, but as I packed up my bag and locked the back exit before leaving out the front door of Saint Securities, I let my mind whisper it.

Maybe I'd ended up back in Silverton for more than just forgiveness.

CHAPTER ELEVEN

Wilder

I had lost my damn senses.

I couldn't think about anything but Sarah this morning. I had fifty things to do before Bruce arrived tomorrow, and I wasn't going to manage any of them, especially not now that my mom was about to show up for her visit in the next five minutes.

But at least I had an excuse to talk to Sarah. *And there it is again.*

Somewhere between her apology Friday and not seeing her for most of the last two days, I'd truly lost my ability to keep my thoughts from her. Especially since she had been here at the building. I had all kinds of security and surveillance equipment set up and had gotten the notification right at eight when she showed up yesterday. I'd resisted the urge to pull up the video feed and see what she had been wearing because *that* would be creepy.

Instead of berating myself for touching her, getting close enough to catch her soft scent, I cast it out of my mind. I'd spent two decades learning the discipline to focus on the mission at hand, and here, today and for the foreseeable future, that was to reconnect and rebuild with my family and get my business up and running.

Apparently, all it took was a few smiles, a minute or two talking about her love of books, and feeling the warmth of her hands, and all my highly trained skills took a trip. I'd kept myself from checking the security cameras, and I'd forbidden myself to get within six feet of her in case that gravitational pull dragged me in like it had earlier this week in the break room.

Wouldn't be as much of a problem to do the same thing by wandering up the hallway and past her desk to prepare for my mother, right? Right.

Decided, I pushed back from my chair right as I heard Sarah's laugh. The sound hit me in the solar plexus at the same time the realization hit me in the face: Mom had arrived. I hadn't headed her off at the pass, which left Sarah to deal with her.

Jane Saint was the definition of a good woman. Even as tense as some of our communication had been over the years, I'd never resented her or even disliked her. If anything, I'd admired the way she'd managed our lives without a spouse to help her in the daily grind. But she was also a meddler. She used to revel in reminding me that I got all my stubbornness from her, and it faded with each generation so she could outgun me any day of the week if she wanted.

In my almost thirty-seven years, I'd learned not to doubt that.

While I had no idea how often Sarah and Mom had

interacted, I couldn't imagine they did with any frequency based on Mom's reaction to her working here. So I needed to get in there and keep things from going sideways.

Jogging to the front, I saw her slim figure clutching her purse, and in a way, that told me she was purely delighted to catch me unprepared. She wore practical boots, jeans, and a big sweater with a light rain jacket over top. The early spring day here would've been downright cold in North Carolina, but I savored the chill every time I felt it, because I'd missed it. Between Carolina winters or deployed stints during the rainy seasons in the Middle East and elsewhere, nothing felt more like home than Utah seasons.

Except maybe seeing that gleam in my mother's eye and being thrust back into my youth, bracing for whatever she had up her sleeve.

"Mom, hey. You're a few minutes early." I rounded Sarah's desk and pulled my mom into a hug.

She held me to her, then released me and glanced over at Sarah. "Such a good hugger, isn't he?"

Sarah's cheeks immediately brightened with a blush. Mine probably would've, too, without the beard. "Mom, you can't—"

"He always was, yes." Sarah's eyes flicked up to mine, then right back down as she ducked her head. Nothing would hide that blush, but she made a go of it.

A bittersweet tang pricked at my gut, the mix of memories of hugging and being close to Sarah, and the unforgettable reason why it'd all stopped. The loss. The grief. The choice to walk away.

"I love seeing you two together. Oh, I know you're not *together*, of course, because wouldn't that be crazy? Just a beautiful, mad confluence of events. Still, though. I love knowing you're here with my Wilder so he's not all alone all day every day, and you're, what? Five minutes from the new bookstore and ten from Guac?"

Oh, she's crafty. She went right for Sarah's favorite things—or two of them, at least that I knew of. The grasping sensation that hit me whenever I thought about the details of Sarah's life that I'd gathered up like an unwilling collector hit yet again, but I buried it when I witnessed her response.

She beamed at Mom and sent an arrow straight into my chest with the smile.

"Actually, yes. I haven't been into the bookstore, but I love that it's finally open! Have you been?"

My mom got this weird smile on her face. "Actually, I was going to check it out after my hair appointment. I've got that at one after lunch with Wilder. Would you want to join me?" Then to me, she added, "She can get off a little early for a bookstore browse, right?"

The look I gave Jane Saint was one I imagined might fell a lesser woman, but she had given me my own backbone of steel, so I couldn't be surprised she only shot me a satisfied little grin before turning back to Sarah.

"That settles it. You'll get off early, and we'll go investigate this new place. Then I'll have some new reading if my date tonight goes south."

I choked on air. "Date?"

Out the corner of my eye, I saw Sarah bite her lip.

"Yes. Wyatt and Warrick haven't told you I'm a woman about town?" She waved a hand like it shouldn't make me feel a little queasy. "They've accepted it. So will you. I'm officially in my *mid-to-late* fifties, and I'm healthier than a horse. I might have another forty years to live, and I've spent the last thirty-some alone. I'm done being alone."

And then her gaze found mine, and I knew this would

hurt. Her expression turned serious and she said, "It's hard to be brave and put myself out there, but I'm doing it. I'm proud of myself, and I think looking for love and companionship is noble."

She meant the words for herself, for sure, but I felt her pressing them into me, urging me to take them for myself. She had been on me for years to find someone, to make a life. When I'd told her I was coming home to set down roots and begin the next phase of my life, she'd rejoiced. I knew this—the idea that I'd find a partner—had been at the forefront of her celebration.

She couldn't possibly understand the barriers that my own life held regarding what she was searching for. I'd never been open to that, not since I was too young to know better and got my heart crushed in the process, both by the brutality and fragility of life and by someone I'd loved to the point of pain.

I'd let no one close since then. It hadn't been a quest to stay away—more like a posture that had me hunched against anything other than a focus on work and maintaining the minimal amount of connection possible. Years of intensity and tragedy had developed the bond a special operations team demanded. That trust became essential in order to keep people alive and complete mission. Only through that time and experience had I ever connected with Bruce and a handful of others.

But a woman? A person I wanted? Maybe it was being here in the same room as the only person I could ever really remember wanting, but I couldn't imagine finding someone else.

"Good for you, Mrs. Saint."

Mom's face cracked into a sly smile. "Come on, Sarah. You're a grown woman now. Call me Jane."

Sarah huffed a laugh, though something about her dimmed for a breath before she spoke. "All right, then. Thank you."

Mom's pleased grin swiveled back to me. "Are you ready?"

With a flourish of fingers in Sarah's direction, she exited, allowing me to hold the door before I dipped my head to Sarah in farewell and followed her out.

"Ah, what a gorgeous spring day," my far-too-plucky mother said, twirling around with her arms out and head up to the sky.

"What has you so cheery?"

She shot me a grin that was pure Warrick—I'd seen that exact expression on his face all my life. Or, all my life save the last twenty years. With that mental caveat, a pang of homesickness hit. That'd been happening more and more, and it didn't make sense that I felt that more now than I had when away.

But even I could tell it was that longing to feel at home here like I used to more than simply occupying space in Silverton. Mom had argued that was all I'd done in the Army. And that would come in time.

"I just love seeing Sarah all grown up. She's absolutely gorgeous."

No denying it. Why deny that the sun is bright? "That she is."

Her slightly raised brow posed her question, but she asked anyway. "You think so?"

I searched for rescue on the sidewalk ahead and to either side of us, but no help came. "You know I do. That's why you're so happy."

She shook her head. "Not at all. I have always wondered how she was doing. When she and Wyatt went out last year, after he explained what happened, I felt like a part of me that'd torn open was sewn shut again. When your brother told me how good she looked and that she'd moved back, it gave me relief. I haven't wanted to pressure her, and there's a mountain of history between us, so I didn't even approach her. But now... now I have a playdate."

Internally, I rolled my eyes at her language even though my gut lurched at the thought of Wyatt with Sarah. Of course, it didn't mean anything, but some stupid, primal, completely misguided instinct had my bones screaming *miiiine* in response to my brother getting to be near her when I hadn't for so long. But there had to be an explanation, and I'd only get it if I asked. Jane Saint was not about to give away the goods for free when she had me in a corner I wouldn't admit to standing in.

I wouldn't be sharing any of that nonsense with my already-too-pleased mother, so externally, I simply took the bait. "Wyatt and Sarah went out?"

She waved a hand. "It was nothing. They accidentally matched up on RuralMatch. It's a fairly small dating pool here, of course."

I could feel her trying to look at me without turning her head, as though I couldn't sense every molecule of her interest trying to gauge my reaction to the news that my oldest brother had gone out with Sarah. Or maybe that the dating pool was small? Either way, there wasn't anything to reveal. As logic had shouted at that animal instinct to rage, Wyatt would never purposefully date Sarah, and though I didn't know her all that well anymore, she wouldn't date him either. Obviously, that was the case since my brother was now happily married to Calla.

That issue closed, I refocused on the more immediate issue. "That's the app you use?"

She sighed. "Are you going to give me grief about it?"

"No. I want you to be happy."

She stopped mid-stride and turned to me, placing one hand on my arm. "I want the same for you, Wilder. I might make light of it, but I'm not going to pretend like Sarah working for you doesn't seem like some kind of cosmic sign. Doesn't it?"

As a man who didn't believe in signs or omens or any of that BS, I answered accordingly. "No. It seems like she needed a job, and we needed an administrative assistant."

She gave me a look that sent me right back to junior high, when I'd been sullen and even more quiet than usual. "Well, what about Bruce?"

I urged her forward and we walked on. "Bruce? What about him?"

She raised her brows like it wasn't obvious. "Maybe he'll want to date Sarah."

I gritted my teeth as we walked into town and made our way to the Elk Street Grill. But she couldn't leave it alone, apparently.

"I can't imagine Bruce is a bad guy, if you've chosen to partner with him."

"He's the best."

She tipped her head to one side as if to say, *See?* "Exactly. So who would you rather have with Sarah than him?"

Magma-hot jealousy ripped through me at the thought of Bruce and Sarah together in almost any way, followed by the film of frustration and shame. Crap. *Crap.*

"Hmm?"

I held the door open for her. She nodded demurely as she passed, and I followed her inside.

"It wouldn't be appropriate for him to date her."

"Why not?"

"Because."

"*Because* why?"

"Just... because."

"Is this how you communicate with your clients?"

I scowled at her. She smiled yet again.

And despite my irritation, I found myself smiling, just slightly, too. "No. I manage to use full sentences when I talk to someone who's paying for my opinion."

Her eyes widened. "Well then."

The hostess welcomed us and guided us toward the back, the area known as the wintergarden, which was enclosed in glass and provided a lovely view of a garden hiding between buildings.

Mom perused the menu and chatted about other things —not my work, or who occupied the building even now, or Bruce's arrival tomorrow. But I couldn't stop thinking of any of those things—big surprise. And now that she'd put the idea in my head, I couldn't shake the dread that Bruce really might like Sarah. In fact, there was no way he wouldn't. She was beautiful and smart and had done a great job so far. She was flexible and responsible, and there was no way I'd get out of this without doing or saying something stupid.

What the hell was I doing? I didn't want Sarah for myself. I'd been through the aftermath of that once already —or maybe not *once* but repeatedly over time as waves of grief over losing a child you never knew hit at the oddest times and missing someone you've loved most of your life despite every damn thing telling you to stop came right along with it.

However much I might not want Sarah, some aching, almost monstrous thing in me *needed* her. I couldn't escape it, no matter how I reminded myself of how she'd walked away and *kept walking*. She'd apologized but it didn't change the past.

But Bruce... Bruce didn't have the baggage. And if I didn't own up to it, then why wouldn't he go for her?

There was just not a chance of escaping this without potential misery forcing my hand.

And when it did? My mother would be first in line to let me hear about it.

CHAPTER TWELVE

Sarah

Jane came knocking at four, and despite my discomfort at leaving an hour early, Wilder insisted I go.

"I'm heading out, too. I would've kicked you out."

I held in a smile because I'd realized all I did was smile around the man. I probably looked like a lovesick teenager. I'd been one of those with him, and parts of my draggy, soft heart still felt like one. It had to be thanks to the apology and sharing all those thoughts with him so recently, but still. Not a good look.

"He insists, and so do I. Come on, darling. Put your things in your car and we're off." Jane blew a kiss to Wilder, then slipped out the door.

I gathered my purse, lunch bag, and water bottle, then signed off my computer according to the protocols I'd learned in the training.

"Have fun," he said, loosing butterflies in my chest.

He hadn't walked back to his office, but since I didn't especially want him to know that I was aware of everything he did when in a room with me, I'd done my best not to think about him standing there. I really could not be having a reaction like this every time he spoke to me.

In fairness, I hadn't, had I? When he insisted on my leaving early, I hadn't found that thrilling. Not entirely, anyway.

"I think maybe you should be saying, 'Good luck.'" I tucked my water bottle into my purse and pushed in the chair.

"Fair point. Good luck."

I shot him a smile this time, my stomach flipping at the exchange. He was so much more talkative than last week. A sad barometer for improvement considering we still didn't speak much, but I'd take the progress. I'd happily accept the silly butterflies in my stomach in place of the dread and heartache that plagued every second of my time here before I apologized.

And if a bit of that lingered... it made sense. Not like my quick apology changed everything between us. The history we shared was still there, miles of road behind us. And my feelings, knotted up into a little ball though they were, lingered, too.

"See you tomorrow." And with that, I left him to lock up while I faced down Jane.

It really was a facing down of sorts. As kind as she was, I knew we'd have to talk about what happened in one way or another. It was one aspect of being here I hadn't confronted in the year-plus I'd lived in Silverton, and I needed to stop avoiding it. I couldn't be certain we'd do that today, but she wasn't one to stay quiet. Thus far, though, she seemed intent on moving ahead, not punishing me for the past. That kind of thing probably wasn't Jane's style anyway, but until we'd confronted our history, I would be... cautious.

"So, what are you reading these days?" she asked as we strolled the short path past the mill building, then the diner, to Silver Street.

"I'm actually between books. I mostly read romantic suspense, though." I'd just finished a ten-book series and felt more than a little bereft.

"Oh, me, too! I'll read a thriller now and then but haven't been in the mood. I also love a good historical fiction."

I smiled to myself, vividly remembering her reading whenever she had a spare moment. She liked to stay busy, but she let herself relax and read every day for at least a little while. I'd loved that about her since my parents hadn't been readers. They watched the news, maybe read the paper, but certainly no leisure reading.

"I always loved that you were a reader," I said.

"I felt the same way about you."

My heart warmed. Part of me wanted to launch into apologies right there and get them out of the way, but a larger portion of my heart and mind wanted to enjoy this time. To savor the moment between this woman who'd felt like a second mother to me, and who'd understood me in ways I suspected my own mom never had. So instead of the lengthy speech I'd need to make at some point, I forced myself back into the simplicity of our current activity.

"Have you heard anything about who owns the new store?"

"You know? I haven't. Just that he's not from here. I'm so intrigued." She flashed her eyebrows up and down, a genuinely curious glint in her eye.

"Well, shall we?" I stepped to the front door and held it open for her.

"We shall indeed."

The familiar scent of books and coffee welcomed us inside, and immediately, I felt at home. Funny how such a thing could happen in an instant, but the space simply reached out and embraced me upon entering.

Shelves lined all of the outer walls, and shorter stacks created delightful little aisles for browsing. Nestled into each corner or nook sat high-backed, upholstered chairs with pillows. I caught Jane's eye right after we saw the checkout counter that looked as though it'd been made of neatly stacked hardback books in rainbow colors.

"It's adorable," she said, a pleased grin on her lovely face.

"It's just perfect. Now I know what I'm doing on every lunch break." It almost felt more like a library than a store— like you were welcome to curl up and read rather than feeling like you must purchase and exit to make space for the next person.

"Oh, yes! You should. Now the real test will be whether they have an actual romance section." She widened her eyes, and I knew exactly what she meant.

How many local bookstores had I snuck into, searched high and low, and found a small handful of romances buried within the popular fiction or bestseller shelves? The town where I'd lived with my parents had featured one local bookstore that stocked nothing but the tear-jerker love stories that'd been made into movies and always featured someone dying, and basically nothing else. Spoiler alert: not romance.

I'd long since stopped apologizing for reading romance, and I wouldn't start now. Of all the problems in the world, not having locally stocked romance novels wasn't a real one, and yet I couldn't help but say a small prayer that the owner of the store got it.

A gasp made me glance behind me at Jane just in time to see her point.

Oh.

In the far corner of the quaint store sat an archway made of books. Jane stood just outside that arch, and even from fifteen feet away, I could see why she'd gasped. The entire curve was a shelf, save the books somehow stacked together to make the top, and inside that archway were all romances.

I hustled over and followed her through the arch to discover neat little signs denoting subgenres. *RomCom. Historical Romance. Sweet romance. Young Adult. Contemporary. Sports. Romantic Suspense.* And on and on. Several more small categories I wouldn't have imagined. Those smaller ones didn't have but ten books in them, but this was a love letter to romance books. Especially for a small town like Silverton...

And yet, no. Because romance novels sold more books than anything else, period. It'd always driven me insane that they were relegated to one rotating display of mass market paperbacks. But here? They were celebrated—delighted in.

There had to be a romance lover involved. There just had to be. I glanced around, still not seeing anyone. Not great customer service, but again, small town. There was probably only one employee working at a time.

"This is just delightful," Jane said, pleasure oozing from her tone.

"Agreed. I love it. I don't even read paperbacks much anymore, but I love them, and this makes me want to buy them all." And after I got paid next week, I would actually be able to afford one every now and then.

"I mostly read ebooks, but I love holding a paperback in my hand. I can't give them up," she said, then reached for something from the historical shelf.

We browsed for a solid twenty minutes before a man's voice stole our attention. "Can I help you ladies with anything?"

"Oh, thank you, we're—"

Jane's voice cut off when she caught sight of the man—fairly tall, middle-aged, nice salt-and-pepper beard, and a full head of hair, in a cozy-looking cardigan sweater and glasses. She blinked like she couldn't believe her eyes and shifted back on her heel like his presence had stunned her.

I jumped in to cover whatever it was that had happened with her. "We're good. This is the first time either of us has been in. We're just loving your romance section."

"Glad to hear it. My daughter insisted I make it appropriately fancy."

Jane finally spoke up at that. "Oh, are you the owner? And does your daughter work here with you?"

He offered a cheesy little bow. "Darcy Malcom, at your service. I am the owner of All Booked Up, and my daughter is a student at University of Utah, but if you stop in often, you will see her at some point."

Jane grinned. "That's nice that she's close enough to visit. Will we see your wife, too? We'd love to welcome her —and you, of course."

"Ah, no. I'm not married. But I appreciate the kind offer." His cheeks pinked, and odd as it may sound, it was adorable.

I do think the man was flustered by dear Jane Saint, and

he could join the club. She was just so darn forthright sometimes.

"I'm sorry if I pried. I'm Jane Saint, and this is Sarah James. You might as well get to know both of us because we're voracious readers."

At this, the man seemed genuinely pleased. "You can imagine there's nothing a bookseller likes to hear more than exactly that. I'll leave you to browse, but don't hesitate to let me know if you need anything. Help yourself to an espresso at the bar if you like—I'm just going to check her out."

Jane's head whipped to where Mr. Malcom had nodded. I followed and saw another woman standing at the small checkout desk. I hadn't heard her come in or seen her. For as small as the shop was, it created such a nice feeling of intimacy and privacy that she might've been there all along.

Malcom chatted with the woman as he rang her up, and Jane's eyes didn't leave him for a second.

I couldn't be certain I was reading her right, but I had a strong suspicion she had a thing for the new bookstore owner. "He's a handsome man."

"He is that," she agreed.

"And he loves books."

She clutched the historical she'd picked up to her chest. "He must."

"Maybe you should ask him out?"

She raised a single brow at me. "I imagine the man has more than enough on his plate with moving to a new place and opening a business."

"True. Though maybe he needs a friend to help him feel settled. Someone who, say, has lived here all her life and knows everyone? Who would help him drum up business and—"

"Sarah Elizabeth James, I'll have you know I'm perfectly capable of managing my own social life."

I didn't smile at her use of my full name, knowing it might launch her into a lecture. "I have no doubt of that."

She narrowed her eyes at me. "You, however, might need some assistance."

A thrill of fear slipped through me. "Absolutely not. I'm all set. And actually, I have to get going. Thank you so much for letting me come with you. I'll, uh, I'll see you soon, right?"

That suspicious look didn't leave her face for another moment, but finally, her brow smoothed out and she nodded. "Yes, you will. We'll do lunch sometime, and I'm sure I'll be in to see Wilder again soon. I need to meet this Bruce, too."

I had no doubt Bruce would be subject to Jane Saint in quick order. While I could still make my getaway without her delving into what she'd do to help my social life and all the ways I was scared she thought she could do that, I got out of there and didn't look back.

We'd have it out about what happened years ago someday soon, I could tell. Maybe closure with her was what I needed to dissolve that little knot in my chest.

CHAPTER THIRTEEN

Wilder

Bruce pulled me in for a hug and back slap, the usual greeting after time apart. We were brothers, in many ways closer than Wyatt and Warrick were to me. I hoped to change that, and I hoped they'd welcome Bruce when he came to live in Silverton permanently.

But for now, I needed to keep an eye on him as he shifted his focus to Sarah.

Sarah. Who'd shown up in a fitted black dress looking all kinds of professional with her hair twisted back into a... well, a twist, held up by a spikey weapon-like thing. The urge to pull it out and watch her hair tumble down around her face gripped me so relentlessly, I had to tuck my hand into my pocket.

"I'm so happy to be here and meet you, Sarah. I've heard wonderful things about you from Wilder, of course, and I've appreciated how quickly you've jumped into this. I know you weren't exactly expecting this kind of work, but we're very glad to have you."

As always, Bruce demonstrated his abundance of *people ability*. Not just skills, but all-around adeptness at managing and talking to and *handling* people. I'd always admired it—found it useful on missions. It'd already been essential to setting up Saint Securities. But I'd never envied it until this moment, when the disparity between his personable energy and my inherent broodiness sat in a spotlight in my mind.

"Thank you. I'm happy to be working here, and it's great to meet you."

She shook his hand, and I chose to ignore the slight brightness to her cheeks. She wasn't embarrassed or excited by his attention. I didn't need to read *interest* into that blush.

Plus, why shouldn't she be interested in Bruce? He was one of the best men I knew. The more she got to know him, the more she'd see that. He would be a good boss, and since she was a great employee, they'd have a nice relationship.

Nice relationship twisted in my gut like a jagged-edged knife. Professional relationship was what I meant, and that's what they'd have. And if I didn't stop thinking about my employee Sarah's future relationships, I was going to be in big freaking trouble.

I needed to own the fact that I was already in trouble. She'd put me in peril from the minute I saw her last December—the second I'd seen her blanching face and realized she'd come back. That we'd be here together again, back where everything fell apart.

"Wilder and I will do a quick debrief with you, then we've got some less interesting ground to cover in private. But I'd love to take you both to lunch somewhere tomorrow

—maybe you could show me around Silverton a bit? I guess it's never too early to house hunt, right?"

I tried not to glare at the man—my friend, my business partner. A guy who was moving to a place he'd never visited until *today* on my word that it was great and we could build our business here. This jealous crap needed to quit. I had no claim on Sarah, even if that idiot animal instinct said otherwise, and I certainly didn't bear any ill will to my best friend.

"How much longer do you have?" Sarah asked.

"A month and change. Really not even that long until I'm done, but then I need to stay in place for a few other details to wrap up."

Interesting that he hadn't mentioned Kiley, his much younger half sister and ward. She didn't finish school until early June, and he didn't want to do anything more than he had to that would create disruption for her.

Again—good man.

"I think looking for a home now makes sense. I've only gone through the buying process once years ago in Georgia, but it took a while to get the details ironed out. Maybe you can find something on this trip and get everything ready before you're back so you can move right in."

I watched Sarah smile like she was standing at the other end of a tunnel—far enough away to be in another zip code. Why would knowing she'd bought a house—by herself? With a partner?—make my stomach tighten and a knot loop around my neck?

It shouldn't. I had no ownership or right to anything of Sarah's, including information about her. I'd had to remind myself of that fact countless times over the years when the temptation to just look her up and do a little recon about what she'd been up to, where she lived, all that, rose to the forefront of my mind.

I hadn't ever abused the access I had to things like records, nor would I now that I had all the PI and law enforcement certifications possible in this business. But the need to have her tell me more about her life clutched at me with an iron grip.

"I'd love it. If you two would give me an update, then we can get to our stuff and maybe fit in some house hunting later," Bruce said, winking at me like he thought he was cute. No doubt he did.

He didn't know exactly who Sarah was to me, but he had the same training I had. He'd known the second he saw us in the room together that we had more than a boss-employee relationship, and that was without any conclusions he'd drawn during our communications the last few weeks since my arrival and Sarah's employment.

We sat at the conference table, and I launched into a brief overview of Bruce's role for Sarah. She'd read this and knew it, but doing it in person seemed helpful because now she could put a face with the name. Bruce and I were co-owners of Saint Securities—poor sap had rightly agreed Camden just didn't have the right ring to it. What I hadn't drawn out for Sarah was the delineation of our work in the day to day when Bruce finally arrived here.

"I'll take the tactical elements of planning security. Bruce'll handle equipment acquisition, client relationships unless they specifically request me, and he'll be the head honcho in the office."

"So you're not planning to be in the office?" Sarah asked, her brow furrowing slightly with the question.

"Only occasionally." I couldn't stay cooped up inside any more than I could stand on my head all day, nor did I want to. I'd always needed an escape hatch, and I planned to use the freedom I had in my own business to enjoy *not* being stuck in an office.

"Can you explain tactical elements? Or, is there something I could read? I'm sorry if this is all really basic. As you both know, I haven't worked in security or anything like it, ever."

Bruce smiled a shiny, brilliant thing at her. *That ass.*

"Don't apologize. We're running our business our way, so even if you'd worked for someone else, it likely would be different. As you may or may not know, both Wilder and I come out of careers in special operations with the military."

"Oh, like the special forces guys who got Bin Laden."

Bruce's smile flashed wider, but there was that gleam. "Uh, well, no. That was Seal Team Six. They're special operations. Special *forces* is a smaller subset of special operations, and is known as 'white' ops—not quite so covert. That's the majority of your Navy SEALs, your Force Recon Marines, special forces Army groups, and so on."

Sarah shifted in her seat and jotted a few more notes on her pad of paper. "Okay..."

"Seal Team Six is black ops, as is the unit where we worked, and of course numerous others no one knows about or talks about. Seal Team Six and Delta Force are probably the most famous black ops military assets, and where we worked grew out of those units."

Sarah blinked at her pad a few times, then her eyes shifted to me. "That sounds dangerous."

"Not to worry. Here we are, safe and sound. But the point is, we've got skills the government trained us to have and then some. We've got over thirty years of operational experience combined, and we've done everything from hostage extraction to... well, we've got a range most small-town law enforcement and many private security companies just don't have."

Sarah's eyes had doubled in size, and she blinked again as she chewed her bottom lip. "Wow."

"All that is to say, there's no reason you should come in knowing what to expect. We'll teach you what we want you to know. Don't ever be afraid to ask questions, and please believe the old adage that there's no such thing as a dumb question." Bruce glanced at me, likely wondering why I hadn't explained all of this in the first place.

I could've. Maybe I should've. But I couldn't have done that until she signed the confidentiality agreements, and that only happened late last week. Then we had the meeting with Grenier, and the last few days had been crammed, so ultimately, I'd decided I'd let Bruce be the information dumper.

And maybe some ugly part of me wanted to withhold things from her. Not exactly a conscious thought, but she'd withheld herself from me for so long, it felt like a reflex more than anything else.

"Agreed. No stupid question," I added, just to make sure she knew.

"Um, sure. I have about a thousand questions right now, but I have a feeling none of them are really applicable to the topic at hand, so I guess just keep going, and I'll chime in if I have anything pertinent."

Her gaze found mine again, and I tried to read what hid behind her now shuttered expression.

Was she scared of me? Or... interested? People had different reactions to knowing a person was in special operations, even if they had no idea just how *special* it was. That information could be everything from an aphrodisiac to a diagnosis, depending on the person receiving the information.

And despite her openness and many tells, I couldn't get her temp on this. Something twisted in my gut at the thought that she'd take either reaction.

"Of course. Now, you've seen the plans and estimates on how many clients we need to bring on in the next few months?"

Sarah responded, and they proceeded with the discussion as I observed them both, wondering what she would think if she knew how I'd spent my time the last twenty years. Wondering why I cared what she thought since she couldn't possibly have had much interest—never mind her apology—or she would've ended the silence between us long before we'd collided here.

CHAPTER FOURTEEN

Wilder

Hours later, after we'd finished our meetings and driven around a bit, Bruce kicked his feet up on my apartment's shabby coffee table and crossed his arms.

"Well, the place is *lovely*, as expected."

I shook my head. He knew what he'd get when he accepted the offer to crash with me for his visit. He didn't necessarily need to penny pinch, but he wanted a nice house for him and Kiley, and he was going to need to make a strong offer if his taste was anything like what it was in North Carolina.

"I thought you might finally hang some pictures, maybe paint an accent wall—something."

"Why would I do that?" I asked, checking the screen for our pizza delivery. Still a few minutes out.

Bruce tucked his hands behind his head and leaned

back. "Oh, I don't know. Because you're back in your hometown?"

"I'm not staying in this place. I'll be moving into my house as soon as it's built." He knew this.

"Mkay. Yeah. Is this the house you're going to be building *yourself*?"

I handed him a beer and took a seat in the chair across from him. "Yes."

"And if I remember right, they're pouring foundation and framing it out in a few weeks, and after that, you're going to do *everything else*."

"Not everything, but most of it."

"And you have a brother who routinely remodels homes and rents them, and you haven't spoken to him about this."

This jerk thought he knew everything. He'd been busy before I left town, and I had, too. He didn't know everything. "No. In fact, he recommended the contractor who's pouring the foundation and doing the framing. He's trying to talk me into having them do more, but I want to be busy."

Bruce gave me one of his dead-eyed stares as though he thought it'd move me. I wasn't some Sergeant waiting to have my ass handed to me by the great and mighty Shark.

Heaving a great sigh, he leaned forward. "I'm not even going to debate you about this because you know how I feel. What I really want to talk about is—"

"Don't."

And at the same time I said that, he, inevitably, said, "Sarah James."

Our gazes locked in a short battle before I had to look away from his smug face. "Nothing to talk about."

"Sure, sure. That's why I could practically *taste* the tension between you after I explained our experience."

"No idea what that was about."

He whipped out his phone and tapped out a text as he spoke. "I think you know that's a load."

"I don't."

"You do."

"I do not."

"Oh heavenly mountain town help me, you are stubborn. Are your brothers this stubborn, too? Is that why you're like this?"

I thought of Warrick and Wyatt, and though I didn't know either of them very well now, I'd known them better than almost anyone for the first seventeen years of my life. "Yes."

He seemed satisfied with that. "Well, that's good. Can't wait to meet 'em. Have you mended fences and such?"

"Ongoing."

He nodded. "Good."

I exhaled, relieved to leave it at that.

"So tomorrow, we'll hit the office for a bit, grab lunch, and then you and Sarah can give me the tour and we'll see a few houses. I'll leave it up to you whether you want to have her join us for the houses or if you want to send her home. But based on the way you keep staring at her—"

"I'm not staring at her."

"Sure. Okay. My bad." He held up his stupid hands.

"Stop with this. We do have history, but we have no future."

His dark brown eyes hit mine in a flash. "You sure about that?"

I nodded.

"How much history we talking here?"

How to sum up what felt like a lifetime of baggage piling up on me lately? I'd tucked it away in an attic somewhere, only for a trapdoor to swing open the minute I made it back here for good. "A lot."

A knock on the door saved me from explaining any more. My neck itched with that alertness I couldn't wish away, and I checked the delivery app to confirm the driver was parked outside. I missed the place I used back at Bragg that would just drop the pizza and go.

When I opened the door, I found Warrick holding the pizza. "Delivery!"

"You delivering pizzas now?"

"No, but I walked up right when the kid was about to ring your bell, and I saved him from facing your surly mug and said it was mine anyway. He knows me so he probably figured I wouldn't be lying and get him in trouble."

I stepped back, making space for him to enter.

"Hope I'm not interrupting—oh. I am..."

"Hey, I'm Bruce. You're Warrick, right?" Bruce must've hopped up the minute he heard Warrick speak, because he was right there, hand extended to my giant of a little brother.

"One and only."

"I'm Wilder's best friend. He won't ever call me that, nor, I'd guess, will you have heard my name, but I'm actually moving out here in a bit."

Warrick's eyes went wide and flickered to me. "Actually, he did mention you the other day. Heading this way for good that soon?"

I nodded as Bruce explained. "Yeah, Saint Securities, despite the name, is half mine. I'm retiring and I'll make my Silverton debut in early June."

Warrick beamed, clearly charmed by Bruce like so many before him. "Awesome. It's great to meet you. Maybe you can tell me some stories about Wilder since I'm sure I'll never hear them from him."

"Oh, I definitely can."

"Did you need something?" I asked, not sure why my reaction was to shut all this down, and yet unable to stop myself or the tightness in my tone. These worlds were inevitably going to collide, but after the afternoon watching Bruce talk with Sarah, I'd had enough of collisions.

I didn't need to look at Bruce to know my response was messed up.

Warrick ditched the pizza box on the counter and held up his hands. "Nothing, really. Just checking in. Thought we could make a plan to catch a movie or grab a drink or something sometime soon."

Guilt and all kinds of crappy feelings fogged up my chest. "Sure. Lunch next week?"

He seemed relieved by that response. "Absolutely. Yes. You choose the day."

"I have an appointment Tuesday, but other than that, I'm good."

So he chose Wednesday, and left after refusing to join us for pizza and beer. As soon as the door shut behind him, Bruce skewered me with a look.

I just shook my head, refusing to drown in the defeat swarming me. "I know."

"Do you, though? Because that was pathetic."

I took a drink of my beer, then set it down a little too hard. "I know."

"He seems nice. Like he actually wants to get to know you again."

I scrubbed my hands through my hair. "I *know*. I don't deserve that."

Without a sound, Bruce sat on the table in front of me

before I realized he'd moved. "I don't want to hear that again."

The swallow of my next gulp was my only response.

"You seeing that psych they recommended for you yet?"

I tipped the neck of the beer toward him. "A few times. Again this Tuesday."

He nodded. "Good. You need it."

At some point, I might've taken offense at that statement—the idea that I needed help to work through my thoughts and feelings. But the interaction with Warrick, and maybe every second I spent around family or even Sarah, reinforced that. I couldn't grit my way through this, or I'd end up living the next twenty years of my life much the same way I had the last twenty. I had to do better with this transition out of a world with very clear boundaries and focus and problem sets, and into this new space where everything felt smashed together. And even though it'd taken me years to admit it, I didn't want that. I wanted more.

So it was time to learn how to take it.

CHAPTER FIFTEEN

Sarah

At the tail end of a delicious lunch at Basta, Bruce set his twinkly eyed focus on me. The man absolutely knew what effect he had on people, and even if I wasn't particularly attracted to him, he was *attractive*. As in, he drew a person in, made you want to get to know him.

Good luck to the single female residents of Silverton when Bruce Camden became a local. Granted, quite a few women had been eying him and Wilder the entire lunch, especially the table of four giggling over their lunchtime wineglasses. They looked ridiculously glamorous and were probably either famous or wealthy or both. They'd probably be more than a little enamored by these two men, who were not just gorgeous but also highly trained expert soldiers. Ex-soldiers? I guess maybe they weren't soldiers anymore since Wilder was retired and Bruce would be any day now, but whatever the case, they were kind of... dangerous.

"Are you up for joining us for the house hunt, Sarah?" Bruce asked as we exited the restaurant, shaking me from my obnoxious thoughts.

I'd never been attracted to anyone like I had been or currently was to Wilder. Knowing that he was very good at what he'd done in the military only increased that. It made no sense, other than the universal appeal of someone who's really good at their job. Apparently, Wilder was good at rescuing hostages and... other stuff.

"I should probably get back to, uh..." How did I bow out of this little excursion gracefully when the two men I'd be with were my bosses?

"Did you send Ms. Reynolds the assessment of her place?" Wilder asked in that low, gruff voice.

My pulse spiked from his words and the feeling that I'd missed the mark. I hadn't realized it was ready to send. "No, but if you've got it finished, I'll send it over this afternoon."

"It should be waiting for you in the drive."

I nodded, relieved to have a legitimate reason for needing to get back and avoiding any more time with these two. The proximity to Wilder that being in a car would necessitate paired with the act of looking at houses itself just didn't sound like something I was up for. "Perfect. Then I'll head back and get that done, and I'll close up at five. I hope you find some really good options."

"That sounds good. I'm just trying to get Wilder here to show me his property, but he won't—"

"There's nothing nearby. We can't be neighbors anyway," Wilder cut in.

His face had shut down to that unreadable blank expression. Something about it made me ask, "You have a house?"

"No."

The sharp slice of the word shouldn't have hurt, but it did. Fool that it made me, it absolutely did. "Sorry. I didn't mean to pry."

The blush heating my cheeks would've been mortifying enough, but the fact that tears pricked my eyes was downright humiliating. I wouldn't let them see that silliness, so I turned and tossed my manners to the curb as I hollered, "See you soon, Bruce!"

I honestly wasn't sure I'd see him again until he moved out here, but that time would come soon enough. I sucked in a breath of the cool spring air and blinked away the tears.

Why would I let him affect me like this? Of course it wasn't just his curt response. It was everything about this situation lately that just felt *hard*. I wanted to enjoy having this job that had already been more interesting than anything I'd done in the last decade and a half of my professional life. I wanted to enjoy being back near Wilder, who had been my best friend before he'd become my love.

But neither of those things were easy to do. Accepting this job appealed to me would do nothing in the long run since Diane would eventually have her baby and finish her maternity leave. I wouldn't have this for long, and then I'd be stuck trying to find a teaching position next year and facing the reality that even if I found the perfect one, I wasn't sure I wanted that anymore. Or worse, maybe that I never had.

Or more likely, that it was time for me to move on from Silverton. If I really did wrap up things with Jane and accept how things were between me and Wilder, what else was I here for?

"Sarah, hold up a minute."

Bruce's voice broke through my internal debate. I

turned to find him a few feet away. Behind him, no sign of Wilder.

"Everything okay?" I asked, because I was not about to ask where Wilder had gone.

He frowned. "I should be asking you that, but I already know. Wilder was needlessly rude back there, and I just wanted to say..." He ran a hand through his hair and looked around him, clearly not taking in any of the small shops or people walking.

"You don't have to apologize for him. I shouldn't have asked him something personal like that—not really appropriate for an employee, right?"

His lips thinned into a more intense version of that original frown. "I think if these were normal circumstances and you were Diane and she asked about his property, he would've responded differently. That getting to know your coworker, and where they live in a small town like Silverton, wouldn't be unheard of or crossing any lines. But I think because you're *you* and he's *him*, for whatever reason, he didn't want to talk about it."

I searched his face for pity or disgust, both of which I'd expect if he knew what'd happened between us. Not a trace of either. Instead, something I could've sworn was concern.

"Well, yeah. You might be right."

He stood taller. "I am right. And as much as I don't want to overstep, I have known Wilder really well for the last decade. I've been there through some nasty stuff, and I've seen him start to change for the better in a few ways, even in the last six months. Retiring from active duty is no small thing."

I offered him a small smile. "I suppose you know what that's like."

He nodded. "I'm in the process of it now, and it's bigger

than I can handle, I'll tell you that. But that's what thera-pists are for, right?" He chuckled and winked.

"I guess so, yeah," I said, more than a little amazed that he spoke so freely about that. My impression of the man was that he had it all together.

"Point is, Sarah, I think you and Wilder have unfinished business."

A wave of something hot and heavy washed over me, and the blush that had barely died down sprang back full force. "Hmm" was all I could say in response, because what did that mean? Did he know what'd happened between us and thought I needed to make a better effort at apologizing?

"All I'm going to say is this. Wilder's a good man. What-ever history is behind you two is just that—history. You should think about what you have in mind for your future."

His brown eyes jumped back and forth between mine like he was trying to read whether I was getting his message. At this point, I couldn't tell either.

"Okay. Thanks." Because, what else could I say? This was definitely the weirdest conversation I could've imag-ined having with Bruce.

"Well, I think I've overstepped enough. Better go find grumpy pants and scout myself a house. See you in June, Sarah."

"Bye, Bruce."

I watched him jog back down the street and round the corner before I started walking again. My mind swirled with questions and a whole slew of emotions I didn't want to sort through, so instead, I focused on taking in the scene around me.

Silverton hadn't quite burst completely into spring yet, especially thanks to the mid-April cold front that'd swept through. Too early still to plant anything since we'd have frosts on and off until the end of May, but little buds had appeared on the cherry trees and all the stores and restaurants had springy décor in their windows.

I needed to stop in at Bloom and see what glorious arrangements Dahlia was working on. I should try to see if she could hang this weekend, or maybe I could help her if she had a wedding to prep for.

After shooting off a text to Dahlia, I unlocked the office door and got settled at my computer. Sure enough, I had an e-mail from Wilder from just before we'd left the office. *No wonder I'd missed it.* But there right above it sat another one, time stamped just five minutes ago.

My heart thumped and I reached for my water and chugged down a few gulps before clicking on the bolded e-mail, which had no subject line. Normally, I'd wonder what kind of psychopath didn't use a subject line, but in this moment, it didn't slow me down.

Inside, I expected the e-mail held a few spare words like every other correspondence I'd received from him, but this one was different.

I shouldn't have snapped at you. I'm sorry. Please let me buy you a drink tomorrow and make it up to you.

My pulse flew into overdrive as I read and reread the message.

He'd snapped at me, shut down my questions, and now he was asking me out for a drink? My gut had two responses. First? *Yeah right, buddy!* Second? *Yes!* I hated that second response, but I understood it. I didn't want this to be a guilt-motivated apology drink, but I understood the need to make things right between us. I'd been looking for that chance for years and years, hadn't I? I'd finally gotten it, and so if this small incident between us could be corrected sooner than later and avoid even more awkwardness, then so be it. One less thing hanging out there waiting to be resolved before I left.

I typed my response and sent it before I could second-guess myself. Now all I had to do was figure out what to wear to an apology drink non-date with Wilder.

CHAPTER SIXTEEN

Wilder

Bruce had departed a few hours ago, and I was left to pace my apartment and try not to hate myself for ever initiating this meeting with Sarah.

Meeting. *Right.* This was not a meeting, and I knew it. We weren't doing this as boss-employee, or it wouldn't be happening at six on a Saturday evening.

No. This was me trying to make up for being an utter jerk to her yesterday for no good reason whatsoever. Or at least not a reason I could explain to her. I couldn't very well say that I wanted her to know everything about that property and yet couldn't bear the thought of her knowing my plans. And since I didn't want to go into work, where I'd think about her, or pace around this lifeless apartment, where I felt caged and annoyed, I threw on my running shoes and took off.

The altitude still had me moving slow, but I ran my

eight miles in less than an hour, and that felt pretty good considering I hadn't run more than three since getting here. After showering, trimming my beard since Bruce had begged me to before meeting with Madeline Reynolds next week and I'd need to do it by degrees since I hated change, and grabbing my keys, I took off to downtown on foot.

I wouldn't be able to walk into town this easily once I moved to my house. I'd never thought I'd enjoy the proximity to other people or really any measure of civilization, but the convenience of walking to meet Sarah wasn't lost on me. Thankfully, it wasn't even a full fifteen minutes from my property, and once I had a house there, I knew I'd appreciate the seclusion.

Craic, the Irish pub where Sarah had suggested we meet, bustled with people. Tall bistro tables were full of weekend revelers sipping drinks and chatting. On the south end, a space for large shuffleboard tables featured what had to be college students cheering each other on for some brilliant move in the game. Just past the tables sat a dart board, currently unoccupied. The dark polished wood bar had people crammed in from one end to another, but in the middle of it all, I spotted her.

More like, my eyes found their way there, like they would in any circumstance, at any time, on any day. My eyes wanted to find and stay with Sarah, and so they did. She wore a pale green dress that left her knees and calves exposed. Her heels looked high, but since she sat on a barstool with her shoes hooked over the footrest rail, I couldn't tell for sure.

My pulse raced as she turned her head and laughed while tucking her long, glossy blond hair behind her ear. *Wait.* Who'd put that smile on her face?

Ah—the man standing in front of her, pouring out

liquor and shooting her a smile she no doubt found dazzling. The bartender. And of course, bartenders were more successful if they flirted, but this one looked genuinely interested. Maybe he'd just said as much.

My heart thrummed in my chest like a jealous idiot, but my legs propelled me toward her of their own accord. Before I knew it, I'd set a hand on her lower back and leaned down to speak into her ear over the clanging loudness of the bar, telling her thanks for meeting me, right there in front of Sir Charmsalot and everyone.

Sarah's startled response wasn't exactly what I would've wanted, but I couldn't blame her. I'd just touched her for the first time since our hands had grazed when I held up her mug last week, and I'd caught a whiff of her delicious scent when I'd spoken into her ear. I shouldn't have gotten that close.

I wanted to get closer.

"Hi," she said and looked at me full on.

Probably best she hadn't done that before I'd reached her, or I might've stormed over here and hauled her over my shoulder. That animal instinct in me wanted to claim her right here, right now, in front of all these idiots and especially this dark and stormy character behind the bar.

"That'll be him, then?" the bartender asked with, of course, a slight Irish accent.

Was this guy for real? I was supposed to believe he was actually Irish living here in Silverton? Though to be fair, the place had diversified exponentially since I'd left two decades ago, and my mom had been bragging on the growth of the town for years now. A small hospital was even going in soon, so why not a true Irish bartender at the local Irish pub?

Sarah beamed back at the man. "Yes, indeed." She

switched her attention to me, and something in me calmed. "I wasn't sure what you'd want, so I didn't order for you."

"I'll have what you're having."

Her brow wrinkled. "Really? I'm committing the mortal sin of having sparkling wine in a pub."

I must've made a face, because she laughed, which sent pinpricks of awareness all over me. She'd always had a great laugh, and she'd done it easily. I'd never been a funny man, but I'd tried my hardest around her.

"I take it back, then. I'll have the Silver Ridge Brewery's spring seasonal."

"Coming right up," the bartender said, lifting a pint glass to the tap at a perfect angle. He'd been doing this awhile—the fluidity in his movements said he'd likely done it for years. At least he knew how to pour a beer.

"Sorry I'm a minute late," I said, unable to keep my eyes from gobbling up the sight of her. The dress, the hair, and that face I had loved—yes, loved. She was everything.

"You were right on time. I was just..." She chuckled and tucked her hair behind her ear again. "I was nervous, so I ended up getting here a little early."

My heart squeezed. God, she was so open and soft. So damned beautiful through and through. "Don't be nervous."

"Can't help it."

I angled closer to her, but not so much that I was crowding her. I didn't want her nervous. "It's just me."

She inhaled, her eyes finding mine. "I know."

And maybe I should've taken that as a bad thing, or a good thing, but all I could tell was that I needed to do my part to make things right between us. "I'm sorry for yesterday."

"It's okay."

Too quick. Her response came too quick, and though I

didn't think she'd tried to lie to me, she had. "It isn't. I shouldn't have spoken to you like that. It was a knee-jerk response. I have no excuse except to say I'm sorry. I'm still working on being open, and it's hard. Being back here. Even with you."

She tucked her lips between her teeth and nodded.

The tightness in her understanding smile made me say, "But I want to."

"What?"

"I want to get to know you. I want to be open with you."

Her brows rose and she bit her bottom lip, which drew my attention for a half second before I refocused on her eyes.

"You do?"

The sheer disbelief and sweetness of her question cut right through any hope I had of maintaining my usual mask. And because it felt right, I let it. My face broke into a smile, and I wanted to pull her to me and hug her more than I might've wanted anything else in my whole life.

"Don't be so shocked," I said, trying to maintain some level of calm and distance.

She turned back to her wine on the bar and raised the glass to her mouth in a motion so slow, it would've been comical if it didn't indicate just how surprised my comment had made her. That didn't bode well for what she thought of me, if my desire to let her know me came as such a revelation.

Though why wouldn't it? I couldn't honestly say I'd been anything but professional with her beyond the moment with the mug and perhaps the fact that my mom commandeered her to go to the bookstore.

As was my way, I stayed quiet, hoping she'd come to me and equally dreading her doing just that. This tactic worked with all manner of people, and since it happened to be my default setting, I used it more often than not. Granted, I didn't dread anyone else doing what I wanted. I did with her because if she came to me, I knew by the way everything in me responded to her that I wouldn't have the strength to push her away.

After a minute, she turned to me.

"Why?"

Fair question, and I'd wondered the same. What in me wanted her to know me after she'd opted out? "I'm not sure."

Her teeth returned to that full bottom lip as her eyes flickered back and forth between mine. "Okay."

My brows jumped in response, a reflection of the hammering heart in my chest. "Okay?"

She nodded.

I waited.

When she didn't break eye contact or speak or give me any hints about what that meant, I broke. "What does that mean?"

A smile flashed, but she tucked it away like she'd made herself promise not to show me. That neanderthal in me that wanted everything of Sarah's to be mine reared its ugly head, but I shut it down with an elbow to the face.

"It means I'd like that—for you to get to know me."

She blinked in a way I recognized, a quick double-blink that I remembered signaled nerves and anticipation.

My stomach twisted low. I'd seen that double blink before and good things always came after it. "Good."

"Here you go, Sarah, love." The bartender set another thin glass flute with bubbling liquid down in front of her.

"So, what do you want to know?" she asked, toying with

the base of the glass now nestled on a Silver Ridge Brewing coaster.

And though I knew it made me seem a jealous jerk, more than an idiot, I couldn't stop myself from asking the least interesting question possible as a way to ease in. "How about why the bartender's calling you *love?*"

CHAPTER SEVENTEEN

Sarah

What on earth?

Was I really hearing that slight twinge of jealousy in his voice? "That's really what you want to know?"

A flicker of uncertainty crossed his face before he shook his head. "No. But I haven't talked to many beautiful women lately, so I might be a bit rusty."

His response had a dual effect. First, my stomach flipped at the compliment. Second, a little streak of jealousy shot through me at the idea that he had, at any point, talked to beautiful women and knew what to say. But of course he had. It'd been twenty years. *Twenty.* We'd both lived separate lives. I'd had my own relationships and made my own mistakes.

Though so many of those mistakes had been with him. Yes, they'd come after a loss I couldn't control, but then I'd hurt him. Yet again, the flimsy apology I'd made, the lack of a real conversation about everything that had happened, threatened to crush me.

But Wilder was here. He'd come willingly, if prompted by Bruce. And he'd confessed how difficult this was—being close. Trying.

So I could move past that niggling unfinished feeling and be here, too.

"Well, you don't have to be anything but you. Rust and all. And in case you're actually wondering, I'm pretty sure he calls anything remotely female *love*."

"False. He hasn't called any of the other women at the bar *love* since we sat down."

"You've been listening?"

"I'm trained to stay aware."

I glanced around, noting a handful of other women at various points across the bar. If the bartender really didn't call anyone else by the nickname, maybe it was notable. But mostly? No. Not newsworthy. "Kieran is an acquaintance and a nice guy, but there's nothing going on between us or anything. I haven't dated anyone since—for a long time."

And at some point, I'd finish the original sentence there, but not right this minute.

As much as I'd been thrilled to hear him apologize so sincerely and declare his desire to get to know me, I wasn't ready to lay it all out there.

"How is that possible?"

My mental defense of what I hadn't told him had distracted me. "What?"

"That you haven't dated. I'm taciturn and introverted—for me, it makes sense. But you?" His eyes skated over my face from hair to forehead, down over my nose and lingering on my lips before sweeping back up along my jaw and cheek to meet my eyes again. That line of his gaze felt like the drag of his fingertips, barely palpable and yet utterly scintillating. "You're more beautiful than ever, Sarah. I mean it."

My stomach swooped low. I thanked the Sarah of an hour ago who'd taken an extra few minutes on her hair and makeup, even though I knew, if he was at all the same man he'd been, those things weren't what drew him to me.

"Thank you."

A big ruckus shot up when someone did something over at the shuffleboard tables. I didn't know the game, so I had no idea what that might be, but I smiled over at them and clapped along with the people who had joined in the applause. It was a good excuse to look away from his intensity and pull in a breath.

Wilder had been studying me, and his eyes didn't waver when I turned back to the bar and caught him. I'd forgotten what it was like to be the focus of his attention, or maybe I'd never known what it was to be this *man's* focus. He'd been seventeen the last time we'd been anywhere together like this.

"So Bruce is a character," I said, hoping to ease the quiet between us.

He gave a half-smile. "He talked to you after I was a jerk."

"He made a compelling case for cutting you some slack."

His brows lowered into a kind of scowl. "He's a busybody."

I chuckled, but the person to my left bumped me and I jolted forward. On reflex, I grabbed the bar with my left hand, and where my right would've flailed around, Wilder's caught it and steadied me. Heat flashed through me at the contact with his skin and that firm grip.

"You okay?"

"Yes. It's just crazy in here, right?" I hoped my searching glance around to indicate the madness of the pub hid how breathless his touch had made me.

"My first time in."

"Ah. Well, it's busier than usual, although I don't normally go out on weekend nights so maybe I'm totally wrong."

He still held my hand, but when I glanced down to see his slightly darker, calloused hand on mine, he released me.

"Should we go?"

"Would you want to see if we could stand outside? It's not too cold, and I bet they have their heaters going. It can be nice." I hated that I felt so unsure suggesting anything to him right now, but I did. I accepted his apology, but I didn't know what to expect with him.

"Let's go," he said, and grabbed his beer, then my hand. He signaled something to Kieran, who gave him a nod of understanding. Apparently, he'd made peace with the man's existence.

I took my drink in my free hand and followed behind Wilder, the touch of our palms and the way our fingers laced together sending little lightning flashes all up my arm. As though he had actually been here before, he stepped through the back door and out onto the deck. Only a few people hung out here, but Wilder led us to the farthest point of the deck and settled his beer on the table right next to a standing heater.

The sky hadn't gotten fully dark yet, but the air had cooled enough that it had grown quite chilly. The heater helped, though.

"It cooled off quite a bit," I said, removing my hand from his and focusing on the drink in front of me again.

There were only so many times I could stare into the bubbles in my glass and avoid the gargantuan feelings pressing in on me, but I'd do it as long as I could get away with it.

"It feels good. Never got like this in North Carolina this late in the year. Is it too cold?"

I studied him in the dimming light. He'd trimmed his beard, though it was still substantial. It cut closer at his jaw now, serving to highlight his alarmingly good looks even more. Just taking him in like this made my stomach hurt a little.

"No. It's fine. Did you like North Carolina?"

His eyes narrowed and he looked up at the glorious view of Silver Ridge Peak. "Parts."

I waited, but when no more came, I let out a breathy laugh. His raised eyebrow was apparently all I'd get in response.

"You're just still so… you."

His intense gaze didn't waver from mine. "Parts of me are. But… Sorry."

"No. No, it's not bad. It's good." How could I explain that I'd loved him? I'd loved this part of him. Of course, it'd driven me insane sometimes, but I'd loved him as he was when we were kids. Being around him outside of work made all those feelings seem very nearby.

He made a little harrumph of a sound. "Sure."

I grabbed at his shirt, narrowly resisting the urge to set a hand against his heart. I'd wished I could hear it beat again —wished with every part of me in those days after I'd left Silverton, and often over the years, too.

"I mean it. I never made you feel like you had to be anything else, did I?" He knew I meant before.

His dark blue eyes looked black in the low light. "No. You didn't."

"Why do you say only parts of you are still you?" I asked, my voice sounding oddly shaky, and my heart feeling that, too.

He shook his head, and I wondered if that was all I'd get. But instead of leaving it there, he explained.

"I'm at a transition point in my life. I've felt a weird mix of lost and found leaving the Army. Being back here gives me that same sense."

The way he said it, the inflection especially, made me ask, "Being here in Silverton, or here with me?"

And it was only a short pause before he confirmed. "Both."

CHAPTER EIGHTEEN

Wilder

Warrick radiated his usual bounding energy as we sat eating lunch. I worked to suppress the nerves that'd come out of nowhere in the last hour as the meeting with the biggest client I'd likely ever have approached. Bit of a rough way to begin things, but considering I'd escorted presidents and celebrities and done about a thousand other things that made me sweat, I shouldn't have been stressing over the Reynolds meeting.

"So you really can't tell me who it is that's got you all fidgety?" he asked after finishing the last bite of his gigantic salad, favoring his injured arm just barely.

Internally, I worked to shut down that observation as though he was a mark I might need to disarm later with this weakness in mind. The default setting of my mind still needed a little work to adjust to civilian life.

"Nope."

"And it's definitely not Sarah? I heard you were out together over the weekend."

That mischievous glint in his eyes had me shaking my head. "Nope."

He blinked back at me over his water glass, his face so unamused, I almost laughed. But I couldn't very well break now.

"Okay, so you're giving me nothing. Why did I bring you to lunch?"

His tone stayed light, but I could feel the honest question in the words.

He'd done most of the talking in the last twenty minutes while we both scarfed down a meal at a table outside Diner. Fortunately for me, the late April day was gorgeous, and Warrick had suggested the outdoor option. I wasn't certain it'd be a problem, but I remembered walking out of the old diner smelling like fries and didn't relish meeting Madeline Reynolds with a cloud of fried food scent floating around me.

I should've nixed lunch today, but Warrick had shown up right on time, and I couldn't bring myself to cancel or reschedule. At eleven thirty, he'd come in the front door and oohed and aahed over the office space after a short tour and then got that expectant look. Time for lunch. Since Reynolds and her entourage wouldn't be arriving until two, I had time and no decent excuse other than wanting to fold in on myself before the meeting. But I was moving past that, working on being more present even when it wasn't convenient. Plus, I'd needed the distraction.

One, because I had actually developed a small twinge of nervousness over this meeting, and two, because Sarah looked predictably beautiful, and our time together Saturday had given me all kinds of ideas.

I had no business getting ideas about Sarah.

Not long after we'd moved outside on Saturday, her sister had called from somewhere overseas, and when I realized it wouldn't be a short conversation unless Sarah made it so on my behalf, I paid our tab and walked her out. Phone still to her ear, she'd given me a look and mouthed, *I'm sorry*.

Definitely an escape the lunatic who'd taken over my brain had needed because if she hadn't gotten that call, I would've walked her home. Definitely would've kissed her if she seemed interested, and I was fairly certain I'd picked that up from her. But maybe it was better we hadn't had the chance after our very first personal conversation.

The physical connection was still there—our bodies were drawn to each other. That was what a seventeen-year-old could not ignore and what a man my age should be able to. But that wasn't all Sarah and I had when we were younger, and already, I could tell things were easy between us in that way they'd been. She wasn't pressing me into a different shape, waiting for my conversational wings to sprout. She wasn't impatient with the internalizing. And along the winding road she'd traveled to get back to Silverton, she'd kept the ability to be kind. To be gentle, even.

Sarah had the ability to connect with people in a genuine way I'd never grasped. I'd learned my fair share of skills, but in a mission set requiring charm or verbal finesse, we sent in Bruce or West, maybe even Waverly. Sarah could do the job though. I'd berated her for the way she spoke with Juliet but that was simply Sarah doing what Sarah did.

Maybe that was why her silence had felt so persistent. Even after I'd grown used to it, I'd wake from a dream and *feel* it all over again.

So yes, I would've wanted to kiss her. I'd accepted since

the first day she'd showed at work that I was pretty much doomed to want that. But it was the other part that should scare me—just what I'd told her. I wanted to know her, and I wanted her to know me. In the same way I longed for my family to know me in ways I hadn't let them since I'd left, I wanted that from her.

Everything had jumbled together, wires with too many ends to be one clear line, and as much as having a mess like that made pressure mount in my chest, I'd learned to carry that around. I'd learned to handle pressure.

Her quick, repeated apology for the call Monday, my running around the rest of the day and being gone much of yesterday, and our too-short interaction this morning before we both dove into preparation for the Reynolds meeting mostly served to keep me only half-distracted.

I had no business thinking about Sarah. I needed to focus on this job—this meeting. Landing Madeline Reynolds would be a killer contract, and though it seemed like it was almost guaranteed based on Grenier's recommendation, I didn't assume. The job isn't done until the mission is accomplished, and the mission right now was landing Reynolds' contract and then nailing the job itself for her.

If I was going to think about anything other than work, it shouldn't be Sarah. It should be family. I'd come back to Silverton to plant roots and repair wounds. Enter Warrick, and I had a legitimate distraction I didn't need to feel guilty about.

Warrick front and center did the job. And I owed him more than one-word answers. He, even more than Sarah, had been at the forefront of my conversation with my therapist yesterday, and though I still felt like I had a mild hangover from the session, I also felt like someone had taken a weight off the top of a large pile.

Finally circling back to his question, which he'd probably given up getting an answer to, I said, "You brought me so I could apologize and clear a few things up."

His brows jumped, but he recovered and waved a hand in front of him. "The floor is yours."

I nodded, a smile pulling at my lips. He'd always had a great sense of humor, even as a kid. Despite most of our conversations being brief over the years, I'd gotten the sense he'd maintained that. I admired it—one of many things about my younger brother I could say that about.

"I'm sorry for keeping you at a distance. It was never because I didn't care about you or want to know you."

His whole demeanor had shifted to something a little smaller, softer.

I forged ahead. "I'm still figuring myself out. Just started, really. But I've wanted to say that for a long time. I haven't known how to be a part of your lives here and still do what I did there. Some people are better at that kind of thing, I think, but I never was. Or maybe, I'm not. But I came back specifically because I want to do better—be a better brother and son. And I hope, at some point, you'll forgive me for everything I've missed—for shutting you out and staying gone."

Face tight, jaw clenched, Warrick blinked a few more times as he studied me. Thanks to years of practice staying stoic in all manners of discomfort, I didn't shift around under the weight of his gaze. I let him look—let him see the mess that sat across from him.

He cleared his throat. "I don't know whether to be more shocked by the content of your speech, or the sheer volume of words you just spoke at one time."

I shook my head, heart crushing under the weight of regret and hope that flooded me. "Either way, I guess."

He smiled. "Thank you. I haven't felt—" His eyes tracked away from the table, over to the still-snowy mountain peaks to his right, then he chugged the rest of his water before facing me with eyes just a touch red. "I haven't felt you owed me an apology, but I appreciate it."

We breathed through the moment together, emotion charging the air and every word spoken. I couldn't find a response to that, though, so I simply nodded.

"You did miss a lot, but I'm glad you're back. We all are."

Another nod acknowledged his words.

Then he smirked. "And at some point, we're going to talk about you and Sarah working twenty feet apart in that office every day with no one to serve as buffer between you."

I scowled. "You think we'll fight?"

He gave me a look like I was truly crazy. "No. I think you're going to go up in flames of passion any day now. I might've been like ten when you guys were together and totally did not get what all went down when she left at the time, but I remember the way it felt to stand in a room with the two of you."

"Yeah? How was that?"

His brow smoothed out and he gave me a grin so wide, I internally braced myself for whatever would come out at the sight of it.

"Like I was learning something. Like at any point, you two would unravel into a heap of what I thought at the time would be kisses, but..." He winked.

Tossing my balled-up napkin at him, I stood. "And with that—"

He burst out laughing and rose to stand as well. The waitress had already cashed us out, so I wandered back toward the office while Warrick followed, cackling with self-satisfied glee the whole way.

When we reached the little yard finally dotted with dark purple and yellow crocus buds along the border of the flower bed, I faced Warrick. "Thanks for lunch."

"Thanks for actually talking."

And then, he stepped forward at the same time I did, and we embraced. My heart clutched, and the welling of years' worth of distance and longing hit with the pat of his ridiculously large hand.

"I've never said anything, because I was young then, but with you back, it's been on my mind. I just wanted to say I'm sorry. For your loss. The baby, I mean."

Like a punch to the gut, the well-meaning words landed their blow, and I exhaled sharply through my nose.

When we pulled back, I suspected we wore identical expressions of feigned composure. The moisture at the corner of his eye and flush of his cheeks were no doubt mirrored on my face.

"See you soon, Wilder."

I nodded. "See you soon, War."

CHAPTER NINETEEN

Sarah

Wilder's lunch only lasted forty-five minutes, but I'd been a nervous wreck the entire time. Not because he'd been gone, but because Madeline Reynolds's assistant had called to say they'd be arriving at one. Not two o'clock, as planned, but an hour early. I'd decided to call Wilder at the last possible minute since I didn't want to interrupt his time with Warrick. The little bit I'd gleaned from Sadie told me they needed the time together.

Thankfully, he walked in at twelve fifty, just in time to make sure we had everything ready. Was I prepared to be in a room however long this meeting would last with this iteration of Wilder? The one who'd arrived this morning in a black designer suit, white shirt, black tie, and trimmed hair and beard?

No. No, I was not. And then, not even touching the fact

that girl power icon and brilliant business mind Madeline Reynolds would be sitting at the same table.

"Everything okay around here?"

He'd asked me to trade off lunchtimes so we had someone in the office throughout the day. It made sense, and fortunately, I'd brought my lunch and shoveled it down the minute I'd hung up with Madeline Reynolds's assistant so that I wouldn't be starving by the end of the day.

I shot to my feet. "The Reynolds meeting is now at one o'clock."

He paused for half a second and his eyes flicked to mine. "Ah. Okay. You ready?"

I nodded. "Just need a quick bathroom break, and I'll get some new coffee brewing."

"I've got the coffee. Do what you need to do, and then hang at your desk until they arrive." He slipped his tie tighter and adjusted it before he stopped even with my desk. "Her assistant is texting you when they park, right?"

"Yes. We'll have a quick heads-up. Assuming they aren't early, that means we've got about seven minutes."

He might've nodded, but I'd already taken off to use the bathroom, making sure it all looked orderly and the soap was full just in case she needed the facilities during the meeting. I could hear Wilder's low murmur into his phone from the break room as he pushed the button to brew the coffee, and finally shuffled back to my desk and straightened out my chair.

"You good?"

I nodded, nerves crawling up my throat and heart racing. I hoped I was. But this was all very intense, and what if I said something wrong? Or what if I *couldn't* say anything because I was too starstruck?

Now that he'd trimmed his beard—and not just a little, but so much that I could actually see the trace of that dimple he had in his left cheek—I could see the corner of his mouth pull up. "You're good."

"If you say so," I felt compelled to add as I stood and took a deep breath.

"I do say so. You'll be fine."

Though part of me wanted to shoot off a sarcastic remark about his confidence, years of doubting myself and my choices rushed back at this, the least opportune time ever.

"Maybe I should go. I'm not sure I won't do something weird or say something wrong."

His dark brows dipped low, and his gaze moved between my eyes, like each one held a different truth. "You're staying. You're fine."

My phone buzzed with the assistant's text. "They're here."

Wilder turned to me. "Tie straight?"

I pressed my lips together. "Actually, no."

He looked down, but of course couldn't see.

"Let me," I said and stepped into his space. I specifically didn't breathe or take any time to appreciate our proximity. Like so many other things, now was not the time.

Careful not to touch anything but his tie, I straightened the knot, then pressed it down. His gaze rested heavily on me, and when I met his eyes, my stomach tumbled. "All set."

"Thank you," he said, low and gruff and don't mind if I do, delicious. The sound, the scent, the visual... all of it.

What is wrong with me? I couldn't stop thinking about him, especially since Saturday. He'd been a befuddling combination of open and heartbreaking. For me, with that man, there couldn't have been a more attractive pairing.

Unless he'd trimmed his beard and worn this suit, maybe. I'd never thought I preferred one style over another, never having truly cared about such things, but my current level of discombobulation over simply standing near him when he looked like this was more than a little ridiculous.

"Incoming," he said, still looking at me, his eyes somehow darker, before he turned just in time to step toward the opening door.

I exhaled, working to steady myself. Why hadn't we had a heated moment like that hours ago, without an audience, when I could break the ice between us and bring up the weekend?

"Mr. Saint?" A thin, surprisingly young man peeked inside and seemed to be shuffling a device and two phones, then opened the door fully as Wilder stepped forward.

"Anthony, is it? Welcome." Wilder extended his hand, and I saw the moment Anthony took in Wilder.

His eyes widened comically, and he gasped loudly enough I could hear it from fifteen feet away, where I stood in front of my desk.

"Oh. Uh, yeah. And this is, uh, is... Ms. Madeline Reynolds."

A woman and an absolute giant of a man stepped inside behind him and the man shut the door. My heart rate rocketed and I willed my cheeks not to flush. There she was. *There she is!*

"Please, come in. We'll be in the conference room this way."

Wilder gestured toward me, and I smiled and forced my lead legs to move. Aside from encountering people around town the last year, I'd never really met anyone famous other than Calla. Certainly not up close like this, and not someone who I admired.

The three followed silently behind me, and I wondered if they'd be so stoic the entire meeting. I still hadn't gotten a good look at the guest of honor because Anthony stood in front of her, and she hadn't taken off her oversized sunglasses.

In the conference room, we'd set out five places as Anthony had told us her retinue would include two others, but no matter. I quickly slipped the two folders into my hands and waved to the table but had to lightly clear my throat before I managed to speak. "Please have a seat. Would anyone like coffee?"

"I'll take some," the larger man said.

"We're all set," Anthony said, apparently in answer for both him and Ms. Reynolds.

"Of course. I'll be right back," I said, and hustled out the door, flashing Wilder a grin as I passed.

A few minutes later, Wilder sat at one end of the table, and I sat to the left with my back to the door. Ms. Reynolds sat opposite Wilder at the other end, her bodyguard on the far side of the table, Anthony next to me. After everyone had settled in their seat and the bodyguard introduced himself as Brad, Ms. Reynolds removed her sunglasses.

Thankfully, I managed to hide the shock that seeing her sans glasses caused. Her familiar, lovely face was shadowed. Removing the shades had revealed dark circles and swelling around each eye as though she hadn't slept in days—maybe weeks.

"Thank you for meeting me," she said, her voice calm.

"Happy to have you. Ms. Christensen gave us an overview but mentioned you'd have some needs you'd only discuss in person. While I respect the need for privacy, I can assure you I'll be able to put together a plan that meets your needs more effectively if I have all the information."

Madeline Reynolds's gaze didn't waver from Wilder's. She took his measure as much as he took hers.

Meanwhile, Anthony bristled. "Ms. Reynolds isn't required to divulge every security challenge she has. She doesn't plan to—"

"It's all right." Her voice cut in, somehow both decisive and gentle.

Anthony's head whipped to her, and after a moment assessing her, he nodded.

All attention focused back on her, and she spoke for herself. "I've taken a sabbatical from work. I'll be in town full time starting in May until at least the end of June."

Wilder nodded, signaling he was listening and already tracking this. Juliet had given us this basic info.

"I've had some trouble with a stalker lately. It has become rather disconcerting, and I'm hoping a change of scene will help. I'm also hoping that adding your security measures will do the same."

By some miracle, I didn't gasp or let my jaw drop like I wanted to. *Stalker?* No wonder she looked like she hadn't slept in weeks—still expertly composed and calm as she reported this messed up situation, but clearly affected. I hated it for her, even though I didn't know her. No one should feel unsafe like this.

"How long has the stalking been going on? And what level of involvement has law enforcement had?" Wilder set his pen down.

"It's been a little over four months now. LAPD and NYPD are both aware of the situation. The FBI is also aware."

The FBI? Whoa. Two police departments and the FBI

seemed to me like a really big deal. Based on the unconceal-able reality of her exhaustion, I wondered what all had happened, worried it was something much worse than this very composed, calm woman indicated.

Wilder didn't seem concerned. "If you're going with us, I'll want you to connect me with your FBI contact. I know a few people there but not anyone close in domestics. We'll want a brief on what that's looked like for you so we're aware."

Brad nodded. "Ready whenever she gives the word. But heads up, I'm keeping man and cyber."

Wilder squinted, assessing the guy. "Is that firm?"

Brad nodded, those giant arms still crossed. "Yep. It's mine. No flexibility."

I wasn't entirely following, but I'd ask Wilder after.

"I understand you're very new. Are you at all concerned about working with my existing team?"

Ms. Reynolds seemed perfectly relaxed in her seat, but I could see signs of strain beyond the darkened eyes—a tight-ness around her mouth, the set of her shoulders that seemed brittle somehow.

"What I'll do for you is not all that different from some of the work I did in the military. One of my specialties is assessing a situation and making a plan. I'll be adding care-fully vetted personnel to the team, and by the time you arrive, you'll be assigned a manager—most likely myself. I'll work with your team as much as they're willing—it won't be an issue on my end."

"I'd like it to be you."

He nodded. "Then it's me. And by the time you're here, your house will have the full setup. We'll run perimeter security, you'll have your man, and anytime you need backup, I'm ten minutes out. We'll put together a plan for whatever your other needs might be."

A ripple of concern crossed her face, but she nodded. "Thank you. And now, could I have a moment with you in your office?"

CHAPTER TWENTY

Wilder

I'd seen this look on other faces. Sometimes good people who'd been hounded by creeps and stalkers like Madeline Reynolds had, and some I'd been sent to hunt down. Like it or not, that'd been a large part of my job. Find the bad guys and remove the threat. Spoiler alert for people outside the black ops community: this rarely entailed capture, and there is no such thing as a tranquilizer dart used on people.

But this woman wasn't an enemy—she needed my help with one. I settled into my seat, and she took one on the other side of my desk. Her posture was stiff in the chair across from me, exactly as it'd been in the other room. Sometimes, people relaxed in a one-on-one setting and others clammed up even more. Madeline Reynolds likely had more experience with meetings of all kinds than I'd have in ten lives, and I'd sat through enough briefings to last at least three lifetimes.

I waited for her to begin. She'd requested the private meeting, and though it wasn't expected, I suspected it wouldn't be unheard of for people like Reynolds who had entourages surrounding her at all times.

"I'm not sure I can trust my current security team. Well, now essentially *former* team, though we haven't fired them outright so that we can figure out what exactly the breach is."

I blinked and dipped my chin, signaling she should continue. I held her gaze but took in details around the periphery—legs remained uncrossed, hair blond but somehow duller than the last interview I'd found online in my search yesterday. Otherwise, every single thing about her was immaculate. Except for those tired, haunted eyes.

"There is no way anyone could know some of the places I've been unless they're inside my circle. I've whittled it down from about seven people to now just Anthony and Brad."

"You trust them?"

"Yes. But I wasn't certain about your assistant. And I've been through enough that..." Her voice shook until she cleared it. "I can't take chances."

"I understand. Sarah is completely trustworthy—I'd trust her with my life. If you trust me, you can trust her and anyone I hire. But your caution is smart, and this helps me know how to proceed. We'll set up some parameters for communication so your usual distribution network who deals with your scheduling, appearances, accounts, and—"

"They're gone. Anthony's here, and Brad. No one else. They'll be with me while I pack up in New York, and then I'm back here with as few traces as possible. I'm not even using my own transportation. Julian Grenier's pilot, Mr. Smith, is assisting me on the way over so that I'm not tracked back here."

All excellent precautions. Brad must be advising her well, and hopefully he was, in fact, capable with cyber protection. I'd known he would stay her physical body guard—I didn't have the staff set up for that anyway. But I'd planned to deal with cyber myself. If Brad insisted and Reynolds was sitting here insisting he was trustworthy, then so be it. I'd have to review the contract and present them with something slimmer, but in the end, it just meant I wouldn't be working as much overtime, and I wouldn't need to hire out my two buddies who weren't active duty to moonlight before they were ready.

If Reynolds only had a few people she could trust, I was glad at least Brad was one and he was making the right calls. Or perhaps it was her brother, an active duty Lieutenant Colonel in the Army, giving her suggestions. Or potentially even more likely, Grenier. He had a knack for security, an interest in it, and his own wealth plus the population he kept company with meant he was more than attuned to the industry and best practices. He'd seeded the money for the refurb of this building and some of the tech we needed to get started beyond what Bruce and I could contribute. Without him, we wouldn't have been able to open for at least a year, if not more, without massive debt.

"We'll get everything set up by the time you're back. You'll be safe here, Ms. Reynolds."

She stood in answer, apparently satisfied with the interaction, or perhaps my assurances that she was safe here. More likely, it was having put a face with the name and having a plan. The unknown was so often what haunted people, and I'd already felt the satisfaction of providing that fix. Exiting the room, we found her staff and Sarah chatting easily in the front.

"If you need anything until you're back, don't hesitate to contact us." I stopped next to Sarah and gave her a look, hoping she'd read it right.

"Yes. And if you need anything in terms of just setting up non-security stuff, or anything, just let us know."

Sarah's bright smile was a little too large, but Ms. Reynolds gave her a small smile in return before catching my eye and nodding. Seconds later, the door shut behind them, and Sarah let out a huge breath and her shoulders slumped.

"Everything okay?" I asked, holding in a laugh.

She brushed a hand over her face. "That was intense. I don't think I've ever been so nervous."

My lips quirked into a smile.

"What, you have?"

A hundred different missions flipped through my mind, little snapshots of the higher-pressure situations I'd faced over the years. Escorting politicians to negotiations. Hunting down actual terrorists. Locating and extracting Americans from various hostage situations in a dozen different countries. "Yeah. I've had a few intense moments."

Her tension cracked the second she made the connection. "Oh. Right."

And then, she laughed. It started as a small chuckle but quickly unraveled into a silent laugh complete with closed eyes and an open-mouth smile.

My heart twisted at this familiar sight. I hadn't seen it in more than twenty years, but it reached out and grabbed me. I couldn't stay stoic in the company of this utter abandon.

So I laughed, too. She bent over and grabbed my arm to keep from falling. Historically, all her muscles gave out when she succumbed to a laugh attack like this. They'd hit at odd times, just like now.

I missed this. I missed her. In this moment, her hand on my arm and her silent laugh somehow filling the space with a bursting kind of joyful energy, I felt the loss of the decades we'd spent apart.

That hand on my arm made me wonder the same thing that'd been crawling through my mind one biting hope at a time and that, thus far, I'd shunned with every ounce of strength I'd had. But with her laughter tapering into soft, audible breaths, I let it come. *Could we possibly try again?*

She righted herself and let go of me, wiping the tears at the corners of her eyes and then bustling over to her desk to grab a tissue and swipe under them. "I'm so sorry. I didn't mean to lose it."

I shook my head. "No apology needed."

"I'm not sure why that felt so high-pressure to me. Obviously compared to the things you've dealt with, that was nothing." She heaved a large sigh as she fully settled back into sobriety.

"It's not a competition. It was intense, especially considering it was our first real client meeting. Grenier and Juliet Christensen's drive-by the other day was nothing."

"True. I guess it kind of threw me. Madeline's so dynamic when I've seen her speak or seen her interviewed. She's always seemed like this incredibly empowered, awesome woman, and she seemed so... small."

I couldn't disagree. "One of the reasons I want to do this job and do it well. We'll keep her safe."

Her bright eyes skated over my face in what felt like an affectionate caress. "She seemed a little better by the time she left."

"Having a plan for her time here probably helps. Obviously, she's seen the equipment and house plans, but meeting us and seeing we're not psychopaths probably helped. She gave us her business based on Juliet's recommendation, and Juliet recommended us based on Grenier's word. Reliable sources, but still removed from her life."

Sarah's demeanor shifted a bit, uncertainty edging in as she leaned against her desk. I made the choice not to admire the way her hip rested against the edge or think of anything related to her and the desk. *No. No. No.*

"I hope I didn't overstep with my last thing. I could've sworn you were giving me a look to say something."

"I was."

Relief visibly washed over her. "Thank goodness. I didn't want to seem over the top, but she's got to be lonely."

My voice came out a little gruff when I said, "You were perfect."

My words hung between us as our eyes locked. God, she was beautiful. Her face was still flushed from her laughter, and her concern for a woman she'd never met was just so *her*. I hadn't been reconnected with her long, but already, I knew she was warm, kind, and even lovelier than she ever had been.

If I set a hand on her waist and leaned forward, what would happen? Would she raise her chin and give me her lips? Let me taste her for the first time in decades, in too long? Would she lean in and put her hands on me? Would she open to me and kiss me back?

She cleared her throat, breaking the moment and shifting to take a seat. "I better get a few things done before I take off."

"Right." I stepped back. "Let me know if you need anything."

Retreating to my office, I shook off the haze that'd

descended in the last few minutes. I didn't know if we had anything ahead of us beyond this working relationship, but the more we interacted, the more it felt like it. And some part of me recognized I might owe it to myself to try with her if she was interested, too.

The other part of me knew what a mistake that would be. She wasn't why I was here. She wasn't why I'd come home.

But wasn't the whole idea that I live a whole life, not just choose one category and immerse myself? Could I be fully engaged setting up work to build the practical logistics of life here while healing my relationship with my family *and* have something with Sarah?

CHAPTER TWENTY-ONE

Sarah

The week had been a good one, and it'd flown. By end of day Friday, I had so much pent-up energy, I decided to go for a run after work. Wilder had been in and out thanks to the no fewer than ten locals interested in having him come out and assess their property's security.

Word about Wilder's business had spread, and I had no doubt his brothers, my friends, and Julian had a great deal to do with that. What it did mean, though, was that Wilder and I hadn't had another moment of downtime. We'd been going in opposite directions, and while I recognized that was probably for the best, I also missed having him around.

I missed that taut energy that rippled between us when we spoke, or stood still, or... *anything*. It'd always been like that with us, but lately, it felt weightier.

For a second after the meeting and my laugh attack, I'd been certain he was going to kiss me. We were inches apart.

If he'd moved any closer, or if I'd lifted my chin just a bit... *whew.* I'd gotten overheated just thinking about my pounding heart and the way my cheeks had flamed before I broke the moment and hid away at my desk.

Since then? Nothing.

So by the end of the week, after Wilder had left to do one thing or another and said he'd see me Monday, I packed up my lunchbox, thermos, and all my tangled feelings, and headed home. With three hours before I'd need to meet my friends, I knew I'd go insane if I sat around. I couldn't go wander through the bookstore, because I'd just want to spend money, and if I really was wrapping up my time here, I'd need to be saving for a move. Just thinking about that had me restless.

Thus, the run. I started off at a light jog, easing my way through the neighborhood and waving to a few high schoolers who lived near my apartment building and had been in my long-term sub class in the fall. No anonymity for teachers in a small town, that was for sure.

Ten minutes in, I made it to the path that stretched along the south side of town and then wound back behind work, the mill buildings, and out into the fields that flanked the little cozy cabins for rent by The Silverton Inn. If I had a little more energy, I might've tried to go farther into the mountains on this warm and bright spring afternoon. Buttery light lit the sky in baby yellows and blues. The trees had taken their cue from the crocuses and dared to bud, ignoring the perpetual threat of another spring storm in favor of working toward their spring blooms.

I rounded the corner into a long stretch and decided to push a little harder than I had to this point. A sprint out to the farthest cabin, then I'd turn back and go hard until I reached the neighborhood and could use that time to cool down. After turning around, I hauled myself forward, arms pumping and chest heaving with the effort. It'd been too long since I'd pushed like this.

And then came the twinge. I'd worked for years to master this knee injury, but I'd never fully overcome it. Times like this, when I got too excited and wanted to show myself what I could do without properly building up, it came back to haunt me.

I reluctantly slowed all the way to a walk as the pain clawed at my knee. Sometimes, I could stretch and walk it out enough to finish at a light jog. My breathing calmed and I decided to stretch a little. I bent into a runner's stretch, then switched to a side lunge.

A brush at my sleeve made me jump and let out a small yelp. When I glanced up from my bent position, I saw Wilder.

Wilder.

My brain stuttered and slid to a stop. Wilder had touched me. Wilder had found me. Neither of these events were particularly surprising. More like I hadn't expected him, had been in my own world and he...

He was magnificent.

Maybe I should've been more circumspect, but I rose to my feet and pulled one earbud out, unable to remember how to make the music stop. He stood with hands on his hips, that severe face eyeing me with an expression I couldn't decipher, especially since his dark hat had been pulled low over his eyes.

Oh, and did I mention he wore sneakers with ankle socks, running shorts, and nothing else except that hat? *Yeah.*

Not to be the most cliché woman on earth or anything, but the man was a work of art. For all his war-hardened roughness, he'd seemed so business-like and focused the last few weeks. But this was more like the Wilder I remembered —no, not shirtless, though I had plenty of fond memories to that effect. It was him, out in nature, cheeks flushed from exertion and skin glowing a golden color like it drank in the mountain air.

His chest and abs were etched in vivid detail—almost brutal in their reality. Those of a man who'd honed his body into a weapon and had then used it. His arms were sleeved in tattoos. I'd seen glimpses at his wrists, but he'd worn long sleeves most of the times I'd seen him until now. Natural scenes, mountain silhouettes, and trees twisted up the length of his forearms and biceps, each vignette a book I desperately wanted to read. A long scar over one pectoral had my fingers itching to trace it, to ask what'd happened, to press myself against him.

Okay, whoa there, girl.

"What'd you say?" I managed.

His eyes narrowed. "Are you okay?"

"Me? Okay? Of course. Why wouldn't I be?"

The amount of disorientation shading my words should've been embarrassing, but more than anything, it felt accurate. I'd always been attracted to him—since I'd known what such a feeling meant. But this was absurd.

"You were bent over in the middle of the path."

If any blood existed elsewhere in my body, it all flooded to my cheeks. "Right. Yeah. I have a little knee-twinge thing that happens sometimes. I was trying to work that out."

"Need any help with it? Want me to take a look?"

His hands were resting on the sharp cuts of muscle that curved from his side and followed his hip then sloped down —*Down.*

A raging, horrible envy for those hands hit me.

"Sarah? Are you dehydrated?"

My eyes shot to his. "What? No. I'm fine. I should've eaten something before I left, I think, but I'm going out with friends tonight and I—you know what? Speaking of that, I'm going to get going. I'll see you Monday, right?"

I turned on one foot and began walking as fast as my angry knee would allow, silently willing him to continue on his merry way.

"I'm not leaving you, so you might as well let me walk with you."

I shot him a scowl that got waylaid by the sight of him with the mountains as a backdrop. *Goodness*, he was handsome. Not a man anyone would ever call pretty, but good-looking in a more unpracticed way than either of his brothers, though they weren't particularly high maintenance men or anything. Wilder just had this aggressively attractive aura that snapped at me, as if baiting me into engaging with it.

The fact that I was walking alongside him on this gorgeous early May afternoon and thinking about his *aura* indicated that I definitely should've had a snack before this run.

"You really don't have to. It's fine to walk on, I just couldn't keep running. I might even be able to jog a bit more soon." I glanced over at him to find his gaze steady on me. My heart tripped over itself and splattered on the ground in front of me.

"I was doing an out and back. This is my last mile anyway. I don't mind cooling down with you."

A memory flickered to life in my mind—this very same path, though it hadn't been paved back then. "Do you remember when you were getting ready to talk to the recruiter, so you trained for the physical fitness test?"

He huffed a laugh and his eyes tracked out in front of

him. "I'd never been a runner. Thought two miles was going to kill me that first time."

"You had the sit-ups no problem. Push-ups took a few weeks." I could see it all so vividly. He'd planned to go ROTC when we graduated high school. We'd go to the same college and he'd start the program, then commission and start active duty as an officer.

Then everything changed. I found out I was pregnant, and he decided he'd get started sooner—enlist and start bringing in a paycheck. We could get married as soon as I graduated. It'd seemed insane, and yet like the right thing. We'd be young but together, and we'd even have health insurance and housing.

An all-too-familiar ache gripped my insides and squeezed. What would life have been like if I hadn't lost the baby? If we'd gone ahead with our plans?

Since he'd gotten back and we'd been thrown together more and more, I'd found myself thinking about who that baby might've grown to be. For so long, I'd shied away from thinking about the what-ifs, but in the last few years, I'd realized that hadn't helped me. It'd only kept me blinded to how I'd continued to hurt the man I loved while also stunting my own healing.

No more of that, now. No more hurting him, or myself. I'd come for peace, on a mission suggested by my therapist in Georgia, and I'd experienced a taste of it. I'd also learned that being fearful about remembering didn't serve me or anyone else.

Maybe she would be in college. Maybe he would've joined the Army, too. Maybe she would've repeated history and had a baby young with her first love, and Wilder and I would've been the happiest grandparents to ever exist.

It wasn't very fair to my heart to think that way, but I'd

accepted it wasn't any more fair to forbid such daydreams. At some point, I needed to find out if he'd ever had similar thoughts.

"True. Though I still hate push-ups." The grit in his voice said maybe he'd gone there, too—back to where everything had unraveled.

I didn't want to stay there when we were *here*. We'd made our choices after the biggest one had been made for us, and beyond that, we'd survived. Somehow, we were back in this place that'd been so formative for us, and yet that we'd both run from for so long. *Too long.*

Maybe that was why I refused to linger in the past and tried opening the conversation again with him. I'd come back because it was the last place I'd felt at home and truly happy. The last place I'd felt fully loved—not just by Wilder but by his family and even mine. I still grappled with feeling that was true, but I'd grieved my relationship with my parents almost constantly the last year and a half since moving here and receiving a steady drip of disapproval from them all along.

Enough of that, because here we were now. A new moment in the mountain air, a chance to move forward.

"How about the running? I guess you made your peace with it?" I looked over right as he did the same.

His gaze made my stomach swoop low again, my heart twisting and twisting in my chest until it felt it might give out. Being around him had been fraught with a crush of feelings since that first time months ago, but this bordered on unbearable.

I wanted to press myself against him, to meld together and share every stunted thought and regret and hope. I needed him to know the way I'd loved him before and how deeply, completely sorry I was for so many years apart.

He stopped walking and his hand, warm and strong, came to my wrist. Those deep blue eyes pinned me in place, all the intensity in the world funneling through them.

"Go to dinner with me."

My breath came out in a rough whoosh and I said the first thing I thought of. "I have plans tonight."

Idiot! I didn't want that to sound like a refusal. I just, I did have plans tonight, and I couldn't cancel them. I needed to process some of the things that'd happened, and now I needed it even more.

"Tomorrow."

"Yes."

His fingers squeezed ever so slightly where they rested against my arm, and then he let go. His head was still dipped down, and for a heartbeat, I thought he'd cover the distance and kiss me. *Yes, please.*

"Tomorrow," he repeated, as though in answer to my body's plea for more from him. Of him. With him. *Anything* him.

"Okay."

We walked another few minutes with only the sounds around us and occasional quiet, surface-level conversation between us for company.

The spring weather—so pleasant.

Where I'd meet my friends tonight—Guac.

How far he'd run—eight miles.

By the time we'd made it back to the neighborhood, that liquid sensation had solidified again, and I'd admitted to myself I'd need to stretch thoroughly and probably even ice my knee. I'd said as much, and he'd seemed relieved by my plan. Then he gave me one of those down-to-my-toes looks I felt race through every part of me before jogging off toward wherever he lived.

I had a girls' night to get to, and by the time I arrived, I was bursting at the seams to tell them everything that'd happened in the last few days.

And tomorrow. Maybe I should've resisted, that sense of something coming to a close nearby wherever I went, but I couldn't say no to him—didn't want to. *Tomorrow* we'd go out. We'd do all the things that one word had promised when he'd said it moments ago.

CHAPTER TWENTY-TWO

Wilder

Warrick's smirky little grin in response to my suggestion we eat at Guac made me want to shove him. So I did.

"Hey! I didn't say anything," he said, faking mortal offense at my action.

"Not with words."

"No, not with words, but you're practically shouting. So tell us, young one, what is it you have to say to Wilder?"

Wyatt's even keel had refereed between us more than once when we were younger, but having him engage now made an unexpected burst of happiness fire off inside me.

"I just happen to know Sadie met her friends at Guac a half hour ago. And I know Sarah is one of those friends."

He wiggled his brows. I shoved him again.

"Stop that," Wyatt said, likely to both of us. "We're

going to Guac, so there's nothing to snipe at each other about."

Warrick chuckled and hid a smile. My giant younger brother called Wyatt out. "Yeah, but we're only going to Guac so you can stare at your woman and then blame it on us."

Wyatt's eyes narrowed to a threatening glare. "Maybe."

Warrick laughed full out, a free, joyful sound that made my heart squeeze. Seemed like a lot of things made my insides twist and squeeze and drop and slow and speed up. I'd been more aware of my heart and its meanderings in the last few weeks than I had in twenty years.

I'd lived by my gut, largely ignoring my heart. Apparently, that was changing, right along with everything else.

Without too much more nonsense from either brother, we soon settled into three seats at the bar since Guac was packed out with a forty-minute wait for a table. The girls, so said Warrick, had made a reservation, so they'd likely had no trouble. We didn't mind holing up at the end of the bar.

"To a reunion twenty years in the making." Warrick held up his tiny glass filled with golden top shelf tequila.

Wyatt and I raised ours to meet it.

"To brotherhood," Wyatt added.

I rounded it out with, "To the Saints."

We each slugged back the burning, tangy liquid, and I questioned my sanity. We were all solidly in our thirties, Wyatt nearly forty, and none of us had any business doing shots. But I wasn't about to be the one who opted out after having done so for most of our adult lives in one way or another.

"So what's going on with you and Sarah?"

Warrick sipped a glass of even nicer añejo tequila. Wyatt switched to water immediately, likely because he had to drive home. I took a burning sip of the same as Warrick, yet again glad I could walk home from the center of town.

Knowing there'd be some kind of upheaval, I resisted the urge to hoard the information and just went for it. "We're going out tomorrow night."

"Ohhhh!" Warrick said, all exclamation.

Wyatt just grinned and slapped me on the back. "Good."

Nerves bubbled in my gut. "I hope. I don't know."

I certainly wanted the time with her, but dividing my attention still felt like a wrong move.

"Don't be stupid. You were made for each other."

I scoffed. "Right."

If that were true, we wouldn't have parted. But even with the bitter singe of that reality, I couldn't have kept myself from asking her to dinner earlier today any more easily than I could've stopped what happened before. The way she'd looked at me, the way I'd known she *wanted* me, and the way I'd honestly never stopped wanting her...

I'd thrown every screaming caution into that gentle spring breeze and gone for it. Having decided that I couldn't simply cut her out of my life now that she lived here and worked for my company—and more so, that if I could on a gut level I didn't want to—I'd given in to the necessity to ask her.

"You do seem well matched. I can understand that you're cautious. That's not a bad thing."

Wyatt's words were always measured, and though he hadn't been one to give me advice very often of late, I still respected his perspective.

"I support that. Slow and steady. But pretending like you guys aren't fire on a dry summer day? It's stupid. So might as well lay the track if you know the train's coming." Warrick raised his glass to no one, then sipped again.

"That was freakishly complex, but I agree," Wyatt said.

Warrick shoved him, one long arm stretching behind me to knock Wyatt sideways. "Shut it, grumpy."

"I'm not grumpy. I'm quite joyful and satisfied. Just ask my wife."

Wyatt's wide smile beamed louder and prouder than anything I'd seen from him, probably ever.

"Oh, you're gross. You should just go home, you old married man."

Warrick's statement came with a full smile of his own, clearly absolutely delighted for our older brother. Wyatt had always wanted love and companionship, and seeing him so head-over-heels gone for Calla felt like a rightness in the world. After all the wrongs I'd seen, all the horrors and brutalities, my older brother's glee at being a husband to a good woman carrying his child?

Damn, but it was beautiful. He'd been steadfast even as a teenager, working hard and waiting for a chance to build his own family. It'd come later in life than I would've guessed and from an unexpected person, that was for sure, but he had it "all" now in the best sense.

"You're not so far off from being an old married man yourself, are you, War?" Wyatt's question came a little quieter and with a pointedly raised brow.

"Shhhh!" Warrick's eyes shot to the table more than thirty feet away where the girls sat.

My own gaze used the excuse of his attention to look there, too. My heart kicked at the sight of Sarah, her head thrown back in a laugh, eyes scrunched shut. She'd always been free like that with friends. At one time, she had been with me—maybe more than with anyone else.

Or so I'd thought.

Earlier today, she had been with me. It'd shifted me from idling into action, and I'd asked before the logic of our situation and history between us could stop me.

"She's not going to hear me from here."

Wyatt's just-above-a-whisper response had me turning back to them.

"So? I don't want word getting out. It's coming up and I'm…" He blew out a big breath. "Nervous."

"What's this?" I asked, realizing I'd missed something.

"I'm asking Sadie to marry me next month." His face had paled, but after a second, he unleashed one of his giant, classic Warrick smiles.

"Congratulations. She seems great." And she did. The family dinners I'd attended had all shown her to be genuine, thoughtful, and completely in love with my brother. "I don't know the details, but I can't imagine she'd say no, from what I've seen."

Wyatt snickered, and Warrick's cheeks went pink before he launched into the story of how the woman he'd wanted to propose to had ended up proposing to him. Our food came and went as he gave me every detail of their history starting with the summer before. I'd known enough to know that Warrick had been hurt and had sworn off marriage, at least to some degree, but I'd had no idea he'd truly believed he wouldn't ever be with someone like that.

That knowledge sank into my gut like a stone.

Warrick must've noted my expression change. "What's that look for? I've changed my ways—you heard me say I'm proposing next month, right? I've got it all planned out."

"I did. And I'm happy for you."

He nudged my shoulder with his. "What is it?"

Wyatt looked on without speaking, but something told me he could read it all on my face.

Whether the tequila had loosened my lips, or the time spent with my brothers the last few weeks allowed me to do it, I couldn't tell. Either way, I responded with truth. "I've missed so much. I failed you too many times by not being here, and I'm sorry."

Warrick swallowed hard. "No more of that, okay? You've said you're sorry. We missed you—we missed you like crazy. And I'm not saying I didn't get upset when you were gone, but that doesn't matter now. You're here, and so far, you seem like you're trying to get to know us again. That's all I need from you."

Wyatt nodded. "Exactly. You're here. You're showing up. That's all we want."

Throat tight, I accepted the generous offering with a burning sense of relief, pain, and gratitude. "All right."

I suspected if we'd been anywhere but a restaurant, they might've tried to hug it out, but I wouldn't have been able to handle that. Physical affection on top of the generosity they'd shown me, the willingness to absolve me for what I viewed as one of my biggest sins, would've toppled me.

"Now let's get back to the real elephant in the room, shall we?" Warrick said, clinking his glass with mine, which I noticed had been refilled during our heart-to-heart.

"What's that?" Wyatt asked, voicing my own question.

The gleam in Warrick's eye should've told me it would be something obnoxious, so I shouldn't have taken a drink right as he spoke again.

"We need to talk about how our beloved mother is on the hunt for the next Mr. Saint, and how I heard my general contractor talking about his plans to ask her out."

The burning liquid shot down my throat as I gulped, his

tone so horrified, the chuckle burst out of me once I swallowed.

Wyatt shook his head, but kept his head down. His shoulders shook, though, so he'd failed to keep calm in the face of Warrick's fake outrage.

"Then Sadie said Sarah mentioned Mom got into a lengthy chat with the new bookstore owner and that the guy was totally charming and into her." He squirmed on his stool.

I just laughed until he swung his focus to me. "You realize people are talking about you, too? About how Sarah was out with Mom, which means you guys are dating?"

"They kind of are, if they're going out tomorrow."

"I guess it's a formal welcome home from the Silverton rumor mill."

And though I didn't love the idea of being fodder for people around town, something about it really did feel like an official homecoming. I wasn't staying on the fringe, hidden and withdrawn. Sure, I hadn't put pictures on my walls, but I wasn't staying in that apartment. I was building a house, laying a literal foundation here in Silverton. I'd already opened the doors to a business.

I'd been working on coming home for years—preparing the way so the very things that were happening now could take place. My brothers' forgiveness had come more quickly than I could've hoped. That Sarah was here, too... it went so far beyond what I'd imagined. I couldn't have guessed that I might be able to pursue setting down those roots I'd been missing, repair things with my family, and reconnect with Sarah. Granted, I didn't expect anything from our date, but I needed the closure in a way I hadn't had it before. As repellent as her being here had seemed at first, now that I'd been forced to accept I couldn't simply segment my life into tidy sections that didn't overlap and deal with them individually, closure with Sarah had become a possibility.

But in my gut, the one that'd never led me astray, I suspected it was more than closure—different. Despite the warning signs and the knowledge that I should pour my energy into my family and business and keep it simple. Sure, that would've been ideal, but I'd learned time and again I could only deal with the problem in front of me, not the one I'd prepared for.

It was time to embrace that the plans had changed and the problem in front of me wasn't the one I'd anticipated. It was, maybe, another part of this beginning.

CHAPTER TWENTY-THREE

Sarah

If Wilder sent me any more scalding looks tonight, I'd end up combusting and burning to ash right here in this shiny little booth.

"Okay, so can we talk about something? Madeline Reynolds is coming to stay in Silverton for like a month," Quinn said, drawing my thoughts, at least most of them, from the broad shoulders of the three men sitting at the bar.

I didn't say a thing, but Quinn looked at me. I gave her an *I can't say anything* look as Calla, Sadie, and Dahlia all chimed in with varying degrees of interest.

"What for, I wonder?" Dahlia asked.

"She was here for a short trip like a year and a half ago. I remember her talking to Aiden at the bar one night." Quinn raised her brows.

Dahlia sighed. "Oh, now that would be beautiful."

Calla snickered. "Okay, little romantic heart."

Sadie nudged her with an elbow lightly. "Seriously, though. Aiden is the best. He's gentle and he's such a good dad."

"I can vouch for Aiden. I work with him on Night in Bloom and he's great. Very professional, very knowledgeable, and if I don't sound like too much of a creep, completely attractive in that salt of the earth way."

Quinn nodded. "He is definitely handsome."

I thought of the man in question next to Madeline. I couldn't see it, but I didn't know either of them. They seemed like total opposites to me, but maybe that's what she'd want, or he'd need. Who knew?

"I'm excited to see her around," I said, not giving away anything I knew or the fact that she was a client at Saint Securities, even though I desperately wanted to.

"Last time she was here, I saw her at the bar that one time and not again," Quinn said.

"She came to the shop once, but I only know that because Garrett had to compose himself for a minute before he went back out and actually delivered her to go order." Sadie's fond expression spoke of how she felt about her most loyal employee. Garrett had been a fixture at Rise and Shine almost as long as it'd been open, from what she had told me. He was a good kid and incredibly devoted to her.

"Maybe she'll get out a bit more. Or maybe she's coming here to hide away. I can't imagine being so public like that," Dahlia said, then her eyes shot to Calla. "I mean, I guess you can."

Calla chuckled. "That I can. But honestly, it's different. I'm famous in one way because of what I do, but she's famous for both what she does and who she is, if that makes sense. Like, she's doing a job few women do as a high-profile CEO, plus she's doing it well, and then she's also targeted for that. I don't know. I am guessing some of our fame experiences overlap, but she's kind of a paragon and I obviously had a different road."

Calla's "road" entailed being publicly derided and blamed for her mother's death, on top of being criticized for basically everything about herself. It was stupid and obnoxious, but all of that brought her here to Silverton, where she hid out... and then she'd met her husband. She had said she didn't regret any of it, and based on the way she kept glancing back at said husband, I believed her.

"Is it a thing with the Saint brothers?" Dahlia asked, tilting her head to one side to study the three men now facing the bar and away from us.

Still a fantastic view...

"Is what a thing?" Sadie asked, glancing over her shoulder to see Warrick eyeing her again.

The heat between those two had already set my cheeks aflame. *Whew.* Especially knowing how much they loved each other, it was basically the best.

"The whole *we give hot looks to our women from the bar* thing? Like, did they come here just to send sexy stares to you guys?" Dahlia scooped a chip into the remaining guacamole on the table, still picking at her plate.

Quinn chuckled but only gave Calla and Sadie a knowing look.

"Hmm. I'd say yes. I mean, it's definitely a Wyatt thing. He's been heating me up with those eyes since the day I met him, even before we liked each other. I wouldn't have thought Warrick had it in him, but having witnessed him look at Sadie... yeah. *Yeah.*"

We all laughed at that, and Sadie flushed a deep red. She only agreed with a "Yeah."

A new round of chuckles passed through the group

before Quinn spoke with a little twinkle in her eye. "And then there's Wilder."

My pulse jumped at his name. Stupid that just his name spoken aloud did that considering all that'd happened today, but that was the truth of it.

"You realize he's looking at you the same way Wyatt and Warrick are looking at them, right? Maybe with a little more desperate heat than satisfied anticipation, but it's absolutely there."

My cheeks flamed, but I couldn't figure out what to say.

Calla shot me a sly smile. "I agree. And based on that blush, you don't mind a bit."

I shook my head, tucking my lips between my teeth as I exhaled. "Can't say that I do."

Sadie's gentle question came next. "You still have feelings for him? I mean, obviously there's attraction."

"Ha, yeah. We can all tell that based on the tractor beam between them," Quinn said, a snarky little brow raise accompanying the smile she sent me.

They knew about the date. As soon as I'd sat down earlier, I burst out with the fact that he'd asked me out. But in the flurry of excitement, we hadn't gotten to this. And *this* was what I wanted to talk about.

"Yes. I'm not sure I ever stopped, but the last few days have shown me there's a lot more between us than just our past. In a good way. I am insanely attracted to him, but that's nothing new. Despite the time apart, I actually still like him, and I like learning who he is now." A thrill of anticipation rose in me. "I can't wait to have some non-work time to do that."

Dahlia clapped, and Sadie and Calla beamed at me.

Only Quinn, ever the voice of reason and pragmatist, had a counterpoint. "I'm not saying this isn't the best thing since Sadie's sunflower whole wheat—I'm not. But I do just want to say, out loud, that if it's not fun, or if it's all physical and you don't click personality-wise, or whatever, that that's okay, too. And that if this doesn't work out, there's someone amazing for you."

"Absolutely true," Sadie agreed. "You're amazing, and if Wilder doesn't recognize that who you are *now* is even better than before, then he's crazy."

A nervous laugh escaped. "He's not. He's solid and reliable and softhearted like he always was, but in a more substantial way. He's definitely not crazy."

That softness killed me. He wouldn't ever call it that, of course, but that desire to help Madeline, to make sure I was okay after my walk, to make peace with his brothers... all of that made up the gooey middle of a man who was uncompromising, stubborn, and a little wild on the outside. That, more than anything, was what told me we had to revisit the past in more depth, but I hoped we'd be able to reconnect a bit more *now* before we did. He'd be far more likely to open up if we broke through a little more of the ice that'd frozen over between us.

"You're adorable. And now, I need to go home. Someone told me I'm supposed to hit a second wind with the second trimester, and it can't come soon enough. So far, it's a few weeks late. Sorry I'm a lame date, ladies." Calla slid from the booth and gave us each hugs. She and Sadie worked their way across the space to Wyatt and Warrick, and both of them stood and abandoned Wilder to his drink in seconds.

"I better get back, too. Julian flies in tonight, and he'll be all needy for my attention."

Dahlia and I laughed at that, unable to imagine Julian Grenier being any kind of needy. Quinn departed and

Dahlia hugged me once more, then nudged me toward the bar. "Go get 'em, tiger."

I rolled my eyes but inhaled a deep, steadying breath before approaching the man at the bar. He stared into the golden liquid in a high ball glass, fingers on one hand lightly gripping the beverage.

"You aren't leaving with your friends?" he asked without looking up.

I slipped into the seat next to him. "Your brothers had plans for two of them, and Quinn has to get back to Julian."

"And the other one?"

"Dahlia? Uh, she thought I might want to come say hi." *Good grief* my nerves were jumping through every limb as though I hadn't talked to him hours ago. Hadn't agreed to spend a whole evening with him.

He finally gave me his attention, and like too many times recently, his dark gaze sent my stomach to my toes. "Hi"

I swallowed. "Hi."

"That's all you wanted? To say hi?"

"Sure." *Unconvincing.*

Dipping his head, he spoke in a low, calm voice. "Shame. I was hoping you had something else up your sleeve."

I blinked and sucked in a breath, my body flushing with heat at the little taunt in his tone and the thrill twining through me. What? "I—I, uh..."

Before I figured out what to say or the moment could linger, he slugged back the rest of his drink and stood. "Walk you home?"

I nodded, because I'd apparently devolved into a speechless ninny. He held his hand out for me, and I took it. He tipped that same hand just a little, a small urging, and I slid out of my seat. With the slightest nod, he sent me ahead of him, deftly shifting so his hand hovered at my lower back, his shoulder just trailing mine.

My heart fluttered wildly. In fact, all my internal organs were fluttering. Every movement of his in the last few minutes had been confident, smooth, and so purely appealing, I could hardly breathe right.

When we exited the restaurant, he slipped his hand into mine and walked toward my place. I hadn't given him my address, but knowing Wilder, he'd seen it on my employee paperwork.

That thought clicked a sharp sense of dread into place.

Somehow, I'd ignored that for weeks now. Maybe it'd been a way to protect myself from this crush of humiliation, this feeling of walking naked next to Wilder Saint.

That thought sent my pulse racing even harder as the realization crashed into me. If he'd seen that, he'd seen the background check. And if he'd read that, he'd know everything—all the anti-climactic non-accomplishments of my life and my many, many failures.

Including the words listed under the section for names used for the background check. *Name: Sarah Elizabeth James. Other names used: Sarah Wilson.*

My mind rioted as we passed people out for spring evening strolls. It was the first warmer weekend evening, and it felt like everyone was out. Between his large, warm hand in mine and the clutching dread of talking through my resume of failures I'd just realized he absolutely knew about, the walk felt like nothing.

At my door, when earlier I might've been contemplating the right angle to tilt my head and get a kiss, I was now scrambling for a way to broach the subject of my divorce. He steered me so I faced him and finally looked in his eyes.

Whatever he saw in mine must not've fazed him, because he simply said, "Tomorrow."

I nodded.

He leaned in and kissed my cheek. "Lock your door when you get inside," he said all deliciously gruff, and then he was gone.

CHAPTER TWENTY-FOUR

Wilder

Sarah's nervous energy announced itself before I ever knocked on the door. It nipped at our heels the whole time we walked to town, and it hounded right up to the table as we sat at Basta.

Soon enough, I'd press her on it. She'd clammed up a bit last night, but I hadn't addressed it then because it hadn't felt right. While dating Sarah James wasn't a mission, per se, there was an element of strategy to it. As much as I'd resisted this mentally, I wasn't about to half-ass it now that we were here.

After watching each of my brothers take their women home, faces besotted with love and wonder when they left the restaurant, my determination to see tonight as a beginning had only grown stronger.

The many logical voices shouting that this couldn't possibly be a beginning when we'd already faced a brutal ending couldn't drown the out and out longing plaguing me. Not an unfamiliar feeling, particularly in the last year as I began to allow myself to look ahead to being here and settling in.

But what I'd felt last night was far more than simple longing or determination. The second I registered her next to me on that barstool, *hunger* had hit. Something primal and ravenous and jarring enough that I'd almost tasted her right there in the restaurant. I'd almost dipped my head and pressed my lips to her neck, her jaw, her cheek.

That couldn't be our first real physical encounter—it couldn't. The animal in me that *needed* Sarah had to be restrained. So I'd walked her home and avoided whatever crowded her mind on the way to also sidestep the impulse to plaster her against the door and take her mouth like I'd envisioned all along the walk.

I'd gotten myself under control thanks to decades of practice with self-control in high stakes situations and insisted it could all wait until today. Whatever was on her mind would have to wait, and so would my desire to be close to her. I didn't assume we would kiss tonight—I wouldn't place pressure on anything between us if I could help it. But I damn well *wanted* to kiss her, be close to her, feel her against me and revel in that contact.

The fantasy of collapsing the space between us running rampant in my head leading up to tonight had faltered at seeing her so closed up. So after barely scraping out a handful of responses to questions I'd asked, just after the waiter brought our main dishes, I went in for it.

"Will you tell me what's on your mind?"

Her eyes darted from mine back to her plate of pasta primavera.

"I'm, um, just enjoying this meal." She held up her fork and smiled—a limp, sickly thing compared to her usual.

"I don't buy it."

"What?"

"I don't believe that the reason you're so clammed up tonight is that you're enjoying the meal so much."

She frowned. "Well, too bad."

"No. Tell me."

The irritated glare was more than she'd given me lately —more real and less nervous than anything I'd seen yet.

"You were always a terrible liar, so just tell me."

Her lashes fluttered for a minute before she set down her fork. "I realized last night when you knew where I lived that you'd probably seen my background check."

Ah. I nodded.

"And that means you know basically everything about me. The places I lived and worked and... names I've gone by."

A pang cut through my torso—one sharp, neat slice at the mention of names. She meant the married name listed on her background check, the one she'd used for approximately eighteen months a few years ago. "I do."

She studied me with an expression that looked a lot like she might be bracing for what I'd say next. "And?"

What could I say? That I automatically hated Aaron Dwight Wilson without setting eyes on him simply because he'd had that part of her life? That I wondered how she'd managed to marry someone while I'd been romantically catatonic for the last twenty years?

None of that would do any damn good.

So instead, I just said, "And?"

"Do you have questions? I mean, you know the barest facts, but you don't really know what or why or how or *who,* and I just want to get all of that out of the way as soon as possible. I hate that you've seen this laundry list of my sins and failures, and I know next to nothing about you."

She fiddled with her napkin in her lap, and I fought the urge to cover her hands with mine. I couldn't reach her lap from across the table, but still. I wanted to touch her, reassure her. Words would have to do instead. "I do have questions, but you can ask me some, too."

She loosed a frustrated huff. "Are you pretending like this doesn't matter? That the fact that I was married has no effect on you?"

Her cheeks, neck, and chest had all turned crimson with her frustration, and the reason why finally clicked. She thought I'd be angry with her for being married, or some other nonsense. "Do you think your relationship history makes me any less interested in being here with you now?"

Some of that ire calmed, and she sat back. "I wouldn't have said it that way, but I guess so. Yes."

I held out my hand. She took it, looking unsure.

"We've both lived a lot of life in the last two decades. I care that you were married because it's a part of who you are. It has undoubtedly played a role in what you want in the future or lessons you've learned. So in that regard, I care. But I don't hold it against you."

If anything, discovering she'd gone through the hardship of divorce made me sad. Angry, almost. When I'd seen that history, I'd wanted to murder the man who'd divorced her, even without knowing what'd happened. And I wanted to shake her now, to force her to understand that what I'd hoped for over the years more than anything else was that she was happy.

In some ways, seeing the proof that she'd been through a divorce and a slew of teaching positions before moving here and taking jobs she didn't seem to stick with very long had hollowed me out. It didn't mean she hadn't been happy—Sarah had a way of finding good things in life, and I held out hope that she'd done that.

The arrogant part of me said that I could've made her happy. That if we'd had the chance to stay together, we could've made a life. And I'd stuffed that twinge of resentment down deep because it had no place between us now.

"Were you ever married?"

Her question jarred me. "No. Not even close."

Her face fell, some part of her evidently hoping we had matching histories in that regard. "Oh. No one serious?"

How could I explain to her that no one had been close to being serious because I hadn't let them? With the exception of the men who'd become like brothers—some closer than my own brothers—and even still, no one had known me like she had.

"No. I dated here and there, but you may have noticed I'm not exactly Mr. Charisma."

She pressed her lips together, but I saw the smile. "Maybe."

"It wasn't a focus for me." After our world fell apart and she ripped my heart out and took it with her, I didn't want anything from anyone for a long, long time.

It didn't escape me that just as I'd returned to Silverton, just as I'd realized *she* was here, I'd started considering something more than living and working here and setting down roots. Despite the temporary nature of her job at Saint Securities and the fact that the town had grown enough, I probably could avoid her fairly well in the future if I put my mind to it.

Instead, for the first time since before I left here, I'd started wondering about more.

CHAPTER TWENTY-FIVE

Sarah

Wilder hadn't become any more loquacious than he'd been growing up, but that only made me savor every word he shared. It wasn't so much that he refused to speak, but he wouldn't speak about himself.

And maybe it made me ridiculous to feel so relieved that he didn't seem upset about my past, but I did. More so, hunger twisted through me despite the delicious dinner in front of me, all of me wishing for more information about him—what did *it wasn't a focus* mean? Nothing serious? Nothing *at all?*

No. That couldn't be true. Wilder wasn't necessarily one to need companionship, I didn't imagine, but everyone needed physical contact, love... everyone.

"You seem troubled."

I grinned down at my plate before letting myself look

up at his handsome face. "Not troubled. Just curious what that means."

"It means just that—I wasn't focused on having relationships. Dating. None of it."

My heart sank. "So you were alone all this time?"

"Not in every way, but romantically? Yes."

I swallowed a bite of the delicious pasta. "That's a long time." A lifetime.

And he was here with me now, making all of this far more intense. And while no, not everything was about me, the possibility that the way I'd treated him had influenced his choice to not try with someone else had my throat tightening painfully.

He didn't demur or make light of it. He simply held my gaze, and with a slight nod said, "It is."

The waiter interrupted to make sure everything was fine—it was. Delicious, even, though I couldn't seem to concentrate on my meal. And after a few minutes of holding back, I let loose. "So you didn't really date or have relationships. What *did* you do?"

He blinked twice as he finished a bite, and one side of his mouth kicked up. His brows raised as if to ask, "really?"

And then I heard it—what my question sounded like. Not simply what had he done with his time, but had he been with anyone in *any* way. My cheeks flushed red for the nth time. "I mean, just, what was your life like? Who are your friends? You know, that kind of thing."

That half-smile deepened before he shook his head. "No, I think it's your turn."

The charm of that expression on his face lost its effect. I wanted to explain and yet dreaded it. I needed him to understand me, but my throat tightened against the words that would help that happen because I couldn't guarantee he would. How could someone so strong, directed, and independent understand anything about my life to this point?

I nodded so he'd know I wasn't ignoring his statement while I gulped down a too-large drink of wine. As always, he waited patiently. I decided to start with the least interesting bits. "Well, you saw that I got my degree and then taught for a few years."

He nodded, full attention on me. No verbal response, and I knew what that meant.

"After a while, I met Aaron."

No reaction.

"He was my mom's friend's son, and they'd always wanted us to give it a try. He'd been living somewhere else but moved back, and so we started dating."

The dip of his chin was the only acknowledgement he'd heard, but it signaled for me to continue. I would've loved to stop now and skip ahead to, well, anything else, but I plowed through and got it done.

"He was nice. We got along well." *And I was deeply lonely and always a little sad, even though it'd been nearly a decade since my life had gone off course when I left you.* "He proposed and I said yes."

"And then?"

Merciless man that he was, he wanted the rest. "And then, that's all it was. Agreeable. Friendly. I should've called off the wedding before it happened, but my parents were so thrilled and..."

His gaze darkened. "You do love to see them happy."

The arrow pierced right where he'd shot it—in the oldest child's heart beating in my chest, the one that'd broken her parents' hearts and had spent years trying to make up for it while also resenting every moment she felt so beholden to them.

"It's been a long road to get to a place where I could tell them no. For so long, I bought into the idea that I didn't know what was right for me. I didn't have strong opinions, not after —not for a long time, I mean, and so I just did what they suggested. Then once I did think about leaving, Eddie left and broke them all over again, and I couldn't stomach disappointing them. But it wasn't like I was strong-armed into marrying Aaron. He was a good man, and he treated me well."

"But that wasn't enough?"

I'd had a few years to make peace with how things had gone with me and Aaron, and for the most part, I did feel peace. But that question would likely always sting because the truth was that I would've let the marriage persist indefinitely if he hadn't ended it, and *that* was something I'd grieved, too. "Actually, it would've been for me, or so I convinced myself. But it wasn't for him."

His brows jumped.

"He came to me one day and said he loved me, but he'd never been in love with me and suspected I felt the same. I admitted I did. He said he'd found someone he thought he could really love and wanted to know how I felt about divorcing." I shrugged. "It was always like that between us— no drama."

"No fights."

The subtext of what he was saying—not like we'd been. We weren't dramatic the way some teens could be, but we were intense. And that dig about my parents came from a real place in that they'd never been comfortable with me and Wilder, even though they hadn't stopped us from being together—at least not until we moved.

"I always felt safe with him, but I always knew marrying him was a mistake." Even before it happened. I'd been so sick on my wedding day, literally sick to my stomach, that I couldn't enjoy hardly anything. But I'd bucked up and smiled and acted like it was the best thing to ever happen to me because the real best thing, the person I'd loved more than anyone on earth, was gone. And I'd been the one to make it that way.

I couldn't have saved our baby, and in retrospect I couldn't have even stayed in Silverton. But we were a year from graduation. I could've called him. Let him call me. I could've done so many things differently, and because I didn't, I'd married a man I didn't l love and wasn't even attracted to.

The only man I'd ever felt passion for had been missing from my life for too long.

Until now.

"Safety is good sometimes," he said, clearly not talking about Aaron. Maybe insinuating he wasn't safe?

"I've been trying to move in a different direction with my decision-making in the last few years."

"How so?"

"I'm trying this new thing where I do what I want? Where I attempt to consider that first and not what would keep me safest or make my parents happy. And I'm trying to allow for the fact that while I thought I was protecting myself by *not* choosing at times, that in itself was a decision, so I might as well be definitive and do what I think is best instead of trying to just... not."

He nodded in approval. "Sounds like an interesting experiment. How's it going so far?"

I huffed out a bemused breath. "Well, I'm in my mid-thirties living alone in a crap apartment in my hometown and working for a temp agency."

"You work for a security company."

I tilted my head to one side, then the other. "If we're taking the Pollyanna spin, then I can say I have made some amazing friends, and I've realized I don't want to teach, and..."

The incline of his head asked for what I very much wanted to give him.

"And I'm here with you."

His eyes flicked back and forth between mine, the air taut around us in an instant.

"So you are."

"So I am."

After a beat, he said, "And is that what you want, Sarah? To be here with me?"

CHAPTER TWENTY-SIX

Wilder

She didn't have a chance to respond to my question—one I wanted an answer to very much—mostly thanks to the waiter removing our plates and then Jane Saint, meddling mother, interrupting us.

"Well, if this isn't an adorable and delightful coincidence!" Mom shuffled up to the table, smile blazing. She wore a nice dress and her hair and makeup were too perfect to be considered casual.

Sarah rose from her seat immediately, and I followed suit. They hugged, then Mom rounded on me and pulled me in, saying softly, "I always knew you were a smart boy."

I shook my head as we separated from the hug but couldn't deny the little jolt of pleasure her approval of me and Sarah being out together caused. No word about what had happened in our past or what might happen in our future, thankfully. Simply happiness at seeing us together.

The scent of her perfume rocketed me back to the past. She'd only worn perfume occasionally when we were growing up, and only when she left the house for church or an outing with friends.

"Are you out with friends, Jane?" Sarah asked.

"Oh, no. I'm on a date."

I admit, I winced. Yes, she had every right to date. I was on a date right this minute. But seeing her out with someone right now seemed weird. I didn't want to know what kind of man she was attracted to. My father had died over thirty years ago, so there was a decent chance whoever she found herself with would be nothing like him.

"Don't be like that, Wilder Saint."

I held up my hands. "We won't keep you, then."

I didn't recall her dating when I was a kid, but realizing she was on a date now made me wonder if she'd ever dated when we were growing up. No doubt I'd been too self-absorbed to think much about anyone other than myself and Sarah.

She scowled but winked at Sarah. "Good luck with this one."

Sarah chuckled and her cheeks pinked in that way that made me wish we were alone. Really alone.

"Sorry about that," I mumbled as my mom twiddled her fingers in greeting to almost every other table she passed on the way back to her own. The man waiting by their table across the room looked decent enough—clothes were orderly and he still had hair. Handsome enough profile. I'd check him out this week just to make sure there weren't any red flags.

"You don't ever have to apologize for your family, Wilder. I've always loved your mom, and your brothers."

I smiled, the genuine sentiment rooting in between my

ribs. She'd gotten along so well with my family. Her parents had tolerated me, and her little sister had nearly worshipped me—often a confusing mix for teen Wilder. In retrospect, I could see how my tendency to be quiet and slow to speak had come off as aloof, but at the time, I'd never understood their general reluctance for Sarah and me to spend time together.

"They love you, too."

I could say it like that because I knew they still did. Obviously, Mom loved Sarah, even if there were things about her absence they needed to discuss. And Wyatt had been more protective of her than me when I'd first gotten back, constantly questioning whether I'd seen her and what I'd said. If I hadn't known he was fully in love with and invested in Calla, I might've thought it was jealousy.

But it'd been that brotherly protection he'd developed for Sarah over the years of our friendship and then relationship.

When she left, I knew my mom had lost something. She'd loved having Sarah around, and neither of my brothers had had steady girlfriends. I got that. But it never occurred to me that Wy and Warrick had lost a sister of sorts. Grandma Tilda had lost a granddaughter. We'd all lost something, and then I'd left them, too.

Guilt etched into my gut. I straightened in my seat, refusing to take in my mom and her date again, then stood and held out a hand. "Ready?"

I didn't mean for it to be a loaded question. I'd meant it as a question about now—was she ready to leave?

But the way her eyes glittered, steady and determined in their focus on me as she set her hand in mine and stood, made all of it feel weightier. And the softly spoken "Yes" did the same.

We exited the restaurant and walked with linked hands under the veil of stars sparkling overhead. My mind had emptied of all thought save one: she was ready. For what, exactly, I didn't know, but for something more than simply leaving dinner, that was for sure.

The closer we got to her place, the more certain I was of her answer to the original question. But I needed her to speak, and I suspected part of her needed that, too—to actually voice her desires. So when we slowly ascended the stairs to her door, I asked again.

"What do you want, Sarah?"

Her throat worked to swallow, and her lips parted as if in slow motion. Maybe my mind was processing it in that way—wouldn't be entirely unheard of for me.

If she couldn't say it, then nothing could happen. I'd ignored all the reasons I had—and there were plenty of them—to resist this between us. She'd run away from me once, and I had no guarantee she wouldn't do it again. No way of knowing how this would go.

But if she could admit to herself and me that this was happening between us, not just in my head or hers, maybe it could work. At least for a while, it could work. And maybe that's all we needed, to try again, now, as the adults we'd become.

She looked down at our joined hands before saying, "I want something with you. If you want that, too."

There was no stopping what came next. I gave her an answer with lips and no words. One hand at her back, one sliding into her hair at the base of her neck, I took her mouth like I'd been dreaming of for hours and days and weeks—and maybe it was time to be honest, years.

The sound she made, something soft and lush, made my

stomach tighten. Her hands sifted into my hair at either side of my head and urged me closer. In seconds, the sweet, exploring kiss had turned to a blaze. This, after all, wasn't our first kiss. We'd kissed a hundred times before, years and years ago. But this was Sarah, a woman with a whole life between now and the time we'd shared, and I was a man who'd been starved for her despite myself since the minute I saw her last December.

In truth, far longer.

Her kisses matched my own—deep, searching, and so delicious I could've died a happy man in that moment.

Being close to her, inhaling the same air and senses filled with her, I lost all measure of restraint. Our connection had always been fire and flame, and the weeks building to this moment preceded by years of separation hadn't done anything to quell that heat.

"Wilder," she said, her breath at my ear as I kissed the curve of her jaw then down the smooth column of her throat.

I made some kind of feral, senseless sound and continued my worship of her neck.

"Wilder, wait."

I froze, her soft words shoving reality back at me.

I had her pinned against her front door, our bodies flush. One hand pulled at the sleeve of her shirt to expose more of her shoulder and the other sat low on the curve of her hip.

Too much too soon, idiot. I immediately let my hands fall away and stepped back. "Sorry. Sorry."

She reached for and grabbed the placket of my shirt, eyes finding mine in the dim light. "Don't apologize for wanting me as much as I want you, please."

Her words registered at the same time her appearance

did—hungry eyes, swollen lips, breathing a little rough. "Okay. Not sorry."

Her face split into a delighted smile. "Fair enough. But I think we need to—"

"Slow down," I said with her, ensuring she knew I was tracking and agreed. Might not've been *excited* for the change of pace, but unraveling her on her apartment front step didn't say... what I wanted it to say.

She smiled again and flattened her hands against my chest. Another pulse of desire shot through me, and I stepped back. "Can't keep that up if we're slowing down."

"Okay. Not sorry." Her brows raised in challenge.

I laughed, genuine joy at her antics and the connection between us. Present after so long and also *new*. "I'm going now. Let me know when we can do this again."

Then I kissed her cheek, and one last peck on her lips because I couldn't help myself, and I left. I didn't look back because if I caught her expression and it held as much need as it had seconds ago, I wouldn't be able to stop myself from turning around.

So I walked on, focusing on the crisp night air and the waxing moon arcing over the shadowy mountains. The scents of earth and a hint of something sweet blooming filled the walk, and I almost prolonged it to be out in the darkness. I'd operated in darkness for so long, it'd become home to me.

Instead of ranging around outside, I returned to my shabby apartment only a few minutes from Sarah's. I locked myself in, the thunk of the deadbolt a reminder that I wouldn't see her again tonight. This wild, animal instinct to be close to her now that she'd said she wanted that too clawed at me, but I moved through the necessities and readied for bed.

Instead of a quiet list of things I'd need to do the next day and a mild anticipation for the oblivion of sleep, I went to bed eager for the day. Sarah hadn't given me a new reason to live or anything so monumental as that, but she'd shifted my focus from tasks to a delicious unknown.

CHAPTER TWENTY-SEVEN

Sarah

To keep myself from texting Wilder first thing the next morning, I occupied myself with cleaning my kitchen and bathroom. Unfortunately, that took very little time—something I normally would've been happy about. But being unable to focus on anything but Wilder had apparently scrambled my brain, and all I could think about were his kisses last night. That intense way he did everything had only heightened with age.

Instead of pacing my tiny living room and wondering if ten in the morning the night after our first date was too soon to call, I went for a run. My knee felt terrible, no surprise, so I kept it short. By the time I'd gotten ready, it wasn't quite noon. But blessedly, the bookstore opened at noon on Sundays. No library option today, so I was glad to have some way to spend time surrounded by books.

The jingle of the bell at the door gave a friendly

greeting followed immediately by the owner's, "Come on in!" shouted from somewhere in the back. I delighted in each curated display table I passed on the way to the beautiful romance archway and quickly collected a stack of books to study in the cozy chair in the corner. I'd decided to treat myself to one book today, so I needed to carefully consider this pile.

"Can I get you a coffee?" Mr. Malcom asked, kind face peering down at me.

"Oh, no, that's fine. Thank you so much."

He smiled, warm and genuine. "Of course. Let me know if you need anything."

After that, I slipped into the world of books and romance, blissfully paging through front and back matter, studying the covers and bios. I loved every part of a print book, especially since I so rarely bought them anymore. Since I'd found the winning title, I tucked into the first chapter and lost another few minutes before Jane Saint's voice recalled me to reality.

"Don't you look cozy," she said, beaming at me.

She appeared typically stylish and relaxed, but somehow tired. Having seen her last night all dressed up for her date, I wondered if she'd been out late with the man.

"How was your date?" I asked, returning to sitting upright like an adult instead of curled into a ball in the chair.

Her lips flattened into a thin line. "Not great."

"Oh. Bummer. I'm sorry."

She sighed. "Such is the reality of my dating life—not great. I'm not ready to give up yet, but I'll tell you, it's tempting."

"I'm sorry. I can understand why it's disheartening, for sure." I stacked the books—keeper and the *I'll own you someday, just you wait* pile—and stood. "Maybe some time with a good book will ease the sting?"

"My thoughts exactly."

We grinned at each other, and just as I was about to escape unscathed, she grabbed my arm to stop me. "It's time I say my piece."

"O—okay." I swallowed hard.

"I can't pretend to know exactly what you felt when you left."

Her blue eyes searched back and forth between mine. My throat tightened, but I nodded to show her I'd listen.

"I do know something about getting an early start on family. Maybe that's why it never scared me—you two being so young, I mean. And I know that wasn't the case for your parents."

Her meaningful gaze made my heart twist. To say they hadn't handled the news of my pregnancy well would be putting it mildly. My mother didn't speak to me for two days, and my father could hardly look at me. I'd had to warn Wilder to stay away.

It'd been Jane who'd embraced us both, tears in her eyes, and asked what she could do to help. It'd been Jane who'd ended up coming to my house and pleading with my parents to allow Wilder to see me and finally, to listen to the plan we had.

Maybe they'd never believed that we would carry out our plan to go to the same school and have Wilder get his commission while I got my degree—part of me had recognized they hoped things would derail and I'd find my way to a path they preferred. But I think the idea of us getting married eased the humiliation of the pregnancy, especially once Jane said whatever she had said when she'd asked me and Eddie to excuse them.

"I never told you how much—" I swallowed convulsively, and she rushed to continue.

"Sarah, dear, let me get this out. I've wanted to tell you I'm sorry for not pressing them a bit more before you left. I failed Wilder, and I failed you. But I also want you to know —" She took me by the shoulders since my hands were full. "I need you to understand that, though it broke my heart, your leaving, I never held it against you."

Tears flooded my eyes and fell in an instant. I sucked in a breath and held it to keep from sobbing, the immediacy of the torrential emotion surprising.

Jane's eyes sparkled with unshed tears of her own. "What I struggled with most was that you stayed away. I loved you, child, and I still do. You felt like my own, like a daughter I'd always wanted. And it was a situation I wouldn't wish on an enemy, much less a seventeen-year-old girl. Any hurt I've felt in these years was rooted in that love, that wishing you would come back to us in some way."

My chest was heavy, and my heart ached with this collision of memories and this moment. I swiped away tears, and she touched her hand to my cheek gently before dropping it.

"I said it back then, but I'm sure you could hardly hear anything in the midst of it all—I'm sorry. I'm so sorry you lost the baby, and it wasn't your fault. It wasn't a punishment or anything but a horrible sadness."

Pain rocked me, the days after losing the baby tunneling back at me. "It was so awful." What else could I say? She knew. She knew exactly how awful it'd been.

She gathered my hand in hers again, a warm, loving expression on her tear-streaked face. "You are welcome here. You are welcome in this town, in our lives, and in my home. I hope you will come to family dinner soon. I should've said this all a year ago, but I wanted to give you time. I didn't want to pressure you or make you uncomfortable or scare you away. I know I can come on a little strong."

Her sheepish grin and wink allowed me to cough out a laugh and some of the pressure building in my chest to ease.

"Thank you. It took... a long time to recover. And by then, I was trying to fit into a new school and bury all the things I'd expected out of life. I didn't grieve losing *you* until a long while later, and it's still something I regret. Deeply."

We stared into each other's eyes, both feeling the loss and grief, but a newness, too. One of understanding and healing. One of hope.

This was why I'd come back. Here was another piece of me fitted back into place.

I'd learned to find hope in small moments and small ideas for years, but this one wasn't all that small. Knowing that Jane didn't hate me for leaving, and maybe even understood a little, brought such sweeping relief, I could hardly stand any longer.

"Thank you," she said, then pulled me in and squeezed around my awkward bulk.

I turned and dropped the books onto the chair and embraced her fully. "Thank you."

I had more to say, but maybe none of it mattered. Especially not when she pulled back, that typical Jane Saint twinkle in her eye, and said, "Now go call Wilder and put him out of his misery."

I chuckled through a little thrill at hearing his name. "Why would he be miserable?"

She smirked. "Because you went out last night, he left you at the door like the gentleman he is deep down, and he is desperate for you."

I laughed outright at that. "I don't think Wilder is the

kind of man who gets desperate, but I appreciate the sentiment."

Maybe the tone I'd affected would keep her from sensing just exactly how much the idea of Wilder being desperate for me affected me.

In case I thought I'd fooled myself, my pulse shot off like a rocket as I remembered his kiss, the firm possessiveness of his touch, and the insistence on saying goodnight.

"I won't pretend to know everything about him. He and I still have quite a bit of catching up to do. But I saw you two together last night, and Warrick saw him running this morning."

"He runs a lot these days, from what I gather," I insisted, resisting the idea that he was waiting around for me.

If I let myself believe her and actually believe he was that enthusiastic about us, I'd probably combust in a raging blush that ended up burning me to an embarrassed, delighted, anticipatory crisp.

"Put it this way. If you call him right now, I guarantee he'll answer."

"He has good manners."

She raised one brow. "Ask his brothers how many times they called him in the last decade and how many of those times he answered. And I'm not talking about him being gone or out of the country."

I waved her silly glare away and turned to get the pile of books. "Time for you to find your comfort read. I'll go check out and—"

"And call—"

"Wilder." We both said it at the same time.

It wasn't like she had to talk me into it. I didn't need convincing. I'd spent the morning trying not to call him and seem overly eager. I wanted to see him again and I'd been daydreaming about sneaking in one more interaction this weekend before we returned to the office tomorrow and everything had to fit within the propriety of the workplace. We probably needed to talk about that, too, I supposed, though as his only in-house employee, maybe not. It might make me a fool to ignore the warning in the back of my mind, that reminder that I'd never planned to stay here for good, but I couldn't find it in me to heed that. Not right now.

Either way, I needed no encouragement from Jane, but I'd take hers and run.

"Have a good day, Jane. And thanks again."

She blew me a kiss and winked. "You have a good day, too, Sarah dear."

CHAPTER TWENTY-EIGHT

Wilder

Sarah's laugh rang out, a grand prize for the efforts of my storytelling.

"I cannot picture this. I might need you to reenact it for me," she said, wiping a laughter-induced tear from one eye.

"I will not."

She beamed. "I think you have to. There's only so much you can tell me about your life and work, right? I think, in this case, you'll need to go all in."

I chuckled, enjoying her delight at the story of my ill-timed car sickness on a mission almost a decade ago that resulted in a black eye for me *and* Bruce. "I will not."

She shook her head. "Maybe I'll ask Bruce and get his perspective."

I shut my eyes in feigned regret. "I knew you two knowing each other would come to haunt me. What have I done?"

She grinned again, then ducked her head to sip some water.

I'd honed my observational skills, among many others, to a sharp point over my time in special operations, and sometimes found it difficult to fully engage in a moment because I was caught up in taking in the details. The rustle of the spring breeze in the newly budded leaves on branches above our heads. The clatter of silverware at nearby tables. A motorcycle zipping down Elk Street, a truck idling on Main. The low hum of conversations, occasional words jumping out at me.

And then, of course, there was Sarah herself. The way her hair slipped over her shoulder when she leaned forward. The darkness under her eyes she hadn't covered up as well today, and I wondered if it was new. The earrings that hung down a half inch and drew my eyes to her neck.

Heat shot through me for the nth time in the last hour. I'd kissed that neck, just there behind her ear, not twenty-four hours ago. The memory of her scent had paled compared to reality. I'd savored our short embrace when we met today and the excuse to kiss her cheek, to get close enough to recapture the essence of her.

All of these things could put me in a posture of gathering data and evidence rather than living in the moment, but whenever my senses tended to tug at me and raise alarm, to say *Hey, something might be wrong here*, her smile, her laugh, that way she bit her lip and then stopped herself like it was a habit she was trying to break, all brought me back.

"He seems like a good guy and a good partner for you. Do you think he'll like Silverton?" She nudged her plate an inch or two away from the edge of the table and sat back in her seat with a little sigh.

I blinked away from a vision of Sarah laying back, replete and satisfied, but not from French toast and fruit. And then I cleared my throat because that was not a smart train of thought, and I had to get my mind under control. "Uh, yeah. Yes. He will. And so will Kiley."

"She's how old?"

I signed the bill on autopilot, refusing to let my mind return to the too-delicious image that'd shot through it moments ago. "Uh, twelve."

"Oh, wow. Yeah, that's a lot of transition for her, right?" Her brows dipped to a concerned vee.

A familiar flood of fondness rushed in. Her concern for a kid she'd never met was one of a thousand reasons I liked her. Not just the memory of her, but Sarah *now*. "You must be a very good teacher."

"What makes you say that?"

"You're so thoughtful. I think kids need that."

I had, certainly. I would've failed English if it hadn't been for Mrs. Wallace's patience. There was more than one teacher who'd ignored what everyone knew was going on in my life when Sarah left, but most of them had cared. They'd done whatever they could to talk me into still going to college, trying to convince me that was the best. But by then, I'd signed a contract, and I couldn't imagine going to college without Sarah. That'd always been the plan.

I didn't have letters from her at basic training. I didn't have her and a rounded belly to come home to, to move to my first duty station with, to learn and grow and build a family with. But I'd cobbled together an existence that I could live with, and for years, until I got to the EMU, honestly, that'd been all I had to give myself.

"I don't know. I mean, yes, I can admit I'm thoughtful. But..." Her lips tucked in like she didn't want to say.

"What?" I prompted, immensely curious for anything she might not naturally share. I wanted all of it.

She pasted on a smile. "I'm just at a crossroads with teaching, I guess." She tossed her napkin. "Ready?"

I saw the topic change for what it was, but went with it. I wouldn't pressure her about that now. There'd be time, maybe even today, to talk about deeper things. So far, we'd kept it light, but I had a thousand questions. I couldn't ask them all today, but I hoped, more and more, we'd get through it.

Because there had to be something that would chafe. There had to be hardship and challenge coming for us. And I wanted to face it head-on, I wanted it addressed and taken care of instead of lying in wait. If my gut was right, and it usually was, something was coming. I hated the feeling, especially when I couldn't tell from where the dreaded *something* would come.

We left the terrace where we'd been seated outside and proceeded back through the Silver Ridge Resort to the main lobby. My mother had conveniently mentioned the resort restaurant featured a spring brunch that had a great menu served until mid-afternoon on weekends and suggested I take Sarah there today, then fifteen minutes later, I'd heard from Sarah.

I'd met her at the resort, a truly impressive version of the old lodge it used to be. I'd seen it in the last few years on my spare visits, but I hadn't been inside. The Morrison family had brought in the big guns, and one of those happened to be Julian Grenier. Warrick might've had mixed feelings about the man, but he certainly made an excellent partner thus far.

Grenier's taste for luxury made even more sense in the context of his part-ownership of the resort—the opulence and quality of everything felt familiar. He'd insisted on wood floors, carpeting, covering the exposed logs of the cabin, the updated break room, the polished wood conference table and upholstered chairs, and much more at our small business. I hadn't objected, aware that his knowledge of upper crust preferences would help Saint Securities land the kind of clients we wanted to serve.

Back outside, Sarah stretched her arms overhead and breathed deeply. My eyes skated over her, gulping down the view before averting my eyes.

"It's so beautiful here. I missed it while I was gone."

"That it is," I said, not caring even a little bit I hadn't looked at anything but her with as much longing.

"Did you like North Carolina?"

"No."

She burst out laughing. "You lived there most of your Army career, right?"

"The last fourteen years."

Her forehead wrinkled. My hand itched to grab hers. Other than the initial hug and cheek kiss, we hadn't touched today. Not that there hadn't been moments when I'd wanted to. At one point, our knees had brushed under the table, and you would've thought she'd slid her hand up my thigh for the way my body had responded.

It'd always been like this before, but I'd chalked it up to teenage hormones. Of course when I was living it, I hadn't thought of it that way. I'd known it was *Sarah*, my love for her. Our connection. The depth of our feelings.

In the years after, I'd made my peace with our connection and the dissolution of it—or I'd tried to—by admitting that love at seventeen could only have so much depth. Granted, we'd both been through a lot, and we'd experienced a lot together. But that rampaging, mind-melting need for her? That'd been hormones.

Except, if that were true, I wouldn't be feeling that way now. And I did. Absolutely. To an embarrassing degree.

"And you didn't like it at all?" She nudged my shoulder and, happily, didn't retreat very far as we walked side by side.

"I've got the west, the desert and mountains, in my blood. The humidity, lack of winter, the bugs..." I shuddered.

She chuckled. "I get that. You could also say you have them on your arms." She glanced at my tattoos, then continued. "I can't tell you how many kids had to go to the nurse thanks to fire ant bites during recess when I taught elementary." She made a face that accurately reflected the horror of fire ants.

"Yeah, you should know. Georgia isn't all that different from North Carolina, and you were there right up until you moved here, right?"

Her expression tightened. "Yeah."

I couldn't read exactly what hid behind the smallness of her response, but I needed to know why she'd come back. "But you came back here."

Her blue eyes met mine. "I did."

"Why?"

A reluctant smile flashed over her features before she asked, "Why did you?"

And though I was still embracing this truth, still developing what it meant for myself in my own mind, I answered truthfully. "I wanted to come home."

CHAPTER TWENTY-NINE

Sarah

Eddie's name flashed on my screen.

"You need to get that?" Wilder said as we reached my building.

"I probably should. She only calls me every few weeks when she can."

Wilder's eyes narrowed. "What's her job, again?"

"She works for the State Department. I can't remember her title. Lots of travel and such, which she loves, of course."

Wilder nodded. "Better get it, then." Eyes dropping to my lips, he moved in a flash and pressed a surprisingly gentle kiss to my lips. "I'll see you tomorrow."

"Okay. Yeah." I answered the call before I lost it but took a minute to raise it to my ear as I worked to focus through the fluttering in my chest and the disappointment that we'd had to say goodbye.

It was smart. I mean, we still had so much to discuss,

including what was even happening between us or what he wanted or how we'd manage things at work, but for now, I'd talk to my sister.

"Eddie? Everything okay?"

"You realize you don't need to answer that way every time, right? I call you all the time, and it's always because I love you and want to talk to you, and not because I've been kidnapped by terrorists or something."

I released a sigh, buckling in for sassy Ed. She had gotten all the sass in the family, but she'd been stealth about it. She'd kept it locked down until she had a chance to get free, and then she'd gone far and wide and never looked back except to call me.

And yes, at some point, I'd probably need to look a little closer at why I considered Eddie leaving home synonymous with her freedom.

Actually, no. I knew exactly why. It was why I'd left and felt weird waves of guilt and shame for not having done so years ago—decades ago.

"I love you and want to know you're safe."

"Completely"—she grunted like she was lifting something heavy—"safe."

I chuckled. "Okay. Good to know."

"Have you told the parents no yet?"

My stomach twisted. "No. They told me to let them know by mid-May, so I'm taking my time."

She made an irritated sound, which I ignored as I slumped onto the couch.

"You got out, Sar. You need to *stay gone*. It's been, what, fourteen months? Don't go back there."

"It's not like I'm incapable of leaving again. I'd book a return flight. I have a life here. Friends, a job." Sure, maybe it was temporary, but it was good. In fact, I loved it, and we'd barely gotten into more complex contracts and client relationships.

Wherever I went after Silverton, I would not be going back to Georgia.

"Yeah? What's the job? Are you teaching?"

Woof. She spit the word *teaching* like it tasted bad. My hackles rose, but I breathed through the defensiveness, reminding myself she was supporting me in her own way, doing what she thought I needed. "No, in fact, it's not. I'm working for Saint Securities."

"*Saint?* I thought you said you were temping last time we talked?"

My pulse jumped. I'd avoided expounding on the job because the last time we'd talked, I'd been... well, I'd been on my heels a bit, knocked back by Wilder's attention and my waterfall of feelings. "Yeah. Wilder and a friend of his from the Army are doing private security. It's a new business, and their admin is on bed rest after like two days on the job or something, so I have until her maternity leave is over."

What I'd do after that, I couldn't wrap my head around. And I wouldn't, for now.

"Wilder? He's out?"

Out of the Army, she meant. "Yes. On his terminal leave, I think it's called? But yeah. His friend Bruce gets here next month. There are some other people involved, but I don't think you'd know them. Anyway, it's really interesting."

She was quiet on the other end for a bit before she finally spoke again. "I can see this for you. I mean, you can't stay an admin or on a temp contract, but I can really see you doing this. I know you have all kinds of guilty feelings about not teaching and saving all of America's children or what-ever, but—"

"I do not! That's ridiculous—"

"The point is, I like this for you. Security is interesting, and you've got a great brain for this. I hope Wilder won't be a typical grunt and assume that, as a woman, you don't know what you're talking about."

Knowing that she'd faced more than her fair share of sexism in her field, though I wouldn't have guessed diplo-macy would be viewed as a man's world, I could understand her comment. But thinking of Wilder, how great he'd been about everything. How wonderful he was...

"He's not." My voice came out soft, and so like her, Eddie jumped on it.

"Ohhh. I'll need you to tell me the whole situation."

I squirmed. "There's—it's—still developing."

The pause in our conversation could only mean one thing—Eddie was figuring out her approach. It meant I'd have no peace until I told her everything. Blowing out a breath to calm myself, I dove in.

"Fine. Okay. We went out last night. A few weeks ago, I apologized for leaving, for hurting him, and things got a lot less awkward. He's still very... *him,* but he warmed to me faster than I would've expected."

Another little sigh escaped because I had fallen fully into the *Wilder is dreamy* feelings and I knew them well. I'd spent most of my days from age twelve until I left Silverton feeling some measure of that consuming ridiculousness. It'd crept in on and off since I'd apologized, though I'd try to ignore it and not get ahead of myself.

"So we're there already—with you sighing over him."

"Um, excuse me? You've been *sighing over* Bri Williamson for like two decades." The woman had been in love with the world-famous popstar her entire life. Completely counter to her anti-romance perspective on life, but one of my favorite little pieces of her.

"As if. Not *two decades*. And stop trying to distract me from Wilder. My point is, if he wasn't such a solid guy, I'd be upset. But this, too, makes sense for you. I just have one thing to say."

Something about her saying he was a solid guy sounded like she knew he was a solid guy. I wondered if she was able to see his military records or they had a friend in common who could vouch for him. But more than that, her silly claim there at the end had me smiling to no one there in my dim living room. A giggle slipped out, because Eddie rarely had just *one thing* to say. "Do tell, brilliant sister."

"I'm glad you apologized. You needed to. But you also didn't need to. You were a seventeen-year-old kid who'd had her world changed overnight, and then it happened again. Our parents pressured you about everything, all the time, and I wasn't so young I didn't see how they treated you until after we moved. *They* are culpable for so much, Sar, and I hope you won't let them off the hook anytime soon."

I sat up, the lazy, chatty feeling gone. "They thought they were doing the right thing at the time."

Even if I always wondered if they'd realized that leaving Wilder had meant leaving my best friend—not just my boyfriend, the guy who'd gotten me pregnant. I'd lost the man I thought I'd marry, sooner or later, and I'd lost the person who knew me best in the world. I'd lost his brothers, who I loved like my own, and I'd lost Jane, his wonderful, caring mother, and Tilda, his oddball, endearing grandma.

"That's the excuse-making nonsense they're going to capitalize on if you try to go to that wedding."

I gritted my teeth. Eddie and I had never agreed about

this, and though I respected her take, even recognized the truth in her words sometimes, I didn't want to do all this again.

"I've forgiven them for my own sake. I don't want the poison of bitterness and blame in my heart—trust me when I say I have lived there, and it's brutal and I won't go back. As much as ending things with Aaron sucked, the best thing that came out of it was talking to a therapist and figuring out how I'd ended up marrying a man I got along with and not much else."

I could think of that marriage without cringing most of the time, too, thanks to therapy. Since I'd had a job with benefits and I'd stayed in Georgia while saving up to move out here, I'd focused on myself. I got mentally and physically healthy again, and then I left.

Eddie's voice came through softer now. "You know I'm proud of you for that. And I don't want to sound like another jerk trying to tell you what to do. I just *hate* when you give them the benefit of the doubt because they don't deserve it. But enough about them. I want a photo of you and Wilder *stat.* Tell him hi for me, and do not elope without inviting me—I'm stateside for a few months, and I'll meet you wherever."

I laughed, love and delight twining through me even as my heart thumped wildly at her words. "That's probably a bit premature."

She snorted. "Sure. Twenty years in the making, you reunite with your first love, who you were torn from in the drama of losing a child you both wanted, and you both happen to be single. You date and... take it slow? Come on, woman. Let's get real."

I shot to my feet, pacing. "I don't have any idea what he

wants. We're just getting to know each other again. He may not—"

"Sarah. I love you, and I love that despite being gaslit and controlled by our parents for way too long, you have maintained your soft, kind heart, but please allow yourself to have this happiness. I don't know if Wilder wants forever with you, but if he's single and asking you out on dates, if he hasn't fundamentally changed who he was—which I grant you is a possibility over the course of time—then he does. He *does*. But ask him yourself."

"I'm not about to—"

"Not tonight or tomorrow. Maybe not even next week. But have the conversation about future plans. Ask him. Because you deserve to be loved well, and Wilder did that. I'm betting, if you both want it, he would again."

I sucked in a breath. "For someone who is patently unromantic, that's a very sweet thought."

She groaned. "Only for you and Wilder. I'll always want you two together, if it's still right."

I loosed a chuckle at that. "Still sweet."

"Hear me, though. *Only if it's still right*, okay? If you keep dating and find out it isn't, ditch the bearded brute and find yourself someone else." A buzzing sounded in her background, and she groaned again, louder this time. "I've got to run. Love you."

"Love you, too."

I slumped back onto the couch, Eddie's words swirling in my mind. She was oversimplifying what it was like to be with someone after *so* long. We weren't picking up where we'd left off, and frankly, I had no desire to. We'd left off at the worst time in my life. But part of what made it so horrible was just that—leaving him.

Wilder had always been certain of us, right up until I left. I didn't know what he wanted for himself now. Did he even want to get married? His brother, Warrick, had planned on staying single forever, though he had his own reasons for that. Maybe Wilder had adopted the same mindset.

Eddie was right, though. If I didn't ask Wilder what *he* wanted and figure that out, I could only blame myself. I hadn't allowed myself to think about staying and being with Wilder long term, but Eddie's words took hold with an iron grip.

And after so long letting other people determine what happened in my life, after being too weak or willfully ignorant to assert myself, I couldn't let things with Wilder go that way.

I wouldn't.

CHAPTER THIRTY

Wilder

Bruce had a way of working magic, and he'd done it, even from afar. Paired with Grenier's vested interest in Saint Securities' success, we had an uptick in work for the week that kept me doggedly busy.

I'd hired three people so far, none of whom could start work yet. Bruce had also hired three. We had one guy coming in end of this month, but until then, it was just me. Since Madeline Reynolds would be arriving next week, I had to get everything possible done so I could provide in-person security as needed, especially if she didn't have her usual bodyguards in place. Her big man, Brad, was obviously trusted and capable, so I wouldn't need to actually *guard* her, but she'd be dropping high five figures at minimum over her six-week stay in Silverton, and if I wanted that to parlay into more, I needed to be completely available to her.

Did I want to be running around town doing system and plans assessments of all of Grenier's wealthy contacts? No. I wanted to be finding excuses to talk to Sarah and stand close enough to catch the scent of her shampoo.

And because I'd had that thought, I'd decided we needed boundaries at work, but how utterly laughable that I ever thought we'd need them considering I hadn't been in the office for more than eight consecutive minutes.

Serving high-end clients, I'd come to realize in the few short weeks since we'd opened Saint Securities, meant bending to their needs. And since most of these people didn't have imminent danger situations or issues like Reynolds's stalker, they wanted me to come to them, check out their alarm system, security feeds, panic rooms, whatever else. They wanted to know vulnerabilities in their fences (usually the whole thing since fences were one hundred percent not an obstacle for a human, though dogs would be deterred). And so far, at least two of the clients were interested in whether I provided bodyguard services... in their bedroom.

Cue the record scratch and... Nope.

Part of the reason I'd been gone so much was that I'd had therapy during my lunch on Tuesday, and had lunch with Wyatt Wednesday. It'd been time well spent—a little reconnecting, prodding him to talk about his growing family and all that unadulterated bliss, and his nudging me to talk about how I was *really* doing. I would've stopped by the office, but instead settled for a scant few texts. I would've asked her to dinner Tuesday night when I realized the entire week was going to go like this, except my mind had been packed full from my therapy session that day.

I'd needed it, too. I'd needed to talk out the gripping sensation that it was all too good to be true.

"Why do say that?" Dr. Corrigan asked in that curious, neutral way.

"I'm happy. She seems happy. Our chemistry is…" My body flashed hot with the memory of kissing her, feeling her pressed against me, hungering for more of her and knowing she felt the same. "Still intact."

The doc nodded.

"But it feels wrong."

"How so?"

I sifted through words, searching for the right ones. "It's too easy."

"Elaborate on that."

Frustration crowded around me, the inadequacy of my explanation so far making me restless. My leg bounced where I sat. "We went through a lot."

She nodded. We'd talked about the history. Then we'd talked about the apology that came after it a bit in another session. She knew a lot of it.

"It's been decades."

She didn't nod then, but she blinked in a gesture I'd learned was like a nod—urging me to continue without interrupting me.

For a man who didn't talk a lot, therapy had been a challenge. I wasn't someone who felt the need to fill the silence, so the first session had been rife with them. But I wasn't resisting it—I just had to work on verbalizing some of what happened inside me. And I'd made progress on that.

"She was my world, and then things fell apart. I'm not sure I let myself grieve very well. I coped by leaving, too. And being back, it feels like I should be more—" I ran my hands through my hair, then leaned forward to rest my elbows on my knees. "Like I should be sadder. Unhappy. That being with her would hurt or I'd feel resentful or angry or wary or stupid or *something* other than happy and so turned on I can hardly see straight."

A smile flashed but she packed it away. "Are you resentful?"

Exhaling through the surge of adrenaline from my last explanation, I searched myself. I'd done that a lot lately, especially where it came to Sarah. "No. After her apology, I wondered if I'd accepted it to get past the awkwardness and keep her from being upset. I could never stand when she was torn up, and I guess that's still true. But I don't. Because we were kids, and her parents were moving, and she'd just lost our baby. She was a mess, and so was I. Ideally, she wouldn't have left, but I'm not foolish enough to think I would've been some expert at helping her deal with all the aftermath of what happened."

And that was true. Simply true. I wouldn't have known how, and who knew how much harder it would've been for her if she'd stayed.

"Are you angry? Bitter? Sad?"

I huffed, seeing her point. "The only thing I'm sad about is realizing the distance I put between myself and my family. And even that is better than I could've hoped for. With Sarah, thinking about the time we've lost makes me sad. Always has. We haven't talked about that much but even though I know we need to, I also want to just not."

She jotted notes in a paper notebook while I gathered my next thought. She was trying to make me see that the absence of those feelings meant maybe it *was* that easy. I got it. I could see where her questions were taking me, obviously. That maybe my life had been on pause, and when I pressed play again, it all fell into place, just like that. But there was more at the heart of this I couldn't ignore.

"I—" I cleared my throat. "I'm not sure I deserve it."

"It..."

"Happiness? Ease? Sarah. My family's forgiveness."

"What makes you say that?"

I pushed back and settled against the couch again. "I walked away. I kept them at arm's length—my family at least. And the work I did mattered, but it didn't have to consume me. I let it—wanted it to. I wanted to live a life separate from things that made me feel too much."

"What's too much?"

I scrubbed a hand down my face. "Doc, you're killing me."

She chuckled gamely. "I'm not trying to. What I'm hearing is that heightened emotions are something you prefer to avoid. I wonder though, did you ever experience anything that you'd qualify as *feeling too much* during your career in the Army?"

"Yes. Not all the time, but yes." I'd witnessed death first-hand. More than one brutal, limb-taking injury. I'd lost friends. I'd grappled with survivor's guilt, with the inability to save them, with the waste of losing them, with the terror of it being me and then another round of guilt for all of that. And then, I'd shut it out and get back to work.

"So you didn't escape that when you left."

"No."

"It sounds like you feel the need to atone for having stayed away, but all the while, you were facing hardships you never would've had if you stayed. Or, if you'd taken up a more traditional military career, perhaps."

My head tipped side to side. "Most of the worst losses were prior to my special ops time."

She nodded, granting me that. "I wonder if you feel Sarah doesn't deserve happiness for having left?"

"Definitely not."

"Do you feel Warrick should have to atone for the time he spent away in the NFL?"

We'd talked enough about Warrick. Plus, the town was small; she knew his history.

"No."

"And what about—"

I waved a hand. "I get it. I do."

We sat in silence as my mind worked through undefinable thoughts. After a while, her timer buzzed with a five-minute warning.

"I'd suggest thinking about ways you can accept what is good."

I made a face, not quite understanding.

She tried again. "Consider that perhaps, after challenging years for you and for Sarah, the ease between you is a blessing. Something to be welcomed rather than wary of."

I loosed a sigh, wondering if I could.

"I'm not saying that means there won't be disagreements or hard moments, but it could also be that your maturity, the work you've both been doing to accept your pasts and participate in the world around you, is allowing this."

Her gaze stapled the point home before she said, "And I'd suggest the same with your family."

I shoved to my feet and nodded before I left. "I'll think on it."

And I would. I had been. But I wasn't ready to see Sarah or anyone, for that matter, until I sorted through it all a bit more.

CHAPTER THIRTY-ONE

Sarah

I ducked my head as though that might keep Wilder from hearing me any better. "It's not the right time."

"When will it be the right time, Sarah? You haven't been back since you left. When are we going to see you again?" My mother's voice took on the familiar tinge of accusation and pleading.

My spine threatened to bend, so I straightened in my chair. "I just started a new job, Mom. I can't suddenly leave right when they're getting things off the ground and expect to keep it."

"Doesn't sound like a very good working atmosphere if you aren't allowed to take time off."

I gritted my teeth, prayed for patience, and pulled in a slow breath before speaking. "It's a very good job. The company is new, and their—well, the point is, I can't take leave yet. I agreed to that up front, so it's not a surprise."

"You've known about your cousin's wedding for weeks. You should be on a teaching schedule, free in the summer so you can—"

"But I'm not teaching. I'm not. I'm doing *this*. And my break is over, so I really need to—"

"If you're not even going to *try* to be here for Angie, I don't know what to say to you."

That bitter shake in her voice made my gut clench. It always had. One of her many tactics, I'd come to realize, and also one I'd learned I was often most vulnerable to. There was always a tremor of emotion that brought me to my knees, eager to solve whatever wrong had been done to her that'd created it.

With Eddie's bolstering words behind me and my own determination in the palm of my hands, I didn't simply hang up. Instead, I said, "That's okay. You don't have to know what to say. But I'm still not going to be able to come."

Silence met me in response.

"I've got to go. Hope you have a good day. Love you." And I hung up.

The usual flood of emotion hit, tears stinging my eyes with embarrassing immediacy. My heart churned in my chest, working to process the glut of regret, relief, and sadness. I shot out of the chair and hustled down the hallway to the bathroom, focusing solely on the restroom and not allowing myself to note if Wilder saw me sprinting by.

He might not've heard. There was a decent chance. And my end of the conversation hadn't been all that damning, had it? Only proof that I'd grown a backbone in recent years—something that'd taken way too long.

I closed and locked the door and leaned against the inside, eyes on the ceiling to keep my mascara from becoming a disaster. Arms folded and tucked against my chest, I attempted to slow my breathing and come back to myself.

It hurt to be on the receiving end of yet another guilt trip. It *hurt*. And not for the first time, the pain made me angry. Why did I still care so much that I'd upset her? I had years of evidence that she used that upset to manipulate me. I'd left in no small part to escape exactly this.

Some of my therapist's words flashed through my mind. *Gaslighting. Exhibiting classic narcissism.*

I'd resisted when she'd originally suggested that my mother was a narcissist, my father an enabler of that behavior, and that they'd manipulated and gaslit me for years, particularly escalating in the years after leaving Silverton.

I'd grieved that as much as I'd been relieved by it—being validated in my feelings that the way they'd dealt with me hadn't been healthy had brought some measure of peace. But I'd had to work through so much shame at having allowed myself to be treated that way, even though of course I hadn't thought, "Sure, this is fine!" as a seventeen-year-old in the throes of depression, or a twenty-two-year-old graduating college on their dime, or a twenty-seven-year-old when Eddie left home and it felt like I was the only one who could *fix* things.

I shook my head against the onslaught of memories. I really did need to get back to work, and my break was well past over. After taking a few calming breaths, I cleaned up my face with a paper towel and smiled widely at myself. Years ago, I'd read that smiling can trigger the release of endorphins, and I needed some right about now. With one last *you can do this* sent to the woman in the mirror, I exited the bathroom and made for my desk. I snuck a glance at Wilder and found him glaring at his computer screen. *Good.*

Maybe he's been absorbed with work and didn't overhear that whole mess.

I dove back into the work I'd been doing when my mother had called. I wouldn't have answered, but I'd just decided to take a quick break and the guilt I was always battling against when it came to her had gotten the best of me. I wouldn't make that mistake again, and like I'd done at different times in the last few years, I'd need to avoid answering her for a few weeks. Conversations after one like we'd had today never went well and always left me feeling even worse, despite knowing exactly what to expect. So, boundaries. I'd said no, and now I would do that again by not answering for a while.

"Come get some coffee," Wilder said, startling me.

"I just took a break." I didn't glance over my shoulder at him, afraid the sight of him would weaken my stance. And frankly, I didn't need to feel any weaker at the moment.

"That was an hour ago. You can take a few minutes."

"What?" My eyes found the clock on my screen. It *had* been an hour—slightly more than, actually. I'd been chasing the rabbit trail of thoughts about my parents while filling out a spreadsheet from one of Wilder's in-person evaluations last week, and the time had flown. "Wow. Yeah, okay."

Still a bit soon for another break, but considering he was the boss and owner, and also considering I really wanted some more coffee, I followed him into the break room. As soon as we stepped through the frame, he turned on me.

"Are you okay?"

My brows jumped, surprised by the sudden whirl to face me and the question. "Yes?"

"That's a question?"

"No. I'm just not sure what you mean."

"Your mother. I heard some of your end. Wasn't trying to, but did."

Embarrassment colored my cheeks and a droplet of shame burned in my chest. I shoved that feeling away, reasoning that I'd stood my ground. "Yeah. It's fine."

His dark eyes searched mine for a moment. "You know you can take any time off you need. Especially now while I don't have quite as much work for you. I've been worried you're bored. You can take time if you need it."

I'd started shaking my head before he'd finished. "No. I —that was an excuse. I'm sure it makes me—" I stopped myself from saying pathetic, working anew to break the patterns of my past. "I'm sure I need to work on coming up with better reasons that aren't lies, but it was the best option to make it clear to her I couldn't come. Even though she's not happy I'm not teaching, on some level, she gets that I have to work and I can't control my big, bad boss."

I flashed him a smile, but his eyes only narrowed. "She fought you pretty hard."

"Yeah. Well... you remember her, right?"

He made a sound not unlike a scoff and a snort combined. "She's unforgettable."

I nodded, not sure what to say. He couldn't know just how far things had gone, but I'd hinted at it a bit so far. "I've been working on how I respond to her. It's always exhausting."

A storm crowded his features, and something in me stood up in response. Not fear—not exactly—but awareness. Like some primal part of me understood a part of him, what it would do for me.

But instead of threatening my parents or telling me what I should've said or done, he spoke softly. "Do you need a hug?"

My heart clutched. "Sure." Like it wasn't the best offer I'd had in recent memory.

His arms came around me so gently, like the aftermath of the call had left me raw and tender. And maybe he was right to move so gingerly, because the moment he held me and I him, the tears hit again. I rested my head on his shoulder and let myself lean on him. I clung to his back and savored the warm slide of his big hands up and down my spine.

"You're all right. You did good."

His whispered words soothed, and though I knew I should be embarrassed by crying in the break room at work, I couldn't summon that feeling. His touch and concern brought me comfort. The delicious tension that followed us wherever we were was absent in favor of care and concern.

Of love.

I wanted nothing more than to stay right here wrapped in him. But at some point, the real world would break in. He'd be swallowed up by the new life he was building after the Army and I would leave. It was always the goal to find peace and closure here, and this hug made a heartbreaking punctuation mark.

My reasons for staying were dwindling. My lease was up this summer, and I'd already stayed longer than I'd originally thought I would.

This safety and acceptance might be a kind of love. I believed we both loved each other in the way people who care deeply about one another do. But enough to build a future on? I'd let others sway my choices for so long—could I look myself in the eye ever gain if I let my feelings for Wilder keep me here?

Wilder

The phone interrupted our hug, and though reluctantly, she ran to get it instead of letting it ring through. I'd wanted to tell her that she didn't need to do that—there was just no reason she needed to run for the phone. Nothing anyone would say on that line was more important than that hug.

If that didn't tell me exactly how far gone I was, I didn't know what would. But between not getting to see her, then the doc's suggestion that it *could* be this easy, and knowing we wouldn't actually get to spend time together until at least Saturday, though we hadn't talked about that... I was in a surly mood, to say the least.

My cell rang just as she hung up, and the afternoon went like that for a while, until almost closing time. When I looked up to find her leaning in my doorframe watching me work, a bolt of pleasure shot through me and I shut my laptop.

"You going to get to leave anytime soon? Seems like you've been working nonstop this week."

The sympathy in her voice did something to me. Maybe I'd been too long without tenderness, or maybe I was just an idiot and her soft, sweet voice made me feel stupid. Either way, I liked it, and I liked her standing there looking at me like she cared I was tired and I'd been working too much.

"I've got a couple interviews with some people overseas coming up tonight, so unfortunately, no."

"I'm sorry." She entered the room and took a seat across from me. "I was hoping we could do dinner."

"Maybe this weekend?" I suggested, wondering how terrible it would be if I canceled the interviews tonight.

Then I could hear Bruce's irritation and see myself wearing thinner and thinner as I worked without help and we did actually grow this business, so I trashed the idea. As much as I wanted time with Sarah, I couldn't cancel.

"Tomorrow?"

Her smiled faded when I said, "Sorry. I'm... busy."

Her brow furrowed and she blinked a few times before recovering. "Okay, maybe Saturday?"

Yes. Saturday. But a nudge from somewhere inside me made me clarify tomorrow. "Tomorrow's the anniversary of some of my friends—of their deaths. And wherever I am, if at all possible, I take some time out to remember them."

Her eyes softened. "I'm sorry for your loss."

I shook that off. "It was a few years ago. But I learned a while back that if I bottle that sh—stuff up, if I close it in, eventually the grief and anger and memories come rolling out when I can't control them. So I make sure to honor them, and honor my relationships with them, by being purposeful." The idea had come from Bruce.

"Do you do it alone?"

I shifted in my seat. "Usually with Bruce, and some-times other guys, when I was in."

A quiet beat passed during which she clearly realized this would be my first time marking the anniversary alone.

"Do you want me to come?"

"No," I said, too quickly. "Sorry, no."

The grief wasn't fresh, but it was familiar. The ritual of the day helped. Remembering my friends helped. But it felt separate from her, separate from *here*, even. The first real vestige of the life I'd only just left, and I wasn't ready to try to wedge it into this new version of things by having her with me. It'd be much too loaded. I might decidedly *act* the fool then.

"It's fine. I shouldn't have even—"

"Sarah, no. It's great that you offered. So thoughtful." I shot to my feet and rounded the desk to take her hand. "I appreciate it more than I can say. But I want to look forward to seeing you Saturday, if you'll have me, and I promise I won't be distracted or moody or anything but completely..." *Yours*. But I settled for saying, "Present."

A small smile appeared on her lips. "You? Moody?"

I gave her a squinty look, and she laughed. I went in for a kiss, lingering with my lips to the smooth skin of her cheek before withdrawing, dropping her hand, and stepping away. "Just let me know when I can see you Saturday, okay?"

"Of course." She smiled broadly, a genuinely glorious sight, and then left me wishing I could cancel everything—everything—and just spend time with her.

Every damn thing had gone wrong today. Everything.

Considering how good yesterday had been—kissing Sarah, making plans with her, knowing we'd have time together in the not-too-distant future—I should've been able to function today without a cloud over my head. But that wasn't the real problem. Today was never going to be happy-go-lucky, and I was fine with that.

It was the number of problems I'd had, the walking through mud sensation I met with, at every step for every action on my list of things to do today, that had my irritation at its peak.

Equipment that should've been here late yesterday failed to arrive. The shipment that did included broken product and in one case, the wrong thing, despite the order being correct. Bruce had called twice while I was out needing information I didn't have about the Reynolds account, Grenier had wanted a one-month financial rundown and I didn't even know what the hell that was, and Sarah had been quiet. Really quiet.

Like she'd wrapped herself into a blanket and dampened every bright, good thing about her.

We'd left things on good terms yesterday, but seeing her seem so *small* just pissed me right the hell off. I stormed up to her when she got back from her lunch break and forced the issue, though I should've taken a vow of silence and the day off if I'd been smart.

"What's wrong?"

"I'm fine."

"No. You're not."

"Um… I'm fine."

I gritted my teeth before going further. "Sarah."

"My parents. They're pushing. It's fine. I didn't get much sleep last night, and that's my fault. But I'm sorry it's affecting my work, and I won't—"

"Don't apologize for them."

She reared back like I'd slapped her. "I wasn't. I was apologizing for me. I didn't mean to seem like something was wrong."

"You were apologizing for them. You tried to when you apologized to me, as though what they did can be forgiven. You said they pressured you into marrying your ex, and I'm guessing any number of other things they wanted you to do to toe the line of their expectations. It's all bullshit, and you shouldn't have to live that way." The snap in my words came out sharper than I ever meant for it to, and yet it barely reflected the rising frustration.

She blinked back at me, absorbing the harsh claim. "I won't apologize for them, Wilder. I apologized for me. And I meant it. I've worked a long time to come to terms with what happened between us, and I'm still making peace with them. Every day, I'm trying."

I gritted my teeth to keep from shaking her. "Why? Why bother? I don't know the full extent of everything between you, but from what I've gathered, their controlling bull—"

"Don't." She swallowed hard. "Please don't. If you want to know, I'll tell you, but don't accuse them or me of anything. Please."

"I'm not trying to accuse anyone. I'm taking what I've observed and trying to free you from worrying about them. Don't go back there in June. Don't go anywhere you don't want to, ever."

She so rarely talked about future plans, and it'd sunken in more and more in the last few days. She lived in an apartment working temp jobs. Didn't seem to want to teach. Yes, she had friends, but was that enough to keep her here?

And did I want her here long term? Forever?

She inhaled sharply, then exhaled a loud breath. Her voice came out steady and firm when she said, "You can't free me from that. Only I can. And I'm working on it."

Guilt and shame twisted in my gut and rose to my cheeks like fire. This day could go to hell, and all the more after I'd hurt her by being a stubborn, judgmental ass. "I'm sorry."

She nodded, lips pressed firmly together. "Don't mention it."

She turned and sat in her seat and immediately began clicking and tapping at her mouse, busy and dismissive of me.

So I left. I stalked through the building, gathered my keys, and left.

Maybe I should've said goodbye or asked if I'd still see her tomorrow. She may well want to cancel on me, and if so, I wouldn't blame her. I'd been a snarling jerk today, and I should've kept my damned mouth shut.

I hated the thought that her parents were still creating guilt and a sense of duty in her. She'd done more than enough. I didn't know the whole story, and I did want to get it eventually, but I knew how they'd left. I knew how they'd responded when we first found out about the baby. I knew how they looked at her like she'd disappointed them—like she'd ruined something. Not just her life, but *theirs*.

From the sounds of her conversation, she hadn't escaped that by moving. They were calling and begging and guilty and *dammit,* it made me want to strangle them. Or slip into their home one night and remind them she was her own person, an adult, and not theirs to control.

But mostly, I needed to shift gears and focus on getting myself straight. I'd gone way out of bounds with her. We were getting to know each other again and I had no say in her relationship with her parents, much less whether she was *free*. I'd lost that right decades ago, and it would take time to gain it back, if I ever did.

I shook my head at myself and decided to jog home. I needed to burn a little energy before I spent the rest of the night memorializing more of what I'd lost.

CHAPTER THIRTY-THREE

Sarah

It took a solid hour for me to calm down enough to think logically. Wilder's words had burned into my brain, and they'd only grown louder when he'd left. No door slamming or storming out, but certainly no farewell. Anger glowed bright in my chest right next to resounding embarrassment and disbelief.

We hadn't fought since reconnecting. We'd been in that sweet beginning stage of a relationship when things were easy, though that wasn't quite right either. We had history—much of it painful. We weren't a normal couple starting to date. But was that even the right word for it—reconnecting?

We were... moving ahead. Toward each other. Together?

But, were we? In truth, I didn't know. How could I, when I hardly knew where I was going?

I shook my head at the thought, frustrated to feel eager about Wilder even while his pushiness irritated me.

He'd seen me upset after the call yesterday, and I'd made clear they'd influenced my time with Aaron. I would have to tell him more—good, bad, and ugly—at some point. But his judgmental approach, like he knew everything he needed to know about how things had gone with my parents before and during what amounted to more than half my life... he didn't.

I'd made mistakes, too. Yes, my parents had held me back, attempted to control me, and I'd been walking a path toward accepting how everything had happened for years. But that was just it, wasn't it? After being entrenched in that relationship and those patterns for so long, after having their focus and support for far longer than I might have had things between Wilder and me not changed, or Eddie not having essentially fled the scene the minute she could, maybe it would've been different. Maybe *I* would've been.

I wasn't. I hadn't. And I'd had to admit there were times I'd let them steamroll me because it was easier—the path of least resistance against them but also in life overall. I'd been lost, and they'd given me direction.

Sifting through all of this had taken a full year of therapy, and even now, I had thoughts and feelings that niggled at me, patterns of behavior and ways of thinking that threatened to slip back down the slope. But I had moved here as a promise to myself *and* to my parents—that I would live my life on my terms. And no, I wouldn't be going back. I'd told them as much and I didn't need him to tell me not to go visit.

Maybe it shouldn't have infuriated me to have Wilder speak to that part of my life like he knew everything just because he'd seen it years ago and now thought he saw the same thing, but it did. I'd made progress, so much progress, and *oh*. That was it. His railing against them made it feel like he didn't see how I'd grown. It felt like he still saw me as this hapless teen who'd follow her parents anywhere, even at the risk of her own mental health. Even at the risk of the most important things in her life.

With a giant sigh, I checked my watch and shut down the computer. Five minutes until Saint Securities officially closed and with no one coming in until next week, safe to say I could shut things down. After that conversation, I wanted to get out of here and go to a movie or do something. On top of all the crap with Wilder, I couldn't get rid of this nagging worry for Madeline Reynolds, a woman I didn't even know and should feel no real feelings for. But I'd seen an article online today about how people were speculating about her sabbatical like it was due to everything from drug addiction to a secret pregnancy to mental incapacity. *Ugh.*

The last major to do had been sending off a list of things we'd done for the Reynolds account, and hopefully Anthony would get back to me on anything we were missing. We'd see her again in-office next week, and I couldn't even dwell on the nerves I knew I'd have thanks to this drama with Wilder.

Actually, despite the confrontation, what I most wanted to do was check on him. He hadn't been himself all day, and the way he'd talked to me only reinforced my suspicion that his issues with my parents weren't really the cause of his mood.

Well, maybe partly. He'd always disliked the dynamic between us and I couldn't blame him—he'd had an outside perspective, even at seventeen. But in the hour since he'd left, I'd remembered. Today was the day—the anniversary of his friends' passings, and he'd mark it by himself for the first time.

I couldn't fathom it. Not the losses in the past or the solitude now. I'd faced hardships alone, but I'd always had Eddie a call away. Here in Silverton, I had my friends. He had his brothers in arms and his blood brothers, but the man was also stubborn as all get out. And based on today, I had to do something.

After securing the building, I pulled my purse over my shoulder and marched straight over to Warrick's gym. He was standing outside chatting with one of his many super fit patrons.

"Sarah James, to what do I owe the pleasure?" He sauntered over and set his hands on his hips. I noticed only then that he had a sheen of moisture on his brow, and the center of his shirt was discolored with sweat.

"I'm sorry to interrupt. I just need a second of your time, if you have it?"

"No interruption. We finished a few minutes ago. What's up?"

Straightening my spine, I met his eyes. "This might sound odd, but I think you should go hang out with Wilder tonight."

That gaze sharpened. "Why? Is he okay?"

I shifted from foot to foot. I didn't want to make a bigger deal of this than I should, but something told me Wilder needed his brothers. I hoped he wouldn't hate me for this. He'd stated very clearly he didn't want *me* there, but I couldn't stand the thought of him alone with this.

"Today is the anniversary of some of his friends' deaths, I guess."

He loosed a breath. "Dang. Brutal."

I nodded. "And he usually is with his Army friends. This is the first year he's out, and I think..."

He snagged his phone from a pocket and dialed as he spoke. "Say no more. I'm on it. Thanks for telling me. I've got this—thank you." He nodded at me and started walking as I heard him say, "Wyatt, cancel your plans tonight and head this way."

I smiled to myself as relief swept in. Warrick would handle this. Wilder would forgive me, and hopefully I'd see him tomorrow and could apologize yet again.

CHAPTER THIRTY-FOUR

Wilder

The whiskey burned, hot and dark, as memories slipped through me. They'd been doing that all day, as though the anniversary's dawning signaled to my brain to pull every moment I'd spent with the men I remembered tonight and march them across my mind in a painful parade.

I should get a dog. Or a cat. Cats were chill. Kind of aloof and quiet—pleasantly standoffish. Wyatt's puppy was a few months old now and he was cute, but annoying. Too much cheery in-your-faceness. *Yeah. I'll get a cat.*

The doorbell made me jump—a clear indication I'd only had two of the five shots I'd take tonight to honor the five men I'd lost. In The Pines, where most of the guys lived back in North Carolina, we'd meet at a bar creatively called Brew and everyone did five shots, sipping beers and sharing memories of the men who'd all passed on the same day. The brutal operation gone wrong and easily one of the worst days of my life.

The repeated ring had me glaring, but I shoved off the couch and padded to the door. The peephole showed not one but two Saints. *What the hell?*

"Open up, Wilder. We can see you eyeing us."

I unlocked the deadbolt and swung open the door. "What're you doing here?"

"We came to check on you," Wyatt said.

"Yep. Just swinging by." Warrick held up a case of beer.

"And why, out of nowhere and with no warning, are you checking on me?"

Warrick beamed. "Sarah mentioned you'd had a bad day."

Wyatt elbowed him and shot him a disapproving glare.

"What? She did. She said very little, only that today was... significant."

A mix of frustration and something sweet, almost like relief, twined together inside me. Sarah had told them. After what a jerk I'd been, ordering her around and talking about her parents like I still knew them or had any right to tell her what to do, she'd sought out *my* family to help me.

I'd been so caught up in my day, I hadn't considered her. I'd thought I should give her space, maybe call her tomorrow and see if she'd still give me the time of day. But the woman had put herself out there for me by asking these two oafs to come check on me. She risked me being a jerk again all because she wanted to make sure I was okay.

My hand not holding the door handle pressed into my chest above my aching heart. I eyed them as they waited for something, until Warrick snorted and shoved past me into the apartment. Wyatt held a giant pizza box.

"We're not letting you be alone tonight," he explained, waiting for me to step farther to the side to let him by.

I glared at both of the presumptuous asses for a moment, but since neither of them even turned to question whether they would stay, I locked up behind them. Plus, if Sarah had sent them, they knew they had cause to be here. I wondered what, specifically, she'd told them.

"Yeah. This is not solo activity time," Warrick said, cracking open a beer and handing it to me.

On reflex, I took it. "This is not family reunion time."

Wyatt had flipped open the pizza box and rooted around in the cabinets until he pulled out three plates. "You're not drinking alone in the dark on an empty stomach."

I glanced around at the dim living room lit only by the lights in the kitchen. I hadn't tried to set it up like this—me sitting in the dark. It'd just felt right. "How do you know I didn't eat an hour ago?"

Wyatt only spared me an unimpressed look as he slopped a cheesy slice onto each place, shoved one in my direction, one at Warrick, and stomped over to the living room.

Each of us settled into a seat—Wy to my left on the couch, Warrick in the chair to my right. I bit into the still-hot pizza and chewed through the scalding toppings, my mind grasping for something to say but failing to find anything. We ate in silence until Warrick shot out of his seat, flipped on all the lights on the panel near the kitchen, and slumped back into the chair.

"Sorry. I get that the mood is somber, for real, but the atmosphere doesn't have to be so completely depressing on top of it." He folded his pizza and took another giant bite.

I let out a breath I'd let compound in my chest.

"Sarah told us what today is," Wyatt said gently.

I nodded, hardly able to summon frustration with her. Only a warmth I now associated with Sarah and only her. A lightness in the midst of drudgery and darkness I hadn't felt in years. "I told her about it. Told her I didn't want her to come. That I would do it on my own."

Warrick set his plate down a little too forcefully. "Yeah? What a shock."

"Warrick."

Wyatt's warning tone should've silenced our youngest brother, but evidently, he had some things to say. Maybe he'd wanted to say them days or weeks ago but now, he wasn't holding back.

"You've got a whole life we know nothing about and a lot of it you can't even talk about. I get that. *We* get that. But I refuse to stay quiet about this. You're not building that house by yourself. You're not living in this crap apartment and sitting by yourself drinking yourself silly in memory of your friends you lost *by yourself.* You aren't on your own here, even though you left your team behind."

Throat tight, I slugged a few drinks of beer. "I know."

"Do you?" Wyatt asked, his volume and tone still calm and low.

"Of course. Why would I move back here if I didn't get that? I know we haven't been close. That's the main thing I want to rectify, my first priority is you and Mom."

Warrick's eyes speared into mine and he shook his head. "It doesn't seem like it. And this is not about us feeling left out, though I can say I have, sometimes. And jealous of Bruce and all your friends you lived this life with—the people you let be a part of it. But we're here now, and you've made an effort, like you said. You came back instead of staying in North Carolina"

I nodded, accepting the statement. In many ways, it would've been easier to stay away. Retire there and figure out what life looked like outside the military while still being surrounded by a culture saturated in it. Many people did, and they loved it.

"Now we're here for you. With you," Warrick said, ducking his head until I met his eyes. "This is us making an effort right back."

"Thank you," I said, rough and scraped over rusty vocal cords. "I'm not opposed to you being here. I just didn't think to ask. It's not a particularly happy evening."

Wyatt set his plate on the coffee table. "We don't need happy, brother. We can't understand everything about your life, but we can listen. You can tell us what you want—about your past, about these men you're remembering."

"You'll have to do shots. If we're doing this right."

Warrick clapped his hands together. "Bring on the whiskey and memories."

For the first time today, a chuckle escaped. "I don't normally do much talking. The other guys take the reins for the most part."

Warrick leaned back in his chair with raised brows. "Obviously, we can't contribute, so you're going to have to man up."

"I'm acceptably secure in my manhood despite not being a Chatty Cathy like yourself."

War's eyes made a slow blink. "Did I just hear super soldier Wilder Saint say the words *Chatty Cathy?*"

Wyatt's laugh came first, followed by an obnoxious guffaw from Warrick. I focused on repouring the two shots I'd had and nudged one of the three I hadn't taken toward them. Their laughter settled and they held their small glasses up. I raised mine and found the words.

"To those we love in life and grieve in death."

They each seemed to swallow hard, like maybe this was a moment for us to grieve not only my friends, but our own father, who we'd all lost before we understood what grieving was. And because I wanted that—the healing for each of us in this moment together, I added one more.

"And to the bond of brotherhood. No distance or time or trial can break it."

Wyatt nodded and Warrick cleared his throat. They spoke in unison. "To brotherhood."

CHAPTER THIRTY-FIVE

Sarah

I'd done my best not to obsess about Wilder. I'd failed miserably.

My knee had been cooperating, so I took a long-ish run before meeting up with Quinn, Dahlia, Calla, and Sadie. I'd texted the group chat to see if anyone was around knowing Sadie might be free tonight since I knew Warrick wouldn't be available. After a few minutes chatting, we nailed down a time and all met at Quinn's house. Thankfully, we wouldn't be going out—I wasn't up for a loud restaurant, and this time of year, despite the ski season being fully over, Silverton was bustling.

Our small town used to be virtually dead in the shoulder season between ski season and summer hiking, and even then, summer was basically nothing compared to winter. But my first year back had shown me this wasn't the small town of my youth with hardly anything open this time of year, thank goodness. More people, more businesses, and more opportunity. The drawback? More people crowding into the delicious restaurants and making a low-key girls' night next to impossible on a weekend.

God bless Quinn for being up for an early dinner before she went and sang. Apparently, she wasn't going in until eight so we had to be out by seven thirty. Sadie needed an early night too since she woke up at the crack of dawn to bake, and I was exhausted by everything this week. And of course Calla was always happy for an early night.

"So the Saint brothers are drowning their sorrows together?" Quinn asked from behind her plate of appetizers.

One of Dahlia's customers had sent her a huge charcuterie board earlier that day as a thank you. A nice gesture, if odd, but serendipitous for us since we could now enjoy the beautiful spread of meats, cheeses, nuts, dips, fruits, veggies, olives... truly, the thing was massive and delicious.

"Don't say it like that. It's a memorial," Calla said, frowning at Quinn.

Quinn held her hands up. "Hey, hey. I didn't mean it to sound sarcastic. I'm glad they're doing it. It seems like a good thing they're together."

I nodded. "I hope so."

My heart hadn't stopped hurting since I'd told Warrick. Something about asking him had unlocked the concern and worry for Wilder that I'd packed away ever since he'd told me about today's significance.

"From what Warrick said a little while ago, it's going well and he seemed glad they were there." Sadie gave me a small smile to encourage, and it did just that.

I nodded at her in thanks as Calla asked Dahlia about the customer who'd given her this spread.

"It's someone who's arriving next week. I'm doing fresh

arrangements for their home. I really don't know much else other than the arrangements are going to be gorgeous, and I can't wait to meet whoever they are. It's all through some company, and instead of delivering like I do for other residential orders, they're picking up."

"How do you know it's for a home if it's a company?" Quinn asked.

"I guess I don't—not for certain, anyway. Just a feeling. Usually, corporate stuff is kind of contained and particular, but this order is..." She beamed. "It's kind of wild."

We all grinned at her expression—part dreamy, part disbelieving. She seemed nothing short of elated.

"Please take pictures so we can see," I said.

"Absolutely. I have a feeling these are going on the website and a few other places if they turn out like I'm expecting."

After talking and eating and catching up for another half hour, the time had come. We all said our goodbyes, and Calla walked out with me.

"I'm glad you told Warrick," she said, eyes searching mine.

"Me, too. I just hope he won't be too mad."

She knew I meant Wilder. "He won't be. As gruff as he can be, he doesn't seem like one to hold a grudge against anyone other than himself."

A sigh escaped. "That's it, exactly."

"I can relate. And I think he and Wyatt are more similar than anyone realizes. Don't worry about them—this will be good for all of them. Are you two...?"

I chuckled. "I think? I'd asked him to hang out tomorrow, but we had a weird ending to our day today. I know it was a difficult one, so I'm just going to check in tomorrow and see how he's doing."

"Good idea." She smiled approvingly. "And if he's up for it, I hope he'll bring you to family dinner on Sunday."

Nerves and hope and immediate refusal jumped through me. "Oh, it's... probably a little soon, right?"

She gave me a doubtful look. "Whatever's right for you, friend." With a quick hug, she released me.

I wandered home from Quinn's house with my mind full of questions and hopes and anticipation. By the time I'd watched a few episodes of the show I'd been bingeing in the evenings, I decided it was time to call it and try to sleep. And just as I laid my head on my pillow a little after midnight, my phone buzzed.

I bolted upright and grabbed for it, scrambling to grip it and squint against the too-bright light in the darkened room. A text from Wilder made my pulse hammer on sight.

"You're too good for me."

I huffed and shook my head, immediately unlocking the phone and typing back. *"No I'm not. There's no such thing."*

"Not sure about that."

"I am. I'm not too good for you. You saw my resume..."

"Your resume's great. You're great."

I laughed at that. Lies, but also, adorable. *"You doing okay? Are your brothers still there?"*

"They left about midnight. Thanks for sending them."

Longing and love crashed through me so hard, I had to steady myself against the headboard. I curled into the phone and typed back. *"Glad you let them in."*

"Me too."

Maybe it was the late hour or the fact that he'd initiated the chatting, but I pushed a little. *"You going to let me in tomorrow?"*

I hoped he knew I meant for our date—that I was referencing the plans we'd kind of made but hadn't firmed up completely.

"I'll let you in whenever you want."

My stomach flipped. *"Good."*

And I thought he'd leave it there. Maybe he'd fallen asleep and we'd talk tomorrow. But then my screen lit up again.

"Not sure I ever let you out."

I didn't know what to say in response, but I held the phone close, cradling it against me like it was him.

Wilder Saint had always been soft on the inside, almost too sweet and gentle to be believed under all the gruff, tight-lipped man. But this whole day had shown me what had been true when we were younger remained so—Wilder wasn't hard or reluctant to feel. If anything, he felt more deeply than most. And maybe, he still felt as much for me as I did him. Maybe staying wasn't just for him, but for me, too.

CHAPTER THIRTY-SIX

Wilder

The morning after a night like last night would normally leave me with an unshakeable malaise. Today felt immeasurably different.

First, because I hadn't been alone. And while I hadn't memorialized my friends alone in the past, I'd still woken up with that isolation. Yes, I had friends who I thought of as kind-of brothers, but they weren't my brothers by blood and childhood. They were important, particularly Bruce and a few others who I hoped would work their way out here when their active time wrapped up in the next few years. But even in those times, I found myself reflecting on missing my family. Feeling like I belonged there, and yet that part of me was held separate.

Last night, that part of me had clicked back into place.

Call it the beauty and brutality of shared grieving or the healing of time or the blessing of vulnerability—call it what you will. It had resulted in a renewed bond between my brothers that I felt as I padded along the path at a lazy pace, the peaks of the mountains ahead of me hidden by clouds.

Wyatt and Warrick had left around midnight, after hours of talking and eating and drinking. Instead of pounding into the grief with the burn of whiskey and solitude, I'd told them stories about my friends—the living and the dead. I'd shared the most difficult moments when the whiskey loosened my tongue, and I'd shared my tears when they did theirs.

I had never imagined crying with my grown brothers would be a necessary event in my life, but this morning, I recognized how essential it'd been. They knew me so much better than they had before because I'd told my stories—ones I only told on days like yesterday. And I knew them better for receiving their compassion and experiencing their grief as we touched on having lost our father. We'd spoken of the baby, too, because we'd also all lost that little one—until the last few weeks, I'd hardly allowed myself to realize how they might've grieved too. It had been good to talk about that.

And then, there was Sarah.

She'd never been more than a breath from my mind all evening, and by the time they left and I'd lain my head on my pillow and wished I could look across and see her next to me, just to rest next to her, I'd texted.

Her response—her welcoming tone despite my failure to apologize for my ass-backward approach to supporting her earlier and my generally piss-poor mood all day—had lit me up. Rereading the texts today, I should've been concerned. I'd put myself out there, shoved my heart right into her hands with that last message.

"Not sure I ever let you out." Hell if that didn't say exactly the truth.

Sitting there with my brothers and knowing she'd sent them to me despite my jackassery of the day, the surety of my feelings for her had wrapped around my ribs and squeezed. Even now, just thinking of her and the prospect of seeing her later today made my normally steady breath come up short.

The day crawled by despite my efforts to distract myself —a tour of the property where they'd pour the foundation this week, weather permitting. Finally, I showed up at my mom's house to burn off some time and to make an effort with her. I'd been so focused on my brothers, I'd rarely had time with just her.

"Your brothers both told me about last night," she said, pouring me a cup of steaming tea.

"What'd they say?"

She turned the delicate handle of her teacup to the side and smiled almost wistfully. "They both said how honored they were to be with you."

Her glance up revealed her eyes were shining, and my throat instantly tightened. Damn the emotions waiting right there at all times these days.

"I was honored to have them with me. Glad they came." Barely scratching the surface, that, but she could see. Mom broadcasted her feelings in every expression, and I could see that joy and relief beaming through her.

"Warrick said Sarah sent him."

I nodded, waiting. She had something to say, and I hoped she'd go ahead with it.

Sure enough, she sipped her tea, then set the cup down with a delicate clink against the china saucer. "Have you forgiven her?"

I swallowed, not sure how to answer. Yes, I had. But in some ways, it didn't feel... finished. I was getting there, more every day, though we hadn't gotten to a full closure on what had gotten us here. But we didn't have to rush it. She was back, and I was, too. I never would've guessed the first few days we were here, not even after her apology, but I believed we'd get there.

I wouldn't say all that to my mom, so I said, "Mostly. Have you?"

Her lips pressed into a smile-frown. "I did a long time ago, but it was different for me. I had to watch you in pain and then watch *you* leave."

My heart pinched. "I guess it should be me apologizing. Can you forgive me?"

She huffed and looked down at her tea. "You never needed forgiving, honey. Never."

"I think I do. I left as a way to survive. I think at some point staying away, staying so separate, was a way of punishing myself for wanting something else. And by the time I'd gotten over that, I didn't know how to fix things."

She reached for me. "But now you have. It won't be perfect, but look at last night. Look at this right here." She shook me where she held onto my hand.

"Thank you for everything you've done. Thanks for standing by me even when I couldn't be here."

She sniffed and cleared her throat. "Always, my son. Always."

We chatted a while longer and finished our tea, and before I left, she hugged me tight. "Welcome home, Wilder."

She'd said it before that first time she saw me when I'd moved back, but the significance wasn't lost on me. I'd physically been home a while, but now, at the risk of sounding thoroughly therapized, I'd come home emotionally, too.

The time finally came to leave for Sarah's. The heavy clouds that'd settled over Silver Ridge Peak and its sisters finally broke open just as I got halfway to her, and by the time I reached her apartment complex and parked, it had turned to near downpour. We needed the rain to help with summer fire danger so no one in the area would begrudge the precipitation, but it fully hampered my plans for us to walk into town together holding hands. At least I'd brought my car in the first place and didn't have to run get it.

"Hey! Come in, quick!" Sarah said, laughing as I bolted in the door, and she shut it behind me. "It's insane out there!"

"Bottom dropped out. I don't think we should walk."

She bit her lip, and her blue eyes caught mine. "How would you feel if we ordered in? I made some appetizers and thought we could get delivery and just hang out here."

Yes. Yes please. Always yes. Did she need to ask? I wanted to be in her space. I hadn't been inside her apartment and seen what her taste was like now. I hadn't been close to her enough, and I couldn't be all that close to her at a restaurant. This was far better than going out, especially on a night like this.

"Sounds perfect."

Her smiled brightened, then faded a touch.

"What?"

Her gaze swept around the room quickly before she met my eyes again. "I'm not sure if I'm allowed to ask, but I've been going crazy wondering how last night went. I don't want to upset you, though."

I closed the distance between us and gently grasped her shoulders, ducking my head to say the long overdue words.

"You can ask me anything. Always. But before you do, I have to apologize for being such a jerk yesterday. I shouldn't have said anything about your folks. I know it's complex."

She swallowed and nodded, hands holding onto my shirt on either side of my rib cage. "Thank you. It is complex, and I'm almost always defensive about it because it's still a tender subject. It's ongoing, but I'm proud of the progress."

I nodded, understanding that completely. "I get it. Not with my family so much as just... figuring out what life is like now and how to be here." I groaned at my poor wording. "That sounds stupid, but it's fairly accurate."

She grinned. "It's not stupid. I know what you mean. I was stuck in so many ways before, and over the last year I've been learning a lot about myself. Just the distance from my parents and the places and people that were entrenched in my life has given me space to figure myself out. But some of that is still coming to terms with the choices I did and didn't make."

I stepped closer, hating the regret in her eyes. "What I mostly wanted to say yesterday but failed to was that you are amazing. If your parents aren't respecting you, screw 'em. If they're great and you want to go visit and that's the right choice for you, then do that. Whatever it is, I support you."

She yanked on my shirt as she stepped into me, rising to her toes to kiss me in a soft, sweet press. "I support you, too."

More than happy to prolong this proximity, I kissed her this time—lingering and slow. We had all night, and nothing about the words we'd just exchanged should've caused the urgency now shuddering through my limbs. I wouldn't push her or anything between us, no.

But I would happily take anything she would give, and Sarah seemed dead set on giving me kiss after kiss that drove my logic right out into the rain. Her hands slipped under my shirt at my waist, and her cool skin pressing against my overheating body felt like heaven. She gasped at the connection of her hands to my sides, and her thumbs swept over the ridges of my abdominal muscles.

"How?" she asked between kisses, pulling back to let her ravenous eyes rake over my face before she returned to steal another kiss.

"How does it feel this good to kiss you?" I asked, lips tracking along her jaw and down her neck.

"No. I—w-what?"

I pulled back to see her eyes flutter open and pin me. A look so familiar and yet something I'd never seen before had me pressing a kiss to her lips again before easing back more fully. "Let's eat some of those appetizers and order dinner. I want to tell you about last night."

And even though a little furrow notched between her brows, this was right. This was *better*. That stutter and flash of desire I'd seen were sign enough she was as lost to the moment as I was. As good as every point of contact and moment of connection between us felt, we'd always done this. We'd always had the physical and it had been decadent and perfect before. Of course, we were kids, but Sarah and I had never been a childhood love story. We'd started our adulthood together, the beginning of facing reality in a way that never recedes. The lives we lived after each other—all of the messy years after—had begun with each other. The more time I spent with her, the more I learned about her, the more convinced of that I became.

And if that was true, then there was no rush to have everything right now—no reason to push past a steadier pace. We were older and wiser now, but the last time we did that, it'd come crumbling down so quickly, I'd never seen it coming. Age and wisdom might help, but some things couldn't be avoided if you ran past all the warnings and logical benchmarks to keep them steady.

So we'd slow down. We didn't have to race into things. We were working our way back to rightness together, and shouldn't let our hands outpace our heads. She'd agree with me as soon as we had a moment to breathe, and in the end, it'd be better. This way, we'd have staying power. This time, we'd last.

CHAPTER THIRTY-SEVEN

Sarah

We moved around each other a little awkwardly after he set me away so easily, and I did my level best not to feel hurt. Really, I tried.

But... had I done something wrong?

"This is really good," he said after chewing a bite of the sundried tomato goat cheese.

"It's from my favorite farmer's market stall. The market just started back up today, and I was so glad to see them back. They have all kinds of cheeses. I tell them every time I visit that they need to open a gourmet cheese shop." *Aaaaaand stop talking! This man does not care about the cheese stall at the market!*

But he nodded as he chewed another bite, then said, "That they should."

We chatted about the farmer's market for a bit—or, I should say, I babbled about it outwardly, while inwardly, I tried to identify what had made him stop kissing me. Certainly, his body language and intensity and the *way* he'd kissed me right up until he'd made space between us had seemed like we were both on track.

"Sarah?"

I shook myself from those musings. "Um, yes?"

"Did you want me to get the door?"

A blush threatened to creep into my cheeks. Had I missed the doorbell? Good grief, the man had addled my brain with his sincere apology and delicious kisses, and now I could hardly stay present for our conversation.

"I've got it. You pour us some more wine." I forced my eyes away from his handsome face staring back at me with a look that said he was working a problem. And knowing Wilder, it was to figure out what the heck was going on in my head, because I was being a weirdo.

A minute later, I returned with our takeout, and we served ourselves and found our places at my two-person table. I'd thought about getting something bigger so I had more seating and space, which would mean I could eventually host girls' nights, but a new table sat fairly far down on the list of priorities.

"Did you still want to tell me about last night?" I hadn't wanted to push, but I very much wanted to hear about his time with his brothers. And since that'd been the topic that inspired him to break our kiss and back away, I wanted to dive in there and see what I could learn.

He finished his bite and seemed to be sifting through his mind for the right words. "It was good."

I bit my lip to stop the laugh that wanted to worm its way out, but I couldn't. It snuck out in a breathy chuckle, which immediately elicited a chagrined expression from him.

"I don't mean to laugh. You just..." *Drive me insane in the best way*. But I wouldn't say that.

"It *was* good though. In a lot of ways. I told them about my buddies who died. And we actually talked about our dad, which was unexpected but really kind of... healing."

"I'm so glad. I'm sure they were so happy to be there with you."

One brow flared up. "I don't know about *happy* because the night was pretty somber, but it felt good to be with them. I realized how my habit of isolating myself from them while I lived away had translated to things like not talking to them about anything real, even stuff between each other like missing our dad or whatever. Things had been getting better, but I feel like it's actively positive now instead of not negative, if that makes sense."

"It does. I'm—" I swallowed the next words, but he pinned me with a look that said he wanted them. So, I complied. "I know I don't have any right to say this, but I'm proud of you."

He squinted as though to see me better but nodded. "I could say the same for you."

I made a *pshh* sound and waved that off. "I'm not sure there's anything to say that about for me."

He caught my waving hand and linked our fingers. "Don't say that. You've made choices, good and bad like everyone. But you're here, building a life for yourself based on what you want. I see that as eminently commendable and something I hope you are proud of."

"I am. Honestly, I think that's part of what made me mad yesterday."

The confusion on his face made me press on. "It felt like you couldn't see that I'd changed—that I'd spent years working on how I deal with my parents and have made crazy strides with them. It made me feel so stupid—like I was seventeen again, in some ways."

He swore under his breath. "I didn't mean to—"

I squeezed his hand and caught his gaze. "No, I get it. I was too sensitive, which is usually how I am after talking with my mom. And you were understandably in a bad mood. Not a great combo for communicating about something difficult, but look." My gaze swept between us and around the low-lit living room where my pointless but pretty fake fireplace was lit. "We're here, and we've made up, and it's all good."

"We've made up. That's a good point." Then he leaned up and over the table to press a quick, searing kiss to my lips.

Heat rushed through me and pooled low in my belly. He was so sweet and hot, and it'd been forever since I'd felt like this. I hadn't wanted anyone like this in... in... well. Since him. Since I was hormone-crazed and unfazed by how insane it was that I'd found the love of my life at fourteen. I'd had him like that a little over two short years and then lost him for two decades, and now here we sat.

"What's that look for?"

The burn in my cheeks matched my hammering heartbeat. I couldn't tell where he was exactly with how he felt about the two of us, but even I knew he wasn't *un*interested. He wouldn't have come if he hadn't wanted to—Wilder simply didn't do things he had no interest in.

"I was thinking how glad I am to be here with you now." I could've said more—how I'd thought about him. Pathetic though it might've made me, I'd wondered how he was and wondered if I'd ever see him again.

I would never say I'd come back to Silverton for him, but I could admit a part of me had come back for the possibility of seeing him. To apologize and right the wrong as much as it could be after so much time had passed.

"I am, too."

After cleaning up dinner, we sat on my small couch, legs touching and my right hand knitted with his left. His thumb swept along the outside of mine in slow arcs and sent a prolonged wave of sensation from my arm all the way through my body each time he did.

Basically, he was torturing me. It felt like every topic we spoke about—his old job, life, friends, and my old jobs, life, and friends—was leading up to what was happening now. What was life like now for us, and what did we want together?

That, and would we actually *be* together? He hadn't kissed me since that quick press of lips at dinner, and though I wanted to climb on top of him and kiss him like the world was ending, I held back.

I'd never been bold like that except with Wilder, and though everything in my body said, *"Get him while the getting's good,"* my heart shuddered at the thought of making the first move. Or, not the first, but the *next* one.

But the more he looked at me with those dark blue eyes, and every time he ran a hand across the close-cropped beard on his jaw, the more I thought about tossing all those doubts to the wind and taking what I wanted. And right as I thought I might do it, he finally looked at me and shifted forward so his face hovered close to mine.

"Thank you for dinner," he said, eyes skating over my face and landing on my lips.

My pulse spiked. "Anytime. I'm so glad you came."

He bit his lip in a gesture so sensual, I would've expired on the spot had it not been for the pained furrow in his brow. But in a blink, it dissolved into a pleasant smile and he reached out, pulled my head toward him, and kissed my temple.

"I'll see you soon," he said with a lingering look that sent fire down to my toes and then hopped up and made for the door.

Um. What?

"Oh-kay, sure, yeah, I'll see you—" I jumped up too and tracked behind him.

One last flash of those eyes and he was gone. Door closed, out of sight, practically disappeared. I would've thought I'd conjured up the whole evening if I didn't still see the leftover trash hanging out of my too-small trash can.

I leaned my head against the panel of wood blocking out the rain and wind, and apparently, a very restless and confusing Wilder. My heart twisted as I parsed through the evening. He was interested—I knew it. But he was holding back.

Not all that shocking, really. I'd left him suddenly, brutally, years ago. Maybe he was scared I'd do it again? I needed to find my voice and use it. Tell him I—

The doorbell rang and I startled back, then whipped it open on reflex. "Wilder?"

The words sprang from my lips as I took him in—rain-soaked shirt plastered to his sculpted chest, dark hair made darker by the moisture dripping off him.

"Do you want me to stay?"

My mouth opened like it'd speak, but the sight of him so

wild-eyed and pulsing with energy and intention had stolen all the words from my brain.

"Sarah. Please. I need you to tell me."

That permeated the desire pounding at my temples and in my neck. Nothing could drown out the longing in his eyes or the desperate leap of my heart in response to him here.

"I want you. Yes, Wilder, I—"

That was all I got out before his arm snaked around my back and crushed me to him. His other hand pressed into the base of my skull, and our kiss set fire to every cell in my body. I pulled at him, desperate for him to be closer now that he'd come back.

Elation and relief welled up and spilled over in a laugh as he maneuvered us over the threshold and into the apartment, kicking the door closed behind us and moving until the backs of my legs hit the side of the couch.

"Let's just—"

"Can I—"

We smiled at each other, kissed again, and I pressed my hand over his heart. "Stay with me."

"Thought you'd never ask."

I shoved him a little, and he clutched me tighter around the waist.

"I didn't know you were waiting on me to ask. The way you ran out of here, I thought..." I swallowed, admittedly still a bit confused by all that.

"Sorry. *Sorry.* I can hardly control myself around you, and I didn't want to rush you." He wore a disappointed look, like it proved a failing he'd had to admit.

If only he could tell what that admission did to me. When I spoke, the sultry, low tone in my voice didn't surprise me. "Don't apologize."

That gaze burned into me for one beat, two, and I shivered at the way the air pulled taut between us like even the molecules around us knew what was coming.

Somehow, his lips were closer but not touching me when he said, "I got you all wet, and now you're shivering."

"You're soaked. Not a surprise."

He brushed his lips over mine, the softest slide that didn't quite qualify as a kiss, but still sent sparks of energy and anticipation racing through me. "What ever should we do?"

I tilted my chin and spoke one last time as my fingers found the button of his shirt. "Better warm each other up."

CHAPTER THIRTY-EIGHT

Wilder

I didn't sleep but a few hours. I'd trained extensively on minimal sleep and could handle just about anything without a full five or more, but I preferred getting at least six. But last night, lying next to Sarah, my heart raced at her nearness.

Her head on the pillow like I'd imagined the night before. Her hair in tangles behind her, her fair cheeks only barely pink in sleep, and her beautiful lips relaxed.

We'd never had this before—hours to simply lay together in the aftermath and revel in one another. I'd never gotten to see her fall asleep sated and exhausted. I'd never gotten to wake up and know I could just stay right here, studying the fan of her lashes against her cheek, resisting touching the smooth skin of her shoulder where it peeked out from under her bright white comforter.

If I thought I'd wanted her before, I'd had no knowledge

of the concept. Being with her last night gave me only a taste of the life I hadn't let myself fully envision. And now?

A soft sigh from her broke my determination to leave her alone. I ran my fingers over her shoulder, tracing the line of her tank top to her back. She hummed, evidently not as hard asleep as I'd thought.

"Did I wake you?"

One blue eye cracked open. "No. Was I snoring?"

I grinned. "No. Wouldn't care if you were, though." She could saw logs all night, and it wouldn't change my desire to be right here.

"Did you need something?" she asked, shifting from her stomach to her side and reaching to run the tips of her fingers along my beard, then down my neck and across my chest to trace the tattoos on my arm.

Her touch had a drugging effect, I'd quickly realized. It was the reason I'd avoided touching her last night for fear of overwhelming her. I'd left in a move I'd wonder about for years, but I'd returned after only about ten steps away from her porch and in the rain. On the off chance I'd read her right and she'd wanted me to stay, and then, God bless Silverton, she'd let me back in.

The process of warming each other up would forever be one of the best nights of my life. Now in the quiet of the next morning, I wanted to tread carefully. We'd taken a big step, connecting like this. It didn't mean forever, but it wasn't without significance. Neither of us could pretend this was casual—not for the kind of people we were to begin with, and certainly not with our history.

But what came next? How to move forward without everything blowing up in our faces? The Doc's words came back—*"Consider that perhaps, after challenging years for you and for Sarah, the ease between you is a blessing."* Maybe it *was* this easy and good and right. Maybe because of that, I could simply step toward what seemed logical in my own mind and we could be together.

"Come to the family dinner tonight."

She swallowed and tucked her lips together, gaze serious. Coming to a family dinner with my siblings and mother was undoubtedly a big step. My stomach clutched in this pause, fear she might say no and I wouldn't know what to do with that creeping in like gasoline into water.

"You don't have to. I know it's a bit more overtly *together* than we've been, but—"

"I'd say we were fairly overtly *together* last night."

I couldn't help the smile that flashed at her playful comment. "And I am very, *very* happy about that. But truly, there's no pressure to come today if it's too soon."

"No. It's good. It'll be good."

Hand threaded into the hair at her nape, I ducked my forehead to touch hers and looked into her bright blue eyes at point-blank range.

"Don't be nervous," I said, easing off the more commanding tone I naturally used at times like this.

When she nodded, I could swear stars burst inside my chest.

Hours later, after a lazy morning and one of the best days of my life to date, I echoed the same sentiment as I stopped the car next to Warrick's in Wyatt's driveaway.

"Don't be nervous," I said again, less commanding this time.

Instead of shaking off my words, I watched the tension winding around her like a rope.

"Hard not to be. It's like a crazy combination of déjà vu and unfamiliar terror." Her gaze slid to the side and took in the large farmhouse just outside the car.

"Terror?" I tilted her chin toward me with my free hand and kissed her soft, sweet lips. "You know everyone in there."

She leaned back and took in the view. The modest farmhouse stood tall and proud in front of us, pastures stretching out behind it before the sharp peaks of the mountains climbed into the sky. The small barn Warrick had refurbished, and where Wyatt and Calla's story had begun last year, sat to our right, vacant of guests for now.

"I know. I just…" She bit her lower lip again, heedless of how it lit my match.

"We can go. I don't want you to feel stuck since we drove together." The forty-five-minute drive back to Silverton made driving separate cars insane. Plus, she was here with me. And I with her. Why would we drive separately?

"No. Let's just get in there and get it over with." She shoved the truck door open and climbed out before I'd started to move.

She'd relax inside. Calla and Sadie would be in her corner, and she'd realize there was nothing to fear here. And if not, I'd make an excuse and we'd leave.

Just before we reached the front door, I said as much. "Say the word, and we're gone. Any reason, any time."

She nodded, then squared her shoulders just as Mom pulled open the door and flung her arms around Sarah.

"My darlings! You're here. We're just about ready to sit down. Come on in," she said, releasing Sarah and pulling us both by the hand inside.

Sarah's eyes met mine, and I gave her a small smile. She beamed a nervous one back at me, and in seconds, we were enveloped in shouted greetings.

"There they are!" Warrick hollered from where he stood dropping rolls into a bread basket.

"Almost ready to eat," Wyatt said, not looking up from his focus on carving what looked like a roast chicken. Wait, *two* roast chickens. With Warrick in attendance tonight, the second was absolutely necessary.

"Sarah! Yay! Come sit with us and talk about my ever-growing diameter," Calla said, waving her toward the living room where Sadie also sat.

"You help the boys finish up, and I'll keep your woman entertained." Mom nudged me toward the kitchen, where *the boys* were apparently on full meal duty.

My woman. I wouldn't even pretend I didn't love that.

In the kitchen, my brothers were busily finishing the meal. Wyatt had learned to cook right alongside our mom and Grandma Tilda. I'd never had much interest, but had learned sufficient skills to keep myself fed when not at work and using the upscale dining facility for breakfast and lunch.

Wyatt's apron—yes, he wore an apron—had retro-looking lettering spelling out *Real Men Garnish.*

"Jealous of my apron?" he asked, still not looking up.

"I was admiring it, yes."

"Calla bought it for me. It's from my favorite food blogger. This is her motto." He fluttered a hand across his torso and gave me a goofy look.

"Guess you'll have to make me a real man and tell me how to garnish, then."

"Oh, you'll need more help than just garnishing," Warrick said with a wink as he gently folded a clean towel over the rolls.

"No. He will not. It's literally all in the garnish. She has *Real Humans Garnish* and *Real Women Garnish* and all kinds of other iterations. I take this to mean you are a real version of yourself if only you garnish." Wyatt's brows flared as he rough-chopped some dark green leaves.

"I didn't realize I'd been missing so much of myself until just this moment," I said, moving to the sink and washing up before diving in to sprinkle the dark greens flecks of parsley over the sliced chicken. Then, he had me add chopped chives to a steaming plate of yellowy spring potatoes shiny with butter.

"That's what coming home'll do for you, Wilder," Mom said as she grabbed the basket of rolls. "Let's eat!"

Everyone piled into the dining area. They'd added a leaf to the table and set it for all of us. Each brother and his date, and my mom at the head of the table. I could hardly remember family meals with my father, but missing him felt natural in a moment like this. I let the sensation seep in between my ribs and mix right along with the sweet, honeyed feeling of being surrounded by people I loved.

Yes. Loved.

There was no denying it—no point in even trying. I'd been a goner the minute I saw Sarah at twelve, and I hadn't ever stopped. This love was old and new. Quiet for so many years, it clanged against my mind, demanding to be spoken and paraded around, demanding outlet and announcement. I grabbed Sarah's hand on my right and Mom's on my left.

Her prayer was brief and vibrant. Heartfelt and perfectly apt to verbalize what the abundant fullness in my chest embodied.

"Bless this table full of love. We thank you for the beauty of life, forgiveness, healing, and especially love."

The *amens* echoed around the table, and then the conversation rocketed off, everyone grabbing the nearest bowl or platter and serving dish. I glanced at Sarah and could see a little bit of the nerves she'd had earlier, but also the genuine smile as she listened to Warrick expound on the glories of the newest personal trainer he'd hired on at Grit.

The conversation stopped after Warrick ended his story and everyone ate Wyatt's ridiculously good food. Some of the sounds Calla made seemed like they should be kept between husband and wife, and we all laughed when Warrick said as much.

Mom shifted as though restless and passed one of the sides to Sarah while saying, "Well, Sarah, what do you have to say for yourself?"

Mom's question split through the lingering chuckles and sent my pulse racing. What was that? What kind of response could she possibly expect to such a random question?

Sarah's mouth opened, then closed, and her wide eyes told me she had the same reaction. Was my mom really doing this now—confronting her about—

"I was going to say, 'What excellent boiled potatoes...'" She nodded to the bowl in front of her.

Mom burst out laughing, a full-on Jane Saint Cackle, TM. "You are my absolute favorite," she said, reaching past me to squeeze Sarah's hand.

Sarah grinned, and everyone else smiled at the exchange. I had no idea what any of that meant, but I'd clearly missed that Mom had set up that response. Why? I had no idea.

"It's from *Pride and Prejudice*, right? Mr. Collins?" Sadie asked, giggling in a way I wouldn't have anticipated was possible.

Mom wiped her mouth primly, as though she hadn't been laughing like a crazy person at a quote that came out of nowhere. "It is. 2005 version of the movie. Utter perfection, and your timing was just..." She did a chef's kiss.

Who was this woman, and how was she joking with Sarah like this? I'd assumed Sarah was nervous about my mom, but she seemed comfortable with her. She seemed comfortable with everyone. Maybe it was simply the knowledge we were moving ahead—that by stepping in here together, it meant something huge. Just like I'd felt when I'd asked her.

Whatever it meant, I could only feel satisfaction as the conversation swirled around me, my brothers, their partners, my mother, and my love entwined in a moment so full of goodness, it was almost unbearable.

CHAPTER THIRTY-NINE

Sarah

The men scrubbed dishes and chatted in the kitchen after dinner while "the girls," as Jane called us, sat in the living room and talked like we had for a few minutes prior to the meal.

Jane had sent me winks and smiles all evening, especially after my boiled potatoes comment. But the way she settled into the couch next to me and took my hand while Sadie and Calla laughed about something I didn't catch told me this was something else. Something I maybe should've braced for.

"I'm so glad you're here," she said, her tone all warmth and loveliness.

"Me, too."

Her expression sobered. "We missed you."

"I missed you, too. All of you."

She smiled though her eyes held pain. "I won't pressure you. I'll just say I hope you keep coming back."

I huffed a laugh. "Thank you. Me, too." Remembering her words from the store last week, the hurt I'd caused by not just leaving but by not coming back until so many years later. "I'm not running away."

She took that just the way I meant it if her soft smile was any indicator. But then it shifted, a little mischief returning when she said, "And if you feel like marrying Wilder and becoming my daughter-in-law, that'd be just great, too."

A full laugh escaped then. "Certainly no pressure."

Face imperious, she shook her head. "None at all."

But here was something I had to say—just had to. To a woman I knew wanted grandkids desperately. Who'd doted on Calla so completely it was nearly suffocating, except that Calla welcomed the affection and love so fully. Much like I would—much like I had years ago. The thought was ludicrous considering Wilder and I hadn't determined what came next beyond him bringing me here, but I couldn't leave this unsaid.

"You know I might not be able to—"

She squeezed my hands. "Just you, dear. All we want is you. Whatever else comes—" she shook her head, then focused on my eyes. "Just you."

Face red and tears just behind the surface, I nodded, begging myself not to cry. "Thank you," I managed to say.

We hugged, needing the closeness. I pulled back quickly, knowing if I stayed in the embrace that felt so warm and accepting and lovely, I'd lose it for sure.

"You two okay?" Calla asked.

"Perfectly fine. Just telling Sarah we've loved having her," Jane said.

"Now we outnumber the boys," Sadie said, agreeing.

"I've loved being here."

"All right, women, the menfolk have cooked and cleaned, and now we demand payment in the form of dessert and other favors." Warrick dramatically slammed his hand on the counter.

Wyatt sent him a glare. "You want *other favors* from your mother? That's sick, *Warbaby*."

"Ew. No! Ew." Warrick swatted Wyatt with a towel.

Everyone laughed at the ridiculousness.

"All right, *menfolk*, sit down and we'll start with dessert," Sadie said, chuckling at her boyfriend's antics, but also clearly loving it.

"Yes. We'll start there and then later, you can—"

"Warrick James, where have your manners gone?"

Wilder shot Warrick a look and Wyatt shoved him into his seat. I just laughed and shared a grin with Calla as we helped Sadie dish up a gorgeous-looking Italian olive oil cake. We all sat down, the boys still ribbing each other, and I thought my heart might burst for all the love filling me up. This was more than I ever could've hoped for.

After a hilarious time enjoying Sadie's delicious dessert, Wilder and I said our goodbyes to the family. The time together had left me strangely raw, and as we drove back down the canyon toward my apartment, my emotions bubbled ridiculously close to the surface.

Actually, it wasn't just the dinner. It was everything that'd happened in the last twenty-four hours—maybe even the last few weeks. Tonight had been the capstone on a series of events that left me reeling. Not in a bad way, but certainly in the sense that so much emotion from the past and the present were entwined and becoming harder and harder to keep inside.

At some point, I'd have to let it out. Though my instinct bucked against that so strongly, I knew now was not the time. I didn't know exactly how I felt beyond *full*, so I couldn't tell Wilder anything anyway.

"You're quiet." Wilder's voice cut into my thoughts.

"Sorry. Just... absorbing it all."

His large, warm hand enveloped mine, his other steering us carefully down the canyon road. "Did you have fun?"

"I did." *Fun* wasn't the right word for something so wholly restorative and soul-filling.

We drove a while longer with only the sound of the road and the car's engine to accompany us. When the motion stopped and I heard the click of a seat belt, I startled back into the moment. "Wow, I was really in my head."

A soft smile was his only answer. He exited the car while I worked on my belt, and by the time I pushed open the door, he'd already arrived at my side and held out a hand to help me down. He kept it, threading our fingers together like he seemed to prefer, leading me to my door.

My mind was moving slow. I knew the evening had held so much significance and emotion, but I didn't want to be thinking through sludgy thoughts. I wanted to be bright and easygoing and ready to invite him inside and spend the rest of the night together.

"We've got a big week," he said, stopping on my welcome mat.

"It'll be great." I smiled.

Apparently, not well, because his brows dropped low and he stepped into my space with a hand on each of my arms. "This has been a lot."

I nodded. Couldn't refute that.

"I think we both need some time to think it through." His gaze was sharp and assessing as he watched me absorb his words. Then he leaned in and kissed my cheek and a trail to just before my ear in a series of quick, soft kisses. "I'll see you in the morning."

My brain finally caught up to his words. "You're leaving?"

His gaze softened even as he stepped back, linked to me by only one hand in mine. "Yes. And not because anything's wrong, to be clear, but because everything in me wants to haul you inside and spend the night in a repeat of last night."

My mouth opened, about to say *Yes, let's do that!*, when he continued.

"But the last day has brought big changes. I don't want us to feel like we've rushed, even though I know it's my fault you came tonight—my fault I stayed last night." He shook his head just slightly, like he was frustrated with himself.

I reached for him, holding his shirt just below his pecs to keep him in place. "I wanted you to stay. And I'm so glad you took me with you tonight."

His eyes killed me. Even in the dusky light, they still made my heart twist and my stomach drop.

"I wanted you there. You belong there."

His words hung between us as my heart flapped around in my chest at the notion. *You belong there.*

What I wanted to say, maybe would've said in another version of my life that hadn't been so hammered by pressure not to assert my own desires, was something like *I belong with you.* I wondered if another version of him would've said something else, too. But tonight, I simply said, "Thank you."

He bent to kiss my lips and groaned as he stepped all the way back only seconds after making contact. "If we keep kissing, I won't go."

"You don't have to."

He huffed and set his hands on his hips as though searching for strength within himself. "I do. But I'll see you tomorrow."

"Okay."

"Now head inside and lock up behind you."

I grinned at his order. "Yes, sir."

He only pinned me with those eyes, hands still on his hips, and watched as I let myself inside, closed the door, and made a point to lock the bolt loudly.

My heart ached and twisted and practically burned in my chest, it felt so full. Talking with Jane had nearly done me in, but thanks to Warrick's ridiculous comments, I'd recovered without blubbering all over her pretty silk blouse.

Everything about the time together had felt good. I hadn't been out of place. No one had wondered why I was there. Obviously, Calla and Sadie were glad to have me, but Warrick and Wyatt were, too. It felt so familiar and good. Sitting at that table—a table at which I'd sat years ago—felt like something coming full circle.

Not something. *Us.* Me and Wilder, coming back to where we always should've been. Where I never should've left.

But if I hadn't, we wouldn't be here now. Who knew where we would've ended up. That didn't really matter because we would never know about that version of our story. What we could know was what happened to us now.

I should've said I belonged with him. I should've said it tonight, no hesitation. At some point, I had to stop waiting for him to prompt me. He needed me to be sure just like I needed him to be. But I was sure—I had no doubts.

If that was true, why did I keep doubting? Was I so conditioned to falter, I couldn't even trust myself to know what I wanted and express that?

I went to bed promising myself I'd be open with him, not scared to say what I wanted. Not nervous about what was to come even if I didn't know what came next. My plans to leave here *could* change. Deviating from the path of leaving when I healed was only a problem if it wasn't what I wanted.

We had Madeline Reynolds arriving for her stay this week. It'd be insanely busy between her and other things popping up on the schedule. But the next time I had a chance, I would tell Wilder. I wanted him. I belonged with him, and he belonged with me.

CHAPTER FORTY

Wilder

S heriff Whitaker, the county sheriff and a good man by all accounts, nodded at me as I approached the giant door to Madeline Reynolds's house.

"She's inside. Shaken up but won't admit it. I had to beg her to let me contact law enforcement. I hope you were right about that."

Anthony chattered nervously as I stepped into the entryway and took in the soaring ceiling. I'd been here before to check out the property, but it impressed every time. A two-story entrance with huge windows letting light and views of the peaks in on one end, and a living room that showcased a view of the sunset in the west. Overall stunning on all sides, even if it seemed insanely big.

My house would have views, too, eventually.

"Has the sheriff seen anything?" I asked, adrenaline still surging in the wake of Anthony's call an hour ago.

Just as Sarah and I were about to head out to lunch, my cell had rung. A panicked Anthony relayed the situation with surprising clarity considering his near-hysterical tone. Madeline thought she'd seen her stalker at the Silverton airport. Anthony had been spooked enough by her saying something, which he mentioned more than once was atypical and she would never exaggerate, and they'd called me immediately.

I'd told him to call the police, but Madeline initially refused. I'd convinced him to convince her, and here we were. I'd taken a careful drive around the airport, town, and neighborhood. I'd double-checked all of her security feeds and circled around the property a few times just for extra assurances while Sheriff Whitaker took her statement.

Sitting at a gray and white marbled countertop with her gaze attached to her phone, Madeline Reynolds tapped with two fingers. Anthony announced me.

"Wilder Saint's here."

She looked up and set her phone down, shoving off the countertop and approaching me with a hand out. "Mr. Saint. Thanks for coming."

"Thanks for taking my suggestion about calling the sheriff. I understand not wanting to alert someone to something you thought you saw, but at this point, you all know more than we do. Your instincts, and your *uh-oh feeling*, can do a lot to protect you. Don't ignore that."

I had my own version of exactly that, and it never boded well. But I needed the full rundown of information, and now that they were back and we were all face to face, I'd finally get it.

She nodded. "Working on it."

"I've checked everything, and if he was there, he avoided getting caught on film."

"He's a crafty one, I'm telling you." Brad came into the room chomping on a chicken drumstick and holding a plate piled with food in his other. "We'll debrief more thoroughly whenever Ms. Reynolds is ready."

The woman in question ran a hand through her now-brown hair. Last I'd seen her, she'd been blonde.

"Let's get it over with. I'm sure Mr. Saint has plenty of other things to be doing." She waved her hands in a gesture I took to mean we should all follow her. Considering her assistant and guard both did, I'd read it right.

"Anthony, can you cancel with the landscaper? We'll reschedule for next week," she said over her shoulder, and immediately her assistant was tapping away on his phone. I got the feeling very few moments in Reynolds's day weren't productive.

I had other things I'd like to be doing—namely, sitting down to a long lunch with Sarah. But we didn't have the luxury of that this week anyway, nor was there technically anyone more important in my life than the woman padding across the gleaming hardwood floors of her multi-million-dollar home. She represented about seventy percent of our paying customers and while I fully accepted the need for time to pass before we had everything in place to help people the way I wanted, I didn't want to give her anything but the best possible security while she was here.

I'd told Sarah I didn't know how long I'd be gone. She had plans tonight, so if I didn't make it back by close, I'd have to wait until tomorrow to see her.

Just now, that seemed like a lifetime away. Pathetic considering we'd gone decades, but after even a day of closeness like we'd had yesterday, keeping my hands off her at work had been challenging enough.

For now, I needed to focus on the problem at hand.

Having Madeline Reynolds's stalker track her down before she'd even gotten settled in would not be a good start to her sabbatical, nor would it do anything for Saint Securities' reputation.

Hours after I'd arrived and long after the close of business, I'd assured Madeline we'd figure this out. They'd come to the office on Tuesday afternoon for a few things, and in the meantime, she'd call the sheriff and then me if anything set off her spidey senses.

Anthony had argued hard for me to be the first call. He had an acceptable understanding of some of my training—that was part of what sold Saint Securities, after all. Experience in the Exceptional Mission Unit was a hush-hush part of a person's resume right until they left the organization and put it on their actual resume. Of course, it would never be confirmed by the military, but considering plenty of generals tagged the unit as part of their history in their bios, Bruce and I wouldn't be above indicating the experience where needed.

I had hundreds if not thousands of hours of weapons training. I was, without arrogance, one of the best marksmen in the world. Compared to the average police officer, whose time training with a weapon was hampered by budget restrictions on everything from ammunition to range time, I was like a god. And again, I meant that in the nicest possible way. The police were focused on a lot of different things. I was trained to find, capture, kill. And maybe a few other jobs that popped up along the way.

Translate that to now? I was trained to find, detain, and call the good guys to come haul them away before they could hurt someone.

Knowing Brad was handling the cyber portion of the job made my role fairly simple. I'd prefer if we had everything in house, but even if I'd had my cyber team in place, I wouldn't have been surprised if Reynolds had wanted her man to stay on it. So no complaints, simply a narrowed role that I'd do as well as I could, even if at times that meant deferring to her team or local law enforcement.

So no, Madeline Reynolds shouldn't call me. She should call the sheriff and let the law enforcement handle it. But I wanted to be that second call so I could assist in any way possible.

My phone buzzed in my pocket as I pulled into my parking spot.

"Miss you tonight. Hope everything went well."

Warmth bled from my fingertips where I held the device all the way to my toes. I tapped a reply before exiting the car. *"I'll catch you up tomorrow. We've got a good plan. How was your thing?"*

I'd planned to talk through things with Sarah at lunch today. Not the most romantic setting, but after the weekend we'd had, it felt like we were together. Solidly committed and moving forward, arms linked. *Plans* linked.

That said, I had no idea if she felt the same. I thought I did, but I couldn't entirely eliminate our history from my mind. Because of that, until I heard her say the words, I didn't know. I wouldn't assume I knew where she was with us.

I'd insisted on going home and not staying the night last night only because the day had been packed full of emotion and meaning, and I could see how close to the surface her emotions hovered. That didn't exactly scare me, but I worried about my own thoughts and needed time to sort through them before we dove back into bed together. And trust, that was exactly where we would've ended. If I had the choice, we'd go there and spend a week without interruption, making up for lost time.

Part of me thought maybe I should wait to talk with Sarah and gauge things until after my therapy session tomorrow. I liked bouncing stuff off the doc at this point, and she was always game to smile and let me work my way through my problem. But that was just it—part of the process was learning to trust myself and my evaluation of my own choices, wasn't it?

Coming back here, I'd felt uncertain of my ability to live life as a civilian. And no, a few months didn't mean I'd wrapped that up in a neat little bow. But good things were happening, and I'd finally started to allow it without questioning it.

This thing between me and Sarah, despite our past, didn't have to be hard or grueling. Or maybe because of how brutal our past was, it'd earned the right to be easy.

I'd always struggled to embrace something I felt I hadn't earned. The Army had given me a perfect, clear system through which to move toward earning my worth—rank, medals, badges, bonuses, etc. Outside of that, life didn't move linearly. There wasn't a rubric for the requirements a given life achievement needed in order to unlock.

But maybe the whole point was that Sarah and I had unlocked the opportunity by simply trying again. We'd toiled through years apart, neither of us finding an acceptable alternative. So coming back together was both a solution and a reward for everything that'd come before this point.

We could be together having earned the right to try again simply because we *had* tried again. There was no other stipulation, no other requirement for suffering before we were allowed to be together and be happy.

And damn if that wasn't the best realization I'd ever had.

CHAPTER FORTY-ONE

Sarah

Dahlia beamed back at me, happiness on my behalf just oozing out of her.

"I just love this for you. I love it. Have I mentioned I love it?"

She'd renewed her sentiments many times, but when she came back from a trip to the restrooms to find me blushing over a text from Wilder, she launched in yet again.

"I'm glad you're so happy," I said, laughing for the nth time tonight and elated to be sharing some of the overwhelming excitement with my friend.

We'd set this meal up a while ago. Her weekends tended to be insane, especially as spring edged its way into summer and more people were getting married or having special events with big floral orders. So a Monday night in late May was all I could get with her, and I'd take it and run. The rest of our friends couldn't make it, but there was something to be said for the one-on-one times, too. I'd only just started getting to know Dahlia and everything I'd learned, I loved.

She was deeply loyal and an incredibly romantic soul, though so far I'd gotten no hints about her romantic past or interests. But based on her reaction to the news that Wilder and I had taken things to the next level to include me attending a family dinner—amongst other things I did not spell out but she clearly inferred based on the amount of eyebrow waggling—she was a true romantic.

"So are you seeing him after this?" she asked, setting her fork to the side of her plate.

"No. He just got back from meetings, and I'm..." I searched for the right words. "Processing."

Her dark eyes widened. "Um, hi. What's to process? You're back together after a dramatic twenty-year pause. Pretty sure you love him. Pretty sure he loves you. His family loves you. He's living here now and so are you. You even currently get to see each other daily because you work for him."

I smiled, but it didn't quite fit. "I know. It feels like a perfect scenario. Though the whole me working for him thing is a little weird, but we'll figure it out."

She tilted her head to eye me. "What is it?"

The knot of feelings tightened. "I'm just a jumble. And at the same time, all I want to do is sink into the chemistry and good feelings and just live there and not worry about the other stuff."

She mulled that over as she took the last drink of her wine. "I get that. But I also see why you're hesitant to do that. I'm just wondering if you've told him that?"

I made a face. "No. Because if I do that, then he'll ask

what I'm worried about, and then I'll have to tell him, and then I have to deal with the reality."

She chuckled softly. "Well, it seems like you might need to do that since it's also keeping you from enjoying the fantasy parts, too." She winked.

I sighed dramatically. "Fair point."

"Sarah James! I'm glad I'm seeing you here. Please forgive my interruption."

Dr. Brown, the principal of Silverton Elementary, smiled down at us, and I fumbled to stand in front of my former-kind-of-sort-of boss. "Dr. Brown, it's great to see you. Do you know Dahlia Price?"

"Please to meet you. You're the owner of Bloom, right?"

Dahlia beamed. "My pride and joy."

"It's just lovely. I can't wait to see what you and Wallace do for Night in Bloom this year."

"Thank you so much," Dahlia said.

Dr. Brown nodded, then turned her focus on me. "Forgive me for interrupting, but I wanted to give you a little nudge that Carmela Ballantine is retiring this summer. There'll be an option in fourth grade and I know you were eager to find something in primary."

A jolt of adrenaline shot through me. "Oh, yes. Great. I'll get my resume ready."

The principal smiled approvingly. "Excellent. All right, ladies, I'm out of your hair. Have a good evening."

"Thank you. You, too!" I slumped back into the seat as soon as she'd exited the wintergarden.

"Why do you look like you were just told you were fired? Haven't you been waiting for an opening like this?" Dahlia rifled through her purse and pulled out cash to set in the little black folder the waiter had slipped onto the table at some point.

It was a valid question. Why did I have a steady base beat of dread running through me instead of pure excitement? Why wasn't this triumph and hope and possibility thrumming in my chest instead of a sharp sense I'd run smack into a brick wall?

"I don't think I can explain it." Not to her. Not to myself.

Maybe I didn't really need to explain it. I'd been barreling toward this reality that I didn't want to teach. I might not have a clear alternative since my current position was temporary and so new, but it wasn't all that complex. I didn't have the heart for teaching anymore.

I'd admitted as much to myself and even Wilder. Still, I expected to feel good about this. Especially now that staying here seemed more and more like the right thing, a full-time teaching job would be perfect. Or, would've been, for another version of me.

Coming face to face with Dr. Brown made me sad, because in some ways, I'd always love the atmosphere of working at a school, and I loved the kids. But the sadness wasn't devastation. It was more a kind of mourning—maybe an acceptance.

Dahlia busied herself with tucking her part of the check into the folder and waited patiently while I did the same. We gave each other the *let's do this* nod, and I followed her out. On the sidewalk, she turned and pulled me into a hug.

Tears welled despite my best efforts, but I swallowed them down when she released me.

"I know we're new friends, but I want you to know that you're amazing. And if Wilder makes you happy and you want to be with him, I believe you can figure it out. Whatever's going on in there to make you doubt or *whatever* this is, don't let it psych you out."

I gave her a pathetic excuse for a smile. "Thanks."

"And same goes for the teaching gig. If you're excited about it, then go for it, balls to the wall."

I laughed freely at that and mercifully felt the tears recede completely.

"But if you don't? For any reason, if you decide you don't want to teach fourth grade at Silverton Elementary, then don't."

I swallowed, nodding to show I'd heard her. I couldn't explain everything behind my walking away from teaching right now, but I appreciated her getting that it might not be right for me anymore. "Thank you."

"Thank me by texting your badass boyfriend and kissing him into oblivion tonight." She winked again and turned with a wave, glancing both ways before she stepped into the street.

"We're talking about your love life next time," I warned as I watched her go.

"Ha! Just make sure you book me for the wedding. Friends and family discount!"

With that, she was off, slipping inside Bloom and leaving me to the mix of warmth from her reassurances and dread of dealing with my confused little brain.

I wouldn't let myself call Wilder and tell him how much I wanted to see him and touch him and dump all my doubts in his lap and pray he wasn't repelled by them. No.

I did tap out a quick message to him, though. *"Can we plan to talk after work tomorrow?"*

A minute or so later, he responded. *"Yes. Looking forward to it."*

Bolstered by his positive response, I firmed my determination for the next eighteen hours. I'd put myself to bed at a normal time like a grown up, and I'd get up and do an excellent job at work with our meeting with Madeline Reynolds. I'd be professional with him while at work, and I'd make sure we sat down tomorrow night and get it all out. No more keeping this nonsense to myself. No more putting off saying what I wanted or what I worried about.

CHAPTER FORTY-TWO

Sarah

Nervous energy coursed through me all morning. Wilder had been here before I'd arrived, talking on the phone for long enough I realized it had to be someone he knew pretty well. He'd then conducted two phone interviews back-to-back. My friend at the school texted to give me a heads up about the job the principal had mentioned the night before and that sent me into an introspective little spiral that had me feeling all kinds of stupid for not jumping at the opportunity.

Wilder wandered up around eleven, eyes dark and expression shrouded in mystery—seriously, I couldn't read him. I could only feel my heart pick up at his approach and every molecule in me lean toward him.

"Still on to talk after work?"

No inflection or body language gave anything away.

Was he dreading it? Excited? Ready to dump me at the door or happy to see me? No idea.

"Yes, if it still works for you. If not, we could—"

"It works."

His phone buzzed in his pocket and he scowled. "I've gotta take this, and probably need to head to my appointment anyway. I'll be back after lunch."

"Anthony confirmed they're coming around twelve thirty."

He nodded. "Anthony has confirmed as much with me three times already."

His expression held just enough chagrin, a laugh slipped through. "I told him we were ready."

His brow furrowed more significantly. "He's anxious. I get it."

That tone sobered me. "Do you think there's really a threat? I mean, obviously there has been, but here?"

His eyes flicked to his watch. "I hope not. But we're ready if there is." He set a hand on the desk next to me and lowered his voice, as though someone might overhear him. "Can I kiss you goodbye?"

A thrill raced through me. No games. No pretending we weren't... whatever we were. Just Wilder's brand of directness and sweetness. "Yes, please."

Needing no more permission, he leaned down and tilted his head. His warm lips pressed against mine and lit fires with the contact. Before it could escalate, he pulled back.

"See you soon."

Anthony burst in the door fifteen minutes early, his anxiety so palpable, like a cloud so thick hung around him, I was surprised he could breathe.

"Everything okay? Come in. Wilder isn't back just yet but should be any minute. Is Ms. Reynolds—"

"I'm fine. He's paranoid or upset I'm *not* paranoid, or something like that, and he was driving me insane at the house so we are here early so I wouldn't commit murder." Madeline's air had a little more vibrancy in it, but maybe only because it had an impatient, almost embarrassed edge.

Anthony shot her a furious glare. "She's probably the most stubborn person you'll ever meet, FYI. Brace yourself if you do end up going to lunch."

Surprise jumped through me, though I supposed it was Anthony's job to remember details like the fact that I'd offered to show her around last time they were here. Or maybe she'd said something? Either way, she smiled at me and ignored Anthony completely.

"Would you mind if we go ahead and sit at the conference table until Mr. Saint arrives? I have a few things to check off my list before we start, anyway."

I waved them along behind me and flipped on the lights to the room we'd be meeting in. "I've got fresh coffee brewing, or you're welcome to water or anything else we have. I can have lunch ordered in, as well, if you didn't have a chance to eat before."

Madeline smiled. "None for me, thank you. Though I think Anthony and Brad were just saying they wanted to get some take out."

I took the cue. "There are a few places really close. I'd recommend the diner—everything's great and it's really close."

Brad nodded and gave Anthony a stare that could only

mean *you're coming with me.* "We'll be back by twelve thirty for the meeting."

Anthony firmed his lips but said nothing as he followed Brad out into the hallway.

"I'll be fine for a few. Please don't feel like you need to stay with me—when everyone's back, I'll be ready to dive right in. Oh, and Julian Grenier's coming to drop something for me when he can—should be just before meeting time."

I smiled, hearing the dismissal, and also looking forward to seeing Julian. It was a gracious send off, and I appreciated her giving me an out while also giving herself a moment alone—a novelty based on what I was seeing.

"That's great. I'll be right out here if you need anything."

She was already focusing on her laptop and diving into work. Fine by me—I scuttled back to my desk and shot off a text to let Wilder know she was here and Brad and Anthony would be back right at our scheduled time. I didn't get a response but hadn't expected to since he'd be here any minute anyway. In the meantime, I finished updating my resume while trying not to wonder about the woman in the other room.

I'd started the resume update to fill time this morning since chatting with Wilder hadn't been an option and most of my essential jobs were done until tomorrow. After Bruce arrived, I'd have more to do consistently, but in these beginning stages, the work really ebbed and flowed.

The front door opened, and a man with a baggy brown suit stepped inside. I didn't recognize him, though I didn't know everyone in town yet.

"Welcome to Saint Securities. How can I help you?"

A fizzy, enervated feeling filled my chest. I hadn't actually helped a customer who didn't have an appointment. I really had no idea what to do with them other than schedule a meeting with Wilder.

"Me? I just stopped by to see what this place was." He offered a smiled as he perused the art on the walls and the stone fireplace.

"We offer a variety of services. As a new company, we're extremely nimble and can meet just about any need as it pertains to personal security, though I will have to refer you to the owner for really detailed questions." I stood and stepped to the side of my desk.

Normally, I stood when people came in because the next step was to show them to the conference room or Wilder's office. It seemed odd to stay sitting while someone was milling around the reception area.

"Is he available today? I do have some unique needs." His eyes flicked to mine, then back to the fireplace.

A wisp of warning snaked through me, but I couldn't figure out why. Even so, I felt strongly I shouldn't tell the truth in response to his question. "He's wrapping up with a client now, but he'll be ready any minute. I can put you on the schedule for later this afternoon and you can come back."

His head snapped up to study me, and I rushed to add, "Or, uh, of course you're welcome to wait."

"I'll wait."

"Oh, good," I said weakly, my throat dry and my heart sprinting. I had no real reason to feel so unnerved by this guy, but as I'd heard Wilder call it, my *uh-oh* feeling was blaring. Maybe I just needed more information—get some details that would help me feel better. Heck, maybe this guy was a long-lost Saint cousin or somebody's uncle from out of town. "What did you say your name was?"

His eyes shifted to the side, then back to me. "Korry Taggart."

"Well, uh... why don't I get you something to drink while you wait? Water? Coffee?"

Evidently pleased by this, he smiled broadly. "Coffee, please. Milk, two sugars, if you have it."

"No problem. Just give me a moment. Feel free to have a seat, if you like." I waved to the couches like he couldn't very clearly see them since he stood three feet from one, but at least my arm moved fast enough he likely couldn't tell how hard I was shaking.

Adrenaline cranked through me as I walked down the hall, and my mind spun. Wilder would be back any minute now. *Right?* My watch said ten minutes until our meeting had been scheduled to start, plus he'd typically be at least a few minutes early.

Any second now, really.

I found a paper coffee cup and slipped it into a sleeve.

"This is a nice room."

I gasped and flipped around. "Oh, Mr. Taggart, we typically ask people to wait in the—"

"Where is she?" His face twisted, morphing from something placid and ignorable to a sneering growl that sent my entire body into overdrive. Adrenaline crashed through me, and it clicked.

"You're—you're—"

His hand came up and revealed a handgun pointing right at my chest. "Take me to her. Now."

CHAPTER FORTY-THREE

Wilder

The doc had let me babble on about Sarah almost the entire meeting. When I'd apologized for talking about her so much, she'd reassured me with, "This time is for you. Use it how you want."

So I did. I ran through how great everything was and how hard I was trying to let something good just be good. But I'd talked through my doubts, too—that it was *too* good. *Too* easy. That something had to give and I hated the sense of impending doom I had about it all.

We'd talked through some of the reasons for that more than once, including an adrenal system that'd been trained to react in certain situations and that might just be leading me astray. I hated the thought that my body might be betraying me, but I'd felt that in very different ways at other times. Namely, my body wanted Sarah's at all times and in all ways, even when my brain said *Pump the brakes, genius. Take it slow.*

I'd failed to take it slow. I'd confessed as much to the doc, and she'd simply asked, "Why do you need to move slowly?"

I stared blankly at her.

"I'm serious. Why do you believe you need to *move slowly*, and I might also ask you to define the term."

She'd done this at least once a session—asked me to define a word or phrase.

"I mean not rushing things—physically, emotionally, whatever. And I believe that because... because isn't that what's supposed to happen?"

She tilted her head to the side, which I knew very well asked, "Why?" without saying it.

I inhaled, summoning the right words. "Because when you care about someone, you do things right. And by right, I mean... purposefully. With the right intentions."

"And you can't do something purposefully if you're moving fast?"

"Slow is smooth, smooth is fast." I cringed as the saying left my lips automatically.

"Explain."

"It's a saying in the special operations community. Move slow, do it right the first time, and it all goes smooth. When things go smooth, they go faster, so you get fast by moving slow."

She nodded as though this really did explain things. "And so you want to move slow in order to go fast with Sarah?"

I groaned and scrubbed a hand over my face. "That sounds like something a teenager would say, doesn't it?"

She cracked a half-smile. "Is it possible that your way of thinking about things with Sarah is informed by how you thought of things with her when you were with her as a teen?"

I slumped back on the couch. "Maybe? Obviously, we didn't move all that slowly considering she got pregnant and I'd planned to marry her before we graduated and join the Army to support us."

"But didn't you tell me you'd planned to go to college together and get married eventually, just not so soon? Couldn't you argue that the years of friendship prior to your courtship would qualify as going slow?"

"Not by her parents' standards, but I don't give a damn about them anymore."

"I might also submit that twenty years between interactions naturally slowed you down. So anything that happens now is, by nature and in an essential, time-bound, inescapable way, moving slow."

I squinted, teasing through that until it clocked. "So you're saying slow doesn't matter."

"Slow. Smooth. Fast. Warp speed. I think what matters is what you and Sarah want. If you're both happy with how things are going—at whatever pace they're moving—I suggest that might be exactly right."

I nodded, letting those words get absorbed, when she continued.

"Have you ever really talked through what happened?"

I shifted, resting my elbows on my knees. "I told you about the apology a few weeks ago. We haven't said much more than that."

I tried to read her response to that, but as usual, she kept any reaction under wraps. "So you have not had a chance to share your perspective."

I tipped my head from side to side, milling through

memories. Fact was, I didn't need to. "No. And as much as I know I need to, I don't want to drag us through it. But maybe that's—" *Crap. There it is.* This was the thing niggling at me, that I kept shoving away instead of inspecting. Instead of facing it head on. "That's what I need to do."

She didn't exactly smile or nod, but something like approval filtered across her face. "When you've done that, I suspect the pace, the timing, won't matter."

The session ended well. In fact, I felt great. Not that I'd needed her permission, but it felt good to feel like I had my own. Instead of dreading the conversation to come, I had faith in us. We could face this together and work through it, and then it was up to us to make the rest of it work. And we would.

"If you're both happy with how things are going..."

I couldn't speak for Sarah, but I was certainly happy, and that was putting it mildly. I hoped her desire to talk tonight would allow us to identify where we both stood on the matter and to dig into things a bit. Look back a little more closely so we could move forward. Plus, I wanted her to tell me she was happy, too, and then maybe I could relax into this.

"Wilder Saint, what's got you smiling in broad daylight?"

I turned at the sound of my mom's voice, noting I had a few minutes before Madeline Reynolds and her crew would arrive at the office. "Hey. Just coming from my therapy session. I have a meeting in ten."

She pushed her sunglasses up onto her head and her soft gaze hit mine. "I'm so proud of you for taking care of yourself."

"Thanks, Mom."

"Really, though. I feel like you're really home, and it—" She glanced away, then back to me. "It fills me with such joy."

I smiled—another genuine one. "It's good to be back. I'm sorry I haven't spent as much time with you as I'd like."

She raised a brow. "Oh, I know who you want to spend time with."

A chuckle escaped, though a thought occurred to me. "Hey, what'd you say to Sarah on Sunday?"

"I said a lot of things to Sarah, why?"

"After dinner. I looked over and you two were hugging. It wasn't a huge shock or anything but it seemed like a moment, or something."

"Ah, yes. I think that's when I told her she could marry you and become my daughter-in-law and that'd be just fine with me."

Her smug look shouldn't have surprised me. "Mom. You can't propose to the woman on my behalf."

Her brows raised in challenge. "Does that mean you're going to propose to her?"

Call me a fool or say I'm having a midlife crisis—call it what you will, but I answered her honestly. "Not just yet, but if things keep going the way they're going, maybe soon."

A beaming smile exploded across her face and she launched at me, squeezing me tight. "I knew it was going well."

Despite the session with the doc, I needed her opinion. "Doesn't seem too fast?"

She shook her head like I was an adorable toddler and

not a grown-ass man who had at least eight inches on her. "Darling boy, no. I'd say it's just right."

And with that, she pinched my cheek just to razz me, told me to get back to work, and reminded me about Sunday dinner this coming weekend and not to come without Sarah. I assured her we'd be there, and then I worked to refocus on the task at hand. Reynolds meeting for the next few hours and then, we'd figure this out.

CHAPTER FORTY-FOUR

Sarah

I wanted to curl up. I wanted to cry. I wanted to scream and beg Wilder to come in *right now right now please right now*, but instead, I spoke loudly. "I don't know who you're talking about. I'm the only one here until Mr. Saint is back, which will be any minute."

"I saw the cars. She's here. How do you think I found her?" His face had gone red, and he grabbed at me, catching my wrist with a cold, clammy hand.

My stomach lurched and I felt dizzy from the scampering beat of my heart. "I don't know who you mean. It's just me."

He shoved me forward and stuck the muzzle of the gun to my spine. I sucked in a breath and prayed he wouldn't shoot. This guy had stalked Madeline Reynolds across the US, maybe all over the world, and I had absolutely no faith that he'd leave without doing something worse.

"All I want is you, Maddie! You just have to come out, and this nice lady goes on her merry way. I just need to see you."

The conference room door swung open, and Madeline appeared in the doorway.

"Korry? What are you doing here?" Her brown eyes hit mine, and I saw the apology and pleading. The *run for it!* Because she didn't realize what he had pointed at my back.

"*LOOK AT ME!*" Korry screamed at her, a vicious, ragged, rage-filled sound that sent terror straight to my gut. This man was not okay.

"I'm looking at you, Korry. You seem upset. My friend Sarah isn't doing anything wrong, so can we let her get back to work?"

He clamped a hand on my shoulder and pressed the gun harder into my back. I bowed away from it as much as I could.

"You coming with me finally? Are you free?" Korry's voice had a creepy softness to it.

"Yes. Just let Sarah get back to work, and I'll talk with you."

"You *come* with me."

Madeline nodded, but couldn't seem to bring herself to say the words. I couldn't blame her, and I wondered if saying she would go with him, wherever he wanted her to go, would make all of this worse somehow.

One thing was for sure: I had no idea how to handle a hostage situation. If I was going to keep this job, I needed more training—for this and any other imaginable situation. We needed emergency buttons in every room I could push to call Wilder or Bruce to me without needing my phone. I needed to learn how to handle a weapon. I needed self-defense lessons and information on how to de-escalate a crazy person who was bent on kidnapping or killing a client.

Korry sighed behind me, then shoved me away with so much force, I stumbled across the hallway and rammed my shoulder into the wall. I hit with an "Oof!" and flipped around to face the man. If he was going to shoot me, he'd have to do it to my face—though I really, *really* hoped he didn't.

"That wasn't very nice," Madeline said, a little shake to her voice this time. She reached out a hand to me and I took it, but this contact made our resident gun-wielding madman unhappy.

"Don't you touch her. Get your filthy hands off *her!*"

I dropped Madeline's hand and gritted my teeth against the tears that came like a flood. "I'm sorry. I'm sorry. I won't."

"Korry, she's my friend. Please don't hurt my friend. You don't want to upset me, right? I—I—"

"We're leaving, Maddie. It's time for us."

"Korry, my friends are about to be back. Why don't you sit down with us and—"

"Don't."

"Sorry?"

Madeline's voice remained calm, though I had no idea how.

"Don't pretend like you're friends with that oaf of a bodyguard and twit of an assistant. I know better. It's why I'm here."

She let out a halting breath, as though trying to steady herself. "Okay. Okay."

"That's enough. I—"

"Everything okay in here?" Julian walked into the hallway, hands raising slowly as he approached.

"Who are you? *Who are you?!*" The shrieking question came out furious.

"He's Julian Grenier. You've seen him on magazines, haven't you, Korry? He's an old friend."

I could see that Julian continued to inch toward Madeline as he spoke—no idea how he'd gotten in here but I was so thankful, and so instantly scared for him.

"That's right. Maddie and I have a few friends in common, and after a while, we got to know one another. She knows my fiancée, too. Quinn thinks the world of you, by the way," he said to Madeline, talking nonstop and not letting Korry have a word in.

"You—you shouldn't be here. You're not supposed to be here. It's supposed to be just—"

"Korry, really. I'm so sorry to interrupt, but I have to insist I have a moment of Sarah and Maddie's time. You understand, don't you?" He slipped fully in front of Madeline who still stood in front of me. Both hands above his head, he spoke as though he had nothing better to do. "Maddie's only in town for so long, and it's rare I get a chance to meet with her in person."

Julian stepped back again, forcing me and Madeline to do the same. We wouldn't abandon him now, especially considering Korry seemed about to lose it if Maddie went anywhere. Julian angled himself and Korry jockeyed side to side, craning his neck to see past Julian's much taller body. Julian wasn't as bulky as Wilder, but he still had inches and pounds on Korry. Eventually, Korry's back was to the door, and he started absolutely raving. I finally understood the term "stark raving mad" and the unadulterated taste of fear that came from witnessing it.

"She's mine now, she already said. She's coming with me. Get out of the way. I don't want to shoot you—you know what it's like. If you're engaged, you know when you love someone, you'd do anything for them. Maddie's mine and when she realizes it, when she stops resisting me, it'll all be better."

All I saw was a flash of daylight in the hallway, and then Korry's rant turned into a weird, strained gurgle, a dull thump vibrated under my feet, and the air stilled.

"Thank God, Saint. I thought he might actually shoot me," Julian said, stepping out of the way enough that I could see Wilder's body crouched over Korry's inert one.

Relief and a rush of dizziness hit. Korry was down. Or out. Or dead? No, Wilder was zip-tying his hands behind his back. Unconscious, it looked like, but not dead. And Wilder was here—he'd come. Even the view of the side of his face, the curve over his shoulder and a glimpse of his ear made me want to cry out and confess my every thought about him, our future, what I wanted.

I'd never want to relive this insanity, but the adrenaline and fear had clarified everything. Any doubts I felt about staying were completely gone. In truth, they'd been gone weeks ago, but I could see it wasn't for anyone but myself. I wanted to stay for Wilder, yes. But not because he wanted me to. I would stay for me to be with Wilder. I would stay for my friends. I would stay to figure out the next right step in my career path. No one else was forcing the issue.

I couldn't spend time wishing it hadn't taken a brush with death to bring me to this place. It wasn't that simple. I'd been inching my way toward this revelation, and in some ways had already had it. Korry Taggart had simply shined a light on the reality I'd been struggling to accept. Now that I saw it clearly, it was so obvious. So completely clear.

"Sorry it took a minute. Had to make sure we had backup." Wilder still crouched down, removing things from Korry's pockets.

I felt like I might scream if I didn't touch him soon—hug him and thank him for coming.

"Are you okay? I'm so sorry. I'm so—" Madeline's voice caught. "So sorry."

I grabbed both her arms. "This was not your fault."

She loosed a harsh sigh. "He never would've come here if I hadn't been here. I shouldn't have—"

I firmed my grip on her arms. "I'm glad you were here. Now he's not a threat anymore. You being here was probably the best thing that could've happened. I'm sorry you had to face him and talk to him. You were nothing short of heroic, trying to get his attention off me."

She grimaced.

"Seriously, you were. Thank you."

A shaky hand rose to brush some hair behind her ear. "I think I'm going to sit down."

I walked her to the table behind us and she sat.

"Where is she? Is she okay? Oh my—" Anthony rushed in and kneeled in front of Madeline. "You're okay?"

She nodded, seeming dazed. I could relate, though instead of numb, I felt... alive. So freaking alive and ready to take on any challenge after surviving an actual madman. Granted, I hadn't done a dang thing to help the situation, but I was still alive and in one piece. Still, this invincible feeling translated to one thing: I knew what I wanted and I was going to take it. That alone was cause for celebration.

I stepped out of the conference room to give Anthony and Madeline a moment. The poor man had been so anxious when they'd come a short while ago—knowing she'd been faced with her stalker had to be a nightmare come true.

New voices filled the space, and the fact that I hadn't been aware of anyone else coming into the building told me my adrenaline-fueled body was starting to miss things. The sensation that had sharpened every sound and movement only minutes ago now made me feel like someone had slid earmuffs over my head and wrapped me in a sheet. My fingers tingled.

"Sarah, can you come talk with the sheriff?" Julian gestured for me to move past him toward the front, skirting a still-passed-out Korry and two police officers to the lobby where Wilder spoke to the sheriff.

My sluggish heart leapt at the chance to be near him. My eyes raked over him, assuring me he was unharmed. Of course he was, but I hadn't gotten to see him standing or even meet his eye until right now.

He turned as Julian and I approached.

"Sarah can do her statement now, and then we'll get to Madeline. I'm sure we don't want to keep her waiting," Julian said.

"No, please do Madeline first," I said, knowing I wouldn't be able to focus until I had a minute with Wilder. "Can I... see you outside?"

I had no idea whether maintaining professional distance mattered to him. I didn't want to collapse into his arms and cry, but for some reason, that was exactly what I felt coming. I needed to touch him and be close to him. I needed him to hold me and reassure me. And I definitely needed to do all those things before I talked through the events of the last... however long it'd been. I had no idea how much time had elapsed between Korry walking in the door and Wilder subduing him.

Thankfully, he needed no other explanation. He took

my hand, entwined our fingers, and walked out the front door.

CHAPTER FORTY-FIVE

Wilder

Years of training allowed me to exit the building, but I made it no farther. I crushed her to me the second the door swung shut, my hands releasing only to satisfy myself that she wasn't hurt.

"Are you okay?"

Her blue gaze met mine as tears spilled over the edge. "I'm okay."

I clutched her to me again, palming the back of her head and rocking her like it might bring her comfort. Or maybe it was me who needed that.

I'd known something was off when Julian texted 911 and a mishmash of letters I assumed were typed without looking. My weapon was tucked in my office safe, and I couldn't guess at the problem, but I figured it out quickly. I came in hard and fast to maintain the advantage and fortunately, Korry Taggart hadn't seen me coming.

"You're okay. You are."

She pulled in a breath and leaned back. "I'm so sorry. I know I messed up, but I'm not sure what I should've done. I really need you to train me for stuff like this if this could happen again, okay?"

A relieved laugh jumped out. "This shouldn't have happened, and you did perfectly. You and everyone else is alive, and that's all we need for now."

And we needed to see Taggart prosecuted to the full extent of the law, which he very likely would be now that he'd made this idiot move. Letting my mind go there prompted me—I needed to tell her what she meant to me. Seeing her in danger had clarified that.

"Can we get your statement now, Ms. James?" One of the deputies peeked out from the front door.

Sarah swiped under each eye and stepped out of my grasp, though I pivoted and rested a hand on her lower back. The idea of leaving her again for any amount of time was untenable. I wouldn't cram in my confession now with the deputy hanging nearby, but at least I could stay with her.

The deputy led her to the couch in the entryway and got situated while she sat. I stood a few feet away to give her space, but I wanted to hear, too. I caught her eye, and she nodded like she understood I needed her to confirm it was okay for me to stay.

And then she started, and the terror I'd felt crystalized into something more real than I'd experienced in twenty years. She talked about Taggart insinuating himself inside and ultimately holding her at gunpoint until Madeline showed her face. And God bless the woman, she should've stayed hidden, but she didn't. I'd need to grovel at her feet for saving Sarah, never mind the fact that this never should've happened to begin with. This guy should've never gotten out of the state of California, let alone here to Silverton, inside my building, to catch Sarah and Madeline alone in the building.

Brad and Anthony would hear from me on the matter, though from the repeated apologies from Brad and the outright tears from Anthony, I doubted I needed to say a word. Their guilt over leaving her to grab lunch would hang heavy on them for a while, I'd guess. The bigger issue was how this had happened in the first place, and we'd figure that out soon enough. I vowed then and there that I'd run the whole show for Madeline going forward, or not at all. For her and anyone else, for that matter. Brad would read me in on everything and I'd get my guy on her protection. Korry Taggart might be off the table now, but this wouldn't happen again on my watch.

We'd create our training courses faster. I'd always imagined teaching self-defense, basic wilderness survival, and other things I'd developed expertise in over the last twenty years, but I'd seen them farther down the line. Maybe Sarah would be the first student.

What felt like a lifetime later, the deputy had all he needed, and Sarah let me fold her into my arms again. My heart hadn't stopped clanging in my chest, beating so hard, I thought my ribs would break with each new detail she revealed.

"Can you come to my office? Do you mind staying for a few minutes?" Taggart had been carted away already so she wouldn't need to worry about seeing him.

"I don't want to leave you," she said, taking my hand in a firm grasp.

Her answer revved my determination, and I returned the hold, marching down the hall, stopping only to give a nod to the people in the conference room. I'd have to deal with them soon enough, and then I'd shut this place down and drag Sarah home with me, and I wouldn't leave her for another second. Maybe ever.

I followed her in and shut the door behind us.

"What did you want to—"

Her small grunt as I swallowed her in another hug made me loosen my hold.

"Sorry. I just... I can't stop thinking about that idiot holding a gun to your head, and it's driving me out of my mind."

"It wasn't my head. It was my back."

I growled. "Not much better. And still a problem. It's not okay. You shouldn't be here. You shouldn't be in this kind of danger, ever."

Her brow furrowed. "I know I didn't handle it well, but I—"

I cupped her face with both hands. Walking into this room, I'd decided *No more waiting*. Because this wouldn't be the only time I said it, and I couldn't risk another minute without her knowing.

But before I said a word, she beat me to it. "I love you Wilder. I need you to know that. I love you so much."

She kissed me, eyes closed and passionate, but I pulled back, chuckling to myself internally as the warmth of our matched hearts knitted mine back together.

"I love you, Sarah. I'm so glad you're okay, and I love you, too."

Her smile broke like a wave on sand. "I love you, too. So, so much."

"You already said that."

She pushed me away but immediately pulled me right back in for another kiss. Knowing that passion and celebration would have to wait, we held each other for a moment.

No tears this time, just relief and joy. I had clarity like I'd never known. Tonight wasn't the time to go back, but we would soon. And in the meantime, I could love her, and I'd tell her every day. *This* day wouldn't be the one that defined us or even started our love story. It would be one of thousands on which I told her the most basic truth.

There were still things to deal with, so we couldn't enjoy the moment much more than a few kisses and a lingering hug that felt so comforting and familiar, I wanted to live in it. But eventually, I pulled back.

"This shouldn't have happened. You shouldn't have had to go through something like this."

"It might happen in this job. You don't think I can handle it?"

"No, no that's not it. I just..." I could hardly form words after everything that'd happened. My exhausted brain scrambled for purchase. "I hate that you were in danger. I don't know if I can handle that again."

Color rose to her cheeks. "You think you'll feel better having Diane, a mom with a newborn baby at home, be in danger instead?"

"What? No. Plus, Diane already resigned. She doesn't want to come back."

Her lashes fluttered. "Wait. When was this?"

"Like two hours ago, one of many things I wanted to talk to you about tonight. But I'm honestly not sure I want to now."

She bit her lip, curbing the rising excitement. "Why? What does that mean?"

I dipped my head, my mind nothing but a useless void. "Because I was going to mention that if you wanted to stay on, we could end your temp contract and start a new one. You mentioned not loving teaching, so I thought it might work. We could bulk up your responsibilities, especially once we have more staff, and—"

She pulled me to her, her lips meeting mine in a frenzied kiss so sweet and exhilarating, I didn't let her pull away when she started to. Devouring her seemed like the best option, the only thing on my list at the moment, until she chuckled against my lips.

"Don't give me that face," she said, clearly referring to my scowl.

"What face?"

"The *Sarah interrupting my kissing* face." Her eyes sparkled with happiness that punched me square in the chest. I flexed my jaw to keep from dumping all my feelings at her feet right then. Not just the love I'd already confessed, but how much of it, how deep, how unbearable it was to love her so much and not know that she'd be mine forever.

"I'll admit laughing wasn't what I was going for," I said, smoothing a hand along her spine before stepping back. "But I'm relieved you can about anything today."

She nodded, a grim set to her mouth returning. I wanted to kiss it into smile again, but we couldn't wish away the last few hours, much as I wanted to.

"We should check on Madeline. She has to be so upset."

"Maybe a little relieved, but yeah. And now that I know you and she are safe, I need to figure out how he found her."

We exited my office and Sarah knocked lightly on the frame of the open conference room. Anthony, Brad, Julian, Sheriff Whitaker, and two deputies sat around the table with Madeline at the center facing the door.

"What can we do?" Sarah asked, edging into the room.

If I hadn't been certain I was in love with her before this moment, this would've clinched it. She'd been held at gunpoint, but walked into this room asking what she could do for others. The strength it took to think of someone other than yourself in a moment like this couldn't be overestimated, and her display of it had me resisting the very strong urge to gather her back in my arms.

"He'd tracked her phone. There wasn't much we could've done to keep him away with that kind of link, but it definitely explains how he managed to find her when we had everything else locked down so tight." Brad shifted, his face all thunder.

His team had been responsible for the tech side of Madeline's security long before we came along, and he'd insisted on keeping that as part of his domain. We'd talk about it another time, not in front of the sheriff, but there was not a chance I'd go for splitting the defense like this again. I'd be unlikely to have a higher-profile client than Madeline Reynolds, so I wouldn't need to worry about precedent. I'd set it now—you work with Saint, you do things our way. I should've insisted from the beginning, and now that was a lesson hard learned.

The sheriff slid his chair back. "This guy wasn't going to stop until he had some face time with you, but this ended the best possible way. He put three people in danger, and we've got evidence out the nose. He's going to jail for a long time, and you can all rest easy." He turned to me and nodded. "Thanks for your call. Looking forward to working with you again."

With that, the sheriff and his crew left to go deal with processing Taggart, and Brad, Anthony, and Madeline made their exit soon after. With the threat of Taggart gone, Madeline's concerns had reverted to far more typical fare, though I suspected our level of vigilance would be even higher than it might've been considering.

Julian walked with us to the front and waited as we locked up.

"You did well, Sarah. Madeline told us how you'd tried to warn her and refused to say she was in the building."

"I'm just glad it's over and she's safe. Thank you for coming when you did. You really are quite heroic."

He shook his head, batting the compliment away. "It was nothing but adrenaline-fueled idiocy. I'm relieved we had a professional nearby to wrap things up quickly before he really lost it."

Julian nodded to me. Never hurt to have our investor witness my skillset, but I would've been happy to skip this little demonstration.

"She's right. Not everyone would've done something like that." I snaked an arm around Sarah's back.

"I'll have to make sure Quinn knows all the details," she said, a grin on her beautiful face.

Julian chuckled reluctantly. "I'm sure she'll demand them. Stay safe, both of you."

With one last look that said we'd have more debriefing another day, he left.

Sarah and I walked hand in hand to her car.

"I could give you a ride home," she said, toying with my fingers.

"Sure. As long as you stay once we get there."

CHAPTER FORTY-SIX

Sarah

Three days after the most insane day of my adulthood, Wilder locked the door to the office and grabbed my hand. We'd spent every spare moment together, as though both of us needed the reassurance of the other's nearness.

We hadn't talked about much, other than some necessary processing of the events for me. He told me his side of things—an odd text from Julian, contacting the police, and coming in hard and fast after he'd caught a glimpse of Korry holding a gun through a window.

Somehow, my brain had allowed me to accept what'd happened and instead of nightmares about what would've gone wrong or even simply reliving the terror of what actually happened, I found the dream version of myself learning Krav Maga and becoming some kind of stealth agent. Ridiculous, but far preferable to being held hostage by Korry night after night.

I'd seen Madeline more than once in the last few days, too. She'd shown up with a giant bouquet of flowers on Thursday and insisted she take me to lunch, so we'd scheduled that. Then I'd seen her at Rise and Shine this morning when I'd stopped in to see Sadie and hug her—she was the last of my friends I'd needed to see and reassure I was okay. Quinn had started calling me Tuesday night once she'd heard a little bit about what'd happened from Julian and I'd filled her in. The next day, long before her store Pluck normally opened its doors, she'd found me unlocking Saint Securities, Wilder by my side, and pulled me into a rough bear hug that told me exactly how worried she was even though everything was done.

For her part, Madeline seemed… relieved. Not necessarily like she had no worries but like maybe she'd been sleeping a bit more, eating a bit more. I didn't know her well, but I couldn't help but feel relieved for her and so thankful it'd all turned out as well as it had.

Wilder and I hadn't discussed *us* beyond simply repeating the beautiful words we'd exchanged that day. He'd been his usual contemplative, word-sparing self the last few days—perhaps even more tight-lipped than he had been before. It was like our bodies were doing the work of reassuring each other—holding hands, hugging, snuggling, nesting together in sleep. Our minds were still working their way through the insanity and that left little room for delving into the history still set on a simmer in the background.

Or maybe that was just me. Wilder had dealt with all kinds of high-intensity situations, and I couldn't say whether this kind of quiet was typical. But he was not a verbal processor, so he wouldn't naturally talk things through. And I knew that if I let myself talk enough, I'd eventually get around to the fact that one of my main fears was not seeing him again and not having a future with him. Yes, we loved each other, but did we want the same thing? We'd loved each other before, too, and we'd been torn apart by life's events and my choices. I finally knew for certain what I wanted—I had to know what he thought.

I'd set my sights on this evening for my confessional and hoped it wouldn't feel out of place for me to say what I planned to so soon after a traumatic event.

We loaded into his truck, and he took off without a word, a wrinkle of determination in his brow. It only took a minute to realize he wasn't going to either of our apartments.

"Where are we headed?" I asked, a little fizz of anxiousness hitting that we might be meeting his family. I loved his family, wanted them to be mine someday like I had always dreamed, but I wanted time with Wilder without the pressures of work or the weirdness of the week.

"Wanted to show you something," he said, eyes pinned to the road ahead.

In another few minutes, his destination became clear. A place I hadn't been to in decades and had forbidden myself to think about. He pulled onto a dirt road, and we fumbled along in his truck through a wooded drive until the space opened up to reveal a stretch of land surrounded by mature trees with Silver Ridge peak towering in the distance.

Without a word, he stopped the car and jumped out. Seconds later, he pulled open my door and held out a hand.

Meanwhile, my pulse threatened to pound out of my throat. This was it. I didn't know exactly what *it* was other than something huge, something we'd never come back from. Something I hoped we wouldn't have to.

"Remember this?"

A breathy laugh tumbled out of me. "Do I remember

the place we used to say we'd buy and build a house on someday? Yes, Wilder, I do."

"I bought this lot over a decade ago. I've been preparing to build a house on it for years, and the foundation's done as of this week. I never let myself admit why I did that. Why I had to have *this* place."

Emotion clogged my throat, and my blood pumped hard enough I grew dizzy. But his hands holding both of mine anchored me. "Why?"

"Because I've never stopped hoping. I never stopped loving you."

A flicker of pain crossed his face, and I took my chance.

"I'm sorry for staying away for so long. I'm sorry it took me so much time to heal. By the time I did, I'd heard through a school friend of Eddie's that you'd gone into the Army. I was terrified to face that you'd found someone else and moved on and too down on myself to dig out of that hole and just... call you. Call your mom. Anything."

He ran a hand over my hair. "The whole time, I kept wondering what I'd done wrong. How I could've been better for you. I knew you were hurting, and I accepted you had to go with your parents, but it hurt so much not to have *anything* of you left."

I choked on a sob. "You couldn't have done anything better, Wilder. You were amazing. You were. And I wish I hadn't left you to grieve alone, but I had to go. What I didn't have to do was *disappear*."

His jaw flexed and he dipped his head. "Mom and Wy helped. Grandma Tilda, too. But God, I wanted that life. I wanted what we'd planned on before with college and ROTC, but the minute you said you were late, I wanted it all with you. It clicked for me—like it was always supposed to be that way."

Tears tracked down my face. "I know. Me, too."

"Losing the baby—seeing you in so much pain and then losing you, too..."

I pulled him close and held him, wishing I could go back and ease the pain for both of us. "I'm so sorry. I'm so, *so* sorry. Can you please forgive me?"

"I don't want us to keep going back. I forgive you for staying away if you'll forgive me for not coming after you."

I huffed through a sound half sob, half laugh. "I had a few daydreams to that effect—that you'd draw on that stubborn streak and just come find me."

His regretful smile was softer than it'd ever been, no line of bitterness. "Part of me wishes I had, knowing what I know now. But after everything, I'm glad we're here."

"I am, too," I said just above a whisper.

We clung to each other as the breeze filtered past, the fresh mountain air wiping the slate clean in the wake of our confession and forgiveness. No erasing the scars, no forgetting. But accepting. Together.

After a few moments, he exhaled and pulled back. With a hand on either side of my face, he spoke. "I love you more now than I ever imagined I could love someone. It's been fast, and I've questioned it. I've doubted it. But after this week, I'll never question it again. I don't want to be without you, ever."

He gripped my hand tightly, and then he was on one knee, gazing up at me.

I pulled at his hands, but he stayed down, stubborn as always. My heart burned with excitement and joy and love, and I hadn't even told him how much. "If you're calling twenty-plus years fast, then I suppose it is."

A smile flashed. "Please, Sarah. Marry me. Let me be yours, and be mine."

I dove into his arms then, clobbering him in the least graceful assault of kisses and desperation to be close. After laughing and crying for a frantic moment, I pulled back and cupped my hands on either side of his face.

"I love you. I love you so much, and yes, I want to be yours. Yes, I'll marry you."

The way he kissed me, then reiterated everything he'd said and done... The heat between us built and built until we were in danger of setting the surrounding trees on fire. We broke then, and resolved to go home. But first, Wilder held my hand and led me around the property, pointing out things he had planned and asking if I wanted to see the plans he'd had drawn up.

"We could do four bedrooms. Or five. Maybe an office instead, though I like the idea of keeping work at work. If you think you'll need an office space, we can plan for that."

He was so chatty, I hated to stop his momentum. But in the wake of all the beauty and joy, I had to make sure he understood.

One hand on his chest, I stopped him. "You need to understand—I may not be able to have kids."

He swallowed. "Okay."

Pain pinched in my chest. "I don't know for sure. But obviously, it didn't work out the first time. I know there's nothing I could've or should've done—but it may be something we need to accept."

His navy eyes flicked back and forth between mine like they so often did, trying to read what I wasn't saying.

"Do you want to try for kids? Did you ever try with—"

"No. I think I always knew it wasn't right—knew bringing kids into it didn't make sense." I'd never had the conscious thought that we wouldn't work, and yet it felt like once he'd initiated the divorce, all I'd felt was relief. Well, that and failure, but I'd long since accepted that it needed to happen.

Wilder nodded. "Have you talked to a doctor?" But before I could answer, he shook his head. "Actually, no. The biggest question is, do you want to try? Do you want to have kids?"

"Yes," I said, my voice tinged with tears. I hated that I was so close to crying, and yet I couldn't not. I'd always wanted kids with Wilder—always.

"Then we'll figure it out. If it doesn't work for us, then we'll look at other options. And if it's just you and me?"

I pressed my lips together, staving off what would most definitely be a sob.

"Then I will live my life a happy man. And we will be the best aunt and uncle Wyatt and Warrick and Eddie's kids have ever had."

That did it. This man was so full of love, and I felt so privileged to be the person who got to feel and see it. Who'd seen it years ago and could see how he'd survived all that he had and still come out able to love so beautifully.

"I love you so much," I said, my voice nothing but a whisper.

"I love you, too."

3 Years Later

Wilder

Mom handed me a pack of glitter glue with a smirk that told me she relished seeing me like this. "You're up, Wilder. Time to show Ella and James your creative prowess."

"Dad, show me!" James's enthusiasm was accompanied by a toddler flail that knocked half the markers and stickers on the ground. He'd hit a two-year-old growth spurt, and it was almost as bad as having a puppy—or so I imagined. But his tiny nose, giant blue eyes, and dark brown hair that curled over his ears and at his neck made him an adorable combination of me and his mother. And according to my mom, he was the spitting image of my dad when he was little.

Sarah and I had never gotten a puppy because it turned out she got pregnant with James on our honeymoon, six short months after I'd come back to Silverton.

"I think I'll leave you and Grandma to it," I said, winking at Mom and bending to kiss my son's head. I'd never tire of it.

"Are you just going to abandon me to these crafts and your mother? Come on, man." Calla gave me an eyebrow raise from across the table, where she sat covered in stickers courtesy of my oldest niece, Ella.

"Callaway, you need to develop your crafting skills or these poor children are going to be creatively useless."

I chuckled as I entered the kitchen to find Sarah, Sadie, and Wyatt doing the same.

"Mom, don't hassle my wife. She's plenty creative."

"Ew, no. No," Warrick said, roused from his new-dad nap on the couch by the double entendre from our oldest brother.

Sadie snickered but kept her focus on mixing some kind of batter that would inevitably lead to something delicious. Motherhood suited her as long as she still got to bake. Warrick's mother hen nature kicked into high gear after the twins were born two months ago, but the more he did for her, the more it drove her crazy. She didn't mind him taking care of her, but when he tried to tell her she could take a break from baking, I think it was the closest to a near-death experience he'd ever had.

"Wyatt! Don't start with me," Calla said as she peeked into the kitchen, her threat completely empty based on the beaming smile she gave him.

I moved to find my lovely Sarah, who'd turned her

attention back to the two babies she held, one of whom would need to eat soon, and the other, which was fast asleep. Warrick's twins were born about six weeks after Wyatt's third child. He and Calla had bred like it was their business, and maybe for a former cattle rancher, that made some sense.

But yes, we liked to give him flack about it. Warrick's favorite line of questioning was how they found the time to make so many babies in between Calla's tours, but it was Wyatt and his full arms, heart, and house who had the last laugh.

Though tonight, it was my full house. The house that Sarah and I had built with the help of my brothers by birth and a few of my brothers by military bond who'd arrived not long after Saint Securities got off the ground.

"I'll take them," Warrick said, reaching for his one little football-sized bundle. He held the snoozing one tucked into his chest like the good former tight end he was, peering down at the other who'd started making tell-tale sounds of discontentment. "This guy's ravenous."

Sarah gave the baby a soft kiss. "Go snuggle your daddy until your mama's ready for you."

Warrick took him and his brother and bustled over to the kitchen to check on Sadie, and I happily took his place right as James ran up and dive-bombed me.

"Whoa, careful, bud. Mom just had your cousins," I said to my son, running a hand over his unruly dark hair.

"Watch her belly baby, too," he said.

My heart threatened to burst. "That's right. Gotta watch the belly baby."

Baby number two was growing steadily in Sarah, and James had started referring to it as the *belly baby* in his tiny voice.

We had just two months left before we met him or her. It drove Wyatt up the wall we were keeping it a surprise.

"Sorry, Dad. I just excited." At only a little over two, it sounded more like "I dus sighted" and it killed me. His complete acceptance and love for me and Sarah had nearly broken me at times. His softness and sweetness, the beauty of having him become ours because he was *meant* to be ours, had made me believe even more that this—all of this—was meant to be.

"It's okay, bud. You going to help Aunt Calla?" Poor woman was contending with her own almost-three-year-old, our Westley, her second child, aka toddler Ella, and Grandma Jane, who we all knew was the biggest handful.

"Gotta go, bye!" he yelled, then bolted off back to the dining room.

Sarah and I grinned at each other, loving his energy and how he'd heard Warrick leave our house once with that abrupt farewell and hadn't stopped saying that whenever he ran off to go do something.

"Hey, I love you," she said, that soft smile on her face just killing me and giving me life all at once.

I scooted down the couch and brushed a finger over her cheek. "I love you, too."

She tilted her head, that signal she gave when she knew I had something on my mind. "What is it?"

I shook my head, wishing I had some other way to say it but knowing I should spit it out anyway. "It's another one of those moments. I can't help it."

Tears hit her eyes in an instant like they so often did these days. "You're too sweet."

I chuckled. "Thinking things are too good to be true isn't sweet. It's stupid. I should embrace it."

She swept her free hand over my shoulder, and I indulged in pressing my hand to her rounded belly.

"You do embrace it, though. Here you are, right now, embracing the beauty by being a part of it. You're not standing on the outside looking in. You're right here in it with me. You're at home here."

I pressed a kiss to her soft lips and breathed a slow inhale. "I am. And I'll never stop being grateful for that."

Thank you for reading Wilder and Sarah's love story! I hope you fell in love with them like I did. For more in Silver Ridge, check out Almost True, starring Madeline Reynolds and Aidan Wallace.

All of You: The Rambler Battalion, Book 5

ACKNOWLEDGMENTS

I've been looking forward to writing Wilder's book since he popped into my head while writing Wells' book *years* ago. I genuinely worried over whether readers could enjoy the story that felt so beautiful and yet so difficult. I tried to talk myself out of the history that rooted itself in my mind for these two, but no matter what I tried, the story wouldn't let me change it. I hope you're coming away from the story feeling satisfied.

Thank you to my editor, Zee Monodee, for helping this book take shape and refusing to let me back off the hard moments.

To Betas—you are amazing and give me help and courage. I owe each of you! Ashley, Amanda, and Genny, you are simply the best.

Thank you to Emma Robinson for making this cover happen in the midst of the madness you've faced this year!

Thank you Amanda Cuff for the proofread. I feel much more confident releasing with your final read in the books!

Thanks to my family and dear friends for supporting my writing even when it makes me angsty. Thanks to the Inkers Crew for your support and friendship.

Thanks to the readers who've supported this series by reading, reviewing, and sharing! Reviews and word of mouth really do make a difference to indie authors, so thank you! I appreciate you more than you can know!

ABOUT THE AUTHOR

Claire Cain lives to eat and drink her way around the globe with her traveling soldier and three kids, but is perhaps even happier hunkered down at home in a pair of sweatpants and slippers using any free moment she has to read and cook. Or talk—she really likes to talk. She has become an expert at packing too many dishes in too few cabinets and making houses into homes from Utah to Germany and many places in between. She's a proud Army wife and is frankly just really happy to be here.

You can also join Claire's facebook reader group for exclusive content and fun: https://www.facebook.com/groups/clairecain/

Website: http://www.clairecainwriter.com

E-mail: Claire@ClaireCainWriter.com

Newsletter sign-up for new releases, exclusives, and freebies, including a free book:

http://www.clairecainwriter.com/newsletter

amazon.com/author/clairecain

bookbub.com/authors/claire-cain

instagram.com/clairecainwriter

facebook.com/clairecainwriter

goodreads.com/clairecainwriter

pinterest.com/clairecainwriter

twitter.com/writeclairecain

www.ingramcontent.com/pod-product-compliance
Lightning Source LLC
Chambersburg PA
CBHW061046190726
48286CB00006B/1632